# *Shrink Wrapped*

Irene Silvers

ISBN: 1541265912
ISBN 13: 9781541265912
Library of Congress Control Number: 2017907490
CreateSpace Independent Publishing Platform
North Charleston, South Carolina

In memory of my mother, who believed…
and with thanks to my family

# *July 23rd*

*I* can imagine what it was like for my shrink when he was growing up: merciless teasing about his last name, *Kisselstine*. It's comical, all right. But this may turn out to be a good thing for me because if Kisselstine endured brutal schoolyard teasing as a kid, surely he developed top notch coping skills and I would be the beneficiary. That's exactly what I need.

I haven't been myself since Renny walked out on me. I can't fall asleep unless I take two Benadryls and even then, instead of quickly sinking into a drug-induced stupor, I'm spooling that fateful conversation with Renny in my head; things I should have said, things I shouldn't have said. It's exhausting. And, I haven't eaten very well—all too often a bag of popcorn for supper at night. I've hardly consumed a proper portion of protein or a complex carbohydrate in weeks and even so, I've lost weight. And the crying. It's humiliating because I'm just not that kind of girl. Last week, when I couldn't drag myself out of bed to get to spinning class before work, I knew I needed help.

So, I found Dr. Robert Kisselstine, an interactive psychologist. He's my new shrink and he's also my one and only shrink. This is a new experience for me— but obviously, in my condition, I simply can no longer rely on my girlfriends, Carla and Natalie, for guidance.

Of course, I Googled interactive psychology before I came to the office. It's about joint problem solving. He's not going to be one of those docs who just sits there and nods his head and says *Hmmm* at strategic points; he's going to be an activist. And I would have to keep a journal after every appointment and literally write down my take on the session and my feelings. I am asked to email it to him within two days of the session. I guess it reads better when it's fresh.

1

Everything about Dr. K is medium. That is, medium build, medium brown hair, medium features. At first glance, two characteristics stand out: his hair is parted on the side and gelled into submission in a retro 1950's look and his glasses are so incredibly thick that I actually can't determine his eye color. Medium?

When he ushered me into his office with its medium décor of beige and taupe and its white noise machine exhaling a medium noise—not too loud, not too soft—I was kind of disconcerted. I had a fleeting thought that his decorator was probably a patient in the throes of a major depression; what else would account for a room that had the personality of a mushroom? He waved me to a very plush chair (beige, of course) and I really couldn't tell if *he* were medium or tall because he quickly sat down in a more austere chair and settled in with a notepad in his lap. When I say "settled" I really mean it: he kind of shrunk into his seat.

"Let's talk about the journal," he said, "because that's really a big part of interactive therapy, Miss Marks. When a session is over, I'd like you to write about it, reviewing anything that comes to mind and very important, writing about how you feel and then email that entry to me. It's a very helpful tool in finding solutions. Are you all right with that?"

"What if I write something awful about you?"

"Don't worry, you wouldn't be the first." He gave me a reassuring smile; I was pleased to note that his teeth were white—not beige. He continued. "So write whatever comes to mind and don't overthink it or try to correct it. Most importantly, don't be concerned about my feelings. Just express yourself as openly as you can." He smiled at me again. "So, that's a plan, yes?"

I smiled back and nodded my head in agreement. "Yes, I will definitely write whatever comes to mind and damn the consequences."

He ignored the touch of sarcasm in my response and went further. "In fact, why don't you get in the habit of keeping a journal even when we don't have a session. It doesn't have to be an everyday occurrence, Miss Marks. But, if you have an experience that you want to think about or one that seems important, just get into the habit of writing about it and forwarding it to me."

I'm not falling for that; I retain the right to edit. So, I'm setting up a folder on my computer with my complete entries and I'm planning to send slightly abridged versions—with necessary deletes—to Kisselstine. He's not going to find out how *medium* he is from me. That would definitely contaminate our relationship.

Actually, I spend a good part of my day at the keyboard as an account executive at Dean Hathaway Chung, a boutique advertising agency in Manhattan. Truly, I'm living proof that English majors can get work. Frankly, I'm not exactly thrilled with the prospect of coming home to write in a journal. It makes me feel as if I'm back in fifth grade and Miss Milbank is standing over me as we write "Our Day"—a daily diary entry required of each of her students.

Miss Milbank, exceedingly prim and proper, was what was called a *spinster* in days gone by. "Sophie, we do not hold our pens in our fist, dear. That's why we have thumbs and forefingers." Dear demure Miss Milbank—until the day I forgot my Peanuts' lunchbox and realized it on my way home from school, so I ran back to my classroom. There I found Miss M sitting *on* her desk with her Peter Pan collared sweater unbuttoned, while Mr. Shandley, seventh grade, was standing between her legs, caressing an exposed breast. Welcome to hands-on sex education.

I knew Kisselstine was going to ask me why I was in his office, but I felt awkward about the whole disclosure process. Maybe not awkward—perhaps embarrassed is the better word. Sad as well. I hoped Kisselstine was the right therapist for me. Then I happened to glance at the wall where he'd placed his framed diplomas and there was Harvard. Harvard! That is categorically not medium.

So, he took notes as I give him basic statistics: age, job, address, medications and family members—that kind of information. Then I told him I was in his office because of Renny, my former significant other, who let me go as easily as turning down a request from a telephone fundraiser.

"How would you describe your relationship with..." he glanced down at his notes and looked up, "Renny? That is, before your break-up."

"Fine," I said. "We were together for three years. Well, together but not living together. I live in Greenwich Village on East 11th Street in Manhattan and Renny is on the Upper East Side on Park Avenue. His address is definitely more upscale than mine, but that's no surprise because he's in finance.

Hedge fund." I exhaled loudly, wondering if I were about to cry, but then I regrouped. I had been worried about going on a crying jag and I'd confided this to Carla, whose solution was for me to imagine my new therapist naked. She was certain that would help. I gave it a try and to my surprise, I started to giggle. He looked up with no change of expression. I quickly clothed the man and soldiered on.

"I think we were as together as you can be with separate condos that are seventy-two blocks apart." I felt defensive. "Look, Doctor, we definitely were a couple." Emphasis on *were*.

"So you lived apart. But did you vacation together? Sleep in each other's apartments?"

I nodded yes. "That was our relationship...although," I confessed, "mostly he'd stay at my place." After three years together, I guess that sounded suspect. "He's not the kind of man who'd let you keep a toothbrush in his medicine cabinet. But he did stay at my apartment many Friday and Saturday nights."

"And you were comfortable with that arrangement?"

What a question! "Oh yes, doctor. It was perfect. We were very happy together."

Kisselstine scribbled on his pad. I waited. Then he looked up at me and said, encouragingly, "Let's talk about the situation that made him your former significant other."

I told him that it started about seven weeks ago when I began to feel sick to my stomach, kind of queasy. I'd open my refrigerator, catch a whiff of some cheese or a hint of leftovers and I'd suddenly feel as if I would collapse from nausea. Just looking at a piece of raw meat made me tremble. At first, I was thinking that maybe I should have gotten that flu shot after all.

When I told Natalie, she laughed. "Girl, you can get yourself a pregnancy test and study the stick—but you heard it here first—you've got a bun in the oven." Natalie has three children so she knows all there is to know about insemination, gestation and delivery. She also has a three-bedroom apartment with two full baths thanks to her late grandmother who lived there for thirty-eight years and no doubt bought it for pennies and then left it to Natalie. My darling grandmother left me an antique diamond and sapphire wedding band, which I have yet to use, and a treasure chest of wonderful memories—not to mention a handwritten recipe book that allows my mother and me to bake the best apple strudel this side of Vienna.

Which reminds me: Renny adored my apple strudel. Before he came over, he always asked me if I'd baked so that he could fine-tune his workout and pump enough iron to indulge his addiction. *Who*—I wonder—*or what*—will satisfy his sweet tooth now?

Anyway, I told Kisselstine that Natalie was correct. I remember sitting on the edge of the tub, holding the evidence—two pink lies on the stick—that would change my life. I felt joyful.

Kisselstine said, "Joyful?" with a slight raise of his eyebrows.

*Joyful*—not a word I would normally use—but in this case it described my feelings exactly. Renny and I had created a baby and I was ecstatic. Frankly, I sometimes have a low grade worry about my aging eggs and my potentially diminished fertility. This usually happens when I go to the supermarket; there's often a tabloid right by the checkout with a screaming headline declaring that a woman in her mid-thirties has eggs that are essentially past their shelf life—just like the month old cottage cheese I am replacing.

But, once I get past the headline, I usually convince myself that thirty-three is still in the fertility safety zone and I really shouldn't be actively worrying until I hit forty. In fact, plenty of women have babies well into their forties. Carla told me that Grandma DeLuca had her eighth child when she was forty-four and probably would have continued to turn out little DeLucas indefinitely if she hadn't finally given up the rhythm method and taken the pill. Carla said her nonna crossed herself and said three Hail Marys every time she swallowed the pill and she counted on the Pope to be privately sympathetic to her plight, so she never bothered to mention it in confession. I don't exactly know why, but I related to Grandma DeLuca's story—possibly because at heart I'm an optimist. I simply believe that the fertility statute of limitations would not run out on me until I hit forty—or beyond.

I always thought that someday Renny and I would have a child. Granted, he didn't melt when he saw an infant, didn't crack a smile at a toddler and barely noticed the sweetness of a kindergartner. But, I truly believed he had potential. Someday, he would want a legacy; someday he would feel the need to nurture and love a child whose DNA he'd created. I always reminded myself to have patience with him. Someday...

Natalie, content in her marriage, wearing it like an old bathrobe that kept her warm and cozy, called me *Someday Sophie*. She'd always contended that Renny would never come around and want children, let alone marriage, and I was deluding myself. Carla seconded the motion.

Now that I was pregnant, *someday* had actually materialized and I was euphoric. I had a strong feeling that now that it was a *fait accompli*, Renny would suddenly be open to the pleasures of fatherhood. I was bursting with pleasure.

"Yes, *joyful*," I repeated to Kisselstine. "I had this gift, this embryo, growing inside me and I embraced my sudden fierce determination to have this baby. I didn't expect it and I hadn't planned on it, but it was wonderful. I was going to be a mother."

I told Kisselstine that Renny was skittish about marriage, having married his college sweetheart right after graduation and then divorcing a few years later. His divorce, as he described it, was relatively painless because he and his wife had neither children nor assets. However, I knew that this unhappy union had definitely left its mark on him and Renny was in no rush to exchange wedding vows. At any rate, marriage wasn't my immediate concern.

"I was honest with him," I explained. "I needed his help so I could raise the baby. I'm doing well financially, but I recognized that I couldn't do it alone. I told him it was his choice to be involved or detached, but either way, I wanted to have the child." And the truth is Renny's positive genetic contribution would have been considerable—brains and looks—but there was no point mentioning that to Kisselstine. It would have made me seem superficial, wouldn't it?

I confess that I started crying at this point in the session. Dr. K handed me a tissue and I wiped my eyes and blew my nose noisily. When I cry my face turns blotchy red and my eyeliner drools. Why can't I cry like actresses do in the movies? Little pearly teardrops softly gliding down high cheekbones, eyes glistening, lashes fluttering, breasts slightly heaving—like the cover of a romance novel—all accompanied by a discreet sob. Well that wasn't the case. I snorted into the tissue again and Kisselstine handed me another. He didn't seem to mind my breakdown; I guess he's seen it all. Anyway, I'm certain that falling apart in a therapist's office is not unique.

However, I wanted to tell him that I never, ever cry like this, that I'm really a strong, independent person, that this breakdown was an anomaly. Instead, I asked him to move the box of tissues closer to me. Then, in between sniffles, I told Kisselstine that Renny and I had dinner together that very night.——the night of the pink stick. It was a Sunday and I had time to cook something special—perhaps a filet with a port wine sauce and roasted vegetables and definitely, my wonderful apple strudel. Mozart in the background—you know, set the stage. I'd tell him the news and he'd take me in his arms, tenderly of course, because I was with child, a delicate flower about to bloom. But he didn't have time to come downtown, so we met at Vinny's Chop House on 45th, somewhat halfway.

"Christ! I can't believe this. That was not supposed to happen."

"Renny, it *did* happen and we're talking about a child we created. I think we've come to the next step. You know…having a baby." I faltered. I had convinced myself that someday he would come around, but as I looked at his sour expression and heard the barely suppressed resentment in his voice, it occurred to me that *someday* might not be in Renny Chapman's vocabulary.

He shook his head. "Sophie, this is something we have to do together." Of course, I reminded him we did do it together, probably when we spent a few days in Connecticut, alternating woodland hikes with large quantities of Chateauneuf du Pape.

"No, Sophie, I mean we both have to want this, be together on this. I can't bring a child into the world because of…what?…a birth control slip-up. Honestly, sweetheart, I really don't want to be a father."

"You don't have to be a father. *Just help me be a mother.*"

He shook his head. "I can't."

"Dr. Kisselstine, this man is thirty-eight years old—a successful Wall Street trader and analyst and he could afford twenty babies," I contended angrily.

Truthfully, I could never figure out exactly what Renny was doing at Headley Capital. I only hoped it wasn't insider trading because I could just picture the front page of *The New York Post*. Renny Chapman on the steps of the courthouse in his Armani pinstripe, his face tight as he towered over his rumpled, portly lawyer who had managed to get him a plea deal. I would be holding up the rear, the loving girlfriend who stood by her man. Except—I was not the loving girlfriend any more.

I told Kisselstine that I'd said to Renny, "Okay, let me take full responsibility for the baby; all you have to do is help me out financially. Just enough so I can swing day-care or a nanny. You don't even have to be on the birth certificate." I'd hesitated at that point because I wanted to express myself very clearly to the obviously reluctant sperm donor of my unborn child. "Renny, you can draw up a contract and arrange for financial help so I can raise the baby and you won't have any other obligation to the child—or to me. We can make it a business arrangement." I took a few deep breaths and made him an offer, my very own Custer's Last Stand: "We can each go our own way, if that's what you want."

He was silent. Incredibly silent. I waited for an answer and, finally, he just shook his head again and then said, "Sophie, I just can't."

Can't what? Love me? Have a child with me? Take some responsibility for creating a life? I could suddenly see the three years we had together dissolving into a blurred memory that was fading before my eyes. Natalie was right. I was a *Someday Sophie* doll, fun to play with, but easily disposable when I didn't conform. He reached into his inside jacket pocket and took out a platinum credit card. I new exactly what he meant. "Please use this," he said. "Please."

The card stayed on the table. I told Kisselstine that I grabbed my purse and left, darting between tables, trying to reach the door before I embarrassed myself with full scale crying. I hailed a taxi so quickly that I had no idea if Renny finally decided to come after me. All I know is that when I walked out I'd left him sitting there, staring at the tablecloth and twirling his wine glass, making no move to stop me. "Dr. Kisselstine, He didn't even offer to take me to a clinic, to be with me for the procedure, to take care of me."

"Yes, that was wrong," Kiisselstine agreed.

"Do you think I asked him for too much?" It was a question I had to pose to my shrink.

"I think you asked for what *you* wanted and needed. You gave him several choices that might have worked with a different man, but unfortunately, not with him." Kisselstine paused and patiently watched me snivel into a tissue as I tried to compose myself. Then he said, "I think he failed you because he didn't take any responsibility for his part in fathering the child and he seemed unable to acknowledge that the three years you shared together required a deeper conversation. And, he wasn't there for you—emotionally."

"Yes, he failed me," I repeated. That's what I wanted to hear. It would have been even better if Kisselstine called him a no-good, miserable bastard. But I guess that's too over the top for my medium shrink.

"Miss Marks, I have to say that your proposal obviously valued the life of the baby and also reflected your desire to celebrate and nurture it. But, from Renny's point of view, it was an unwanted child. He probably realized immediately that any contract you agreed on could be nullified in court because the child had his DNA. Think about it: if he were to marry in the future, the child might pose a problem to his new family. And the child's financial needs might increase beyond his ability to pay—if, for example, he lost his job."

Whose side was Kisselstine on?

He continued. "So, it's not exactly a black and white picture." He paused and then said in a kindly manner, "Something to think about, right?"

I'm thinking. I'm *thinking* that this is not exactly what I came here for.

"And I assume you're no longer together."

I nodded my head. "Other than a very brief "Take care of yourself" text the next day and a couple of similar ones in the next two weeks, Renny has gone missing." I shredded three tissues with this humiliating admission.

Just like all those doctor shows on television, Kisselstine asked me how I felt about that. I flashed him an irritated look. "Are you serious?" I replied, incredulous. "I felt betrayed."

I glanced at my watch. Time was almost up and I'd barely begun my story. And then Kisselstine closed his notebook to signal that my fifty-minute hour was over.

"You know, Miss Marks, there's no easy answer to this. Some women would have the child with the intention of bringing up the baby and then sue for support. Others would have the child because of their religious beliefs and then give it up for adoption. Some would indeed choose to terminate the pregnancy because as single mothers they would worry they couldn't do right by the child." He paused and then said gently, "We have to determine which woman you are."

I realized then that I hadn't given him a clue that I was no longer pregnant.

"We'll talk about this next time," said Kisselstine

At that moment, I felt exhausted. I didn't feel as if I had the strength for "next time." Nevertheless, when I came home and started the journal and had time to think, I decided to give *Harvard* one more chance.

And, I made up my mind that I'd call him "Dr. K" from now on—unless I heard an objection from him. *He* might be medium—but his name was extra long.

# July 27th

$\mathcal{N}$ext appointment. Today, I told Kisselstine that I'd lost the baby three weeks later. How could I have dealt with this at the last session when time was almost up? And Kisselstine had blindsided me with his take on Renny—which was perilously close to sympathetic. I guess I have to get used to being in therapy and baring my private life to a total stranger, and I definitely have to reorganize my thinking and accept the fact that my therapist is not going to automatically agree with me—even though I'm the one writing the check.

So, I began again. I told him that at the time of the miscarriage, early on a Sunday morning, I had not been sure of what was happening to me. The pain and the stomach cramps made me feel like I was knocked out by a powerful flu, so I called Carla and asked her to take me to the ER. By the time I arrived at the hospital, I was staining and then I knew exactly what was happening. It was ugly for a while and then it was over. Our baby was gone.

Suddenly there were no decisions to make about whether I could handle being a single mother; no worries about having enough money for the nanny or nursery school or dancing lessons or Little League uniforms. Suddenly nothing. I'd never know if Renny would have fallen in love with the baby after it was born. I was heartbroken.

I admitted to Kisselstine that the only thing I knew for certain is that I'd misjudged the man I'd been dating for three years. Why? I don't know. I'd ignored the signs, engaged in assumptions that had no basis in reality and basically leaned on a "someday" philosophy that was infused with optimism but was actually quite naïve. If I'd listened to my mother….if I'd listened to Carla and Natalie…

I told Kisselstine that Carla came to my apartment the day after I lost the baby, carrying beer and pizza to fill up the empty space in my tummy. She was bursting with anger. "He's a dick. What kind of guy gets his girlfriend pregnant and then disappears?" She had never really liked Renny because she had concluded that he was unlikely to commit to marriage and I would grow old being his girlfriend. "Let me refine that," Carla had asserted when Renny and I became a couple. "When you started showing signs of age, you would definitely be replaced by a younger model whom *he also wouldn't marry*."

My response: I'd simply ignored her prediction because Renny was smart and interesting and I enjoyed being with him and I thought we were a good fit that *eventually* would lead to permanence—notwithstanding certain mixed signals. However, I had to concede to Kisselstine that in our three years together, Renny had never actually said that he loved me. At different times, he had said I was wonderful, smart, beautiful— all things I liked to hear. But, never the L word. Of course, as a matter of principle, I never lobbed the L word into his court. I knew the rules of the game.

Despite *The Big Three*—that is, my mother, Carla and Natalie—I'd always believed Renny would come around. At any rate, I was in no hurry. I had someone in my life, a significant other, as they say, and that meant a lot to me. I ticked off the benefits to Kisselstine: I had an escort for the company Christmas party, I had a date for Saturday night, I had someone who listened to me talk about my work (although he was far more absorbed in *his* work), and I had an energetic partner who liked to hike and kayak and enjoy fine wine afterwards in Connecticut or upstate New York country inns. True, many times Renny sometimes couldn't spare a weekend or had to cancel dinner during the week because of challenges at the office, but on the whole, the relationship was working. I was fifty percent of a couple—no small feat in a city bursting with attractive single women on a mission.

"Dr. K, I was enjoying the present with Renny, and I believed that there would be a future for us. Um, someday."

"So, you were a couple, but you never discussed marriage or children? Is that right?" Kisselstine had a way of synthesizing my words and getting to the bottom line.

"Well, I guess that's true," I replied

Kisselstine shook his head. "Generally, I would say it's a good thing to have an optimistic and positive outlook on life, but perhaps you carried it kind of far. Three years together—and never a word about something obvious: marriage. Never a mention of how much you looked forward to having children. That's most unusual."

"So, tell me, Dr. K, can you cure me of self-delusion? I don't want to be *Someday Sophie* anymore. That's what Natalie and Carla call me."

"What I can do is help you make healthy choices. As we work together, you'll find that the more you understand yourself, the easier it will be to make decisions that are right for you."

I hope he's right. Last night, when Carla was consoling me with beer and pizza, I was thinking that she could use Dr. K's services as well because her five-year affair with a married man also had its "someday" component. I pointed out to her how ironic our situations were. "You faulted Renny because he didn't commit, but you've been seeing Jake on and off for five years and he hasn't left his wife. Or should I say he leaves his wife every once in a while and then goes back to her after she threatens to commit suicide or his daughter terrorizes him until he surrenders."

Carla lifted her can of beer in a toast, accompanied with a self-satisfied smile. "He left Audrey last week and this time it's for good."

"How can you be sure? Look at his track record," I cautioned her. "He's tried that before and it hasn't worked."

"Well, Jake's daughter just turned eighteen and she's off to college in Boston in September and right now that's all that matters to her. So, Jake is finally free." Maybe. Jake has always been a rubber band, snapping out of the marriage and then snapping right back into it. Clearly, Carla and I, when discussing our fractured relationships, have a lot to talk about.

"Are you relieved or terribly sad about the baby?" Carla asked.

Funny, that's exactly what Dr. K had asked me today. I'd told him the truth: a little bit of both—and I feel very guilty about that. I wanted the baby. I hadn't realized how important it was to me until I was actually pregnant. But, bringing up a child alone—could I have handled that?

Kisselstine had been sympathetic. "I understand how you feel and it's quite normal. You have strong maternal instincts but it's perfectly reasonable to worry that you might not do right by the child if you're a single parent. You really shouldn't feel guilty about your sense of relief, Sophie. That's exactly how someone in your position would feel."

I nodded gratefully. Afterwards I wondered why he didn't call me Miss Marks as he had done previously. Perhaps if I didn't cry in the office, he wouldn't get so paternal. But at this session, he did make me feel better. We talked for a while about my feelings and I realized that just talking to Kisselstine had a calming, soothing effect on me and I was almost sorry when he told me the session was concluded. I was getting used to him.

As I write this entry, draining the last drop of Carla's care package, I'm thinking that Kisselstine is like your very first taste of beer. Ugh. You think it's not something you're going to like, but somehow, after a while, when you're watching football with your significant other, nestled on the couch on a sleepy Sunday afternoon, the beer tastes quite good.

Dr. Robert Kisselstine…my very own Bud Light.

# July 30th

"Tell me what Renny was like. Whatever comes to mind." Kisselstine steepled his fingers and waited patiently for my reply.

Good question, but it wasn't easy to answer. How do I describe a complicated man like Renny? "Well, he's quite interesting. And he can be very challenging—oh, but not in a terrible way. He has such a retentive mind that I always felt I had to work hard to keep up with him, but I found that kind of exciting. Dr. K, What's that expression about not suffering fools gladly? That would be Renny." I suddenly realized that I had to choose my words carefully or I'd make him seem less likeable than he was. "I think that he's very witty, although I would never call him funny. Do you understand what I mean?"

"Yes, I think I do."

"He kept me on my toes—but it was stimulating. He wasn't exactly a romantic man, although every once in a while he made a gesture or said something really nice..." Then I blurted out, "And he's good-looking." After I said that, I had a flash of embarrassment because Kisselstine is such a bland, plain looking fellow with his plastered hair and thick glasses and his fifty shades of beige wardrobe. I wondered if I'd hurt his feelings, but I couldn't tell because his default expression is always neutral. However, I surely will delete that sentence in the journal entry that I forward to him. Yes, I'm keeping two sets of books. I'll edit for Dr. K so that he won't get to read my musings about his nondescript persona.

"So, this interesting man who kept you on your toes and was a bit challenging and not a romantic was the one you wanted to spend the rest of your life with? Is that right?"

"Wait a minute! You're twisting my words."

15

"Well, then, let me rephrase that. You believed Renny was the one whom you wanted to spend the rest of your life with?"

"Yes."

"Sophie, last session, you asked me to help you because you didn't want to be "Someday Sophie" anymore. Well, I think the first step is to figure out *why* you convinced yourself that he was right for you and would eventually marry you. Did you ever consider that perhaps—perhaps—this no-strings relationship was something that *you* wanted?"

"What I wanted? I wanted to be married and have a child someday." Wasn't that obvious?

"In your three years together, did he ever give you a clue that he was evolving? Looking more favorably on a permanent relationship?"

"Well, not exactly. But it could have happened. I mean, that's the kind of thing that develops organically, as time goes on, right?"

"Let's try another tack. Do you know if he's ever had other long term relationships since his divorce so many years ago?"

"I see what you're getting at and the answer is Renny didn't stay in relationships very long. But, ours was different because it was three years, much longer than the others. I really believed he was getting ready to settle down. Someday soon."

Kisselstine pondered my response for a while and then said, very gently, "Sounds like *Someday Sophie* was a bit of a dreamer who was fairly content with the status quo."

"I have to disagree," I answered crisply. "I think you're mistaken."

"Of course, feel free to disagree. We're just exploring different possibilities right now and I value your input. I respect your point of view."

I was placated. Sort of.

"Sophie, did *you* have a long term relationship before you met Renny?"

"Oh, I've dated on and off, but I've had only one other long term relationship, actually. When I was about twenty-four, I dated a really sweet man for about three years."

"Tell me about him."

"Well, David was very nice, very caring and really attentive. He was about thirty-two years old when we first started dating and he'd gone through a difficult divorce that was financially disastrous for him. When we first met, his daughter was five and his son was seven and they were not handling the divorce well and, frankly, they were quite territorial about their father. The kids were extremely challenging and played one parent against the other, so David could be anxious and stressed at times. He'd been divorced for three years when we started dating and he still wasn't able to establish a working relationship with his hostile ex-wife—even though *she* was the one who'd initiated the divorce and she had a boyfriend. I felt so sorry for him because he was really a good person who was trying very hard."

"How did that relationship end?"

I sighed. "I was the one who ended it. David often had problems to solve and at times, it was exhausting for me. And as much as I cared for him, I knew that it would be years before he would have a healthy separation from the kids. Sometimes, I felt as if *we* were in therapy together, with me being the therapist and him being the patient." I wagged a finger at Kisselstine. "I was doing your job and let me tell you it wasn't easy."

He smiled. "I've heard that before. I understand where you're coming from."

"You know, Dr. K, I think mine is a classic New York story. We single women who don't marry young, say when we just get out of college, eventually find that the pool of eligible prospects consists primarily of divorced men who have so much baggage that it just weighs on our relationship. I guess that's what happened with David and me. "

"He asked you to marry him?"

"We hadn't exactly gotten to that point yet…but, he did say he loved me," I answered defensively. How could I explain that David was needy and wanted me in his life for support, encouraging me to bond with his kids—but was unable to look beyond his immediate situation: paying out too much of his salary for alimony and child support, dealing with demanding kids and worrying about what his vindictive ex-wife would think up next to make him more miserable. I explained to Kisselstine, "While I was dating David, he was in no position to think about another marriage."

Kisselstine nodded his head, apparently in agreement. "So, at what point did *you* come to that conclusion?"

I had to be honest. "Probably about a year into our relationship, I would say."

"And yet, you stayed with him for two more years." Dr. K waited for me to respond, but I had to think about my answer. We sat in silence for a while and then I explained, "Look, Dr. K, we had our good moments, on and off. I guess I figured someday, those problems would fade away."

"Let's see if I can sum up what you've told me. You realized after a year that the relationship would not lead to marriage in, shall we say the near or even distant future; you were convinced it would be years before he would be free of his financial and family issues. Yet you continued to date him for two more years because things *might* work out. I sense some confusion here. Do you?"

"Really, Dr. K," I admitted, "now I don't know what to think."

Kisselstine was silent for a while and then changed the subject. "So, when you met Renny, it must have been a relief to be with someone who had no ties, no encumbrances; someone, I imagine, who required just a contained emotional response from you."

"Why, yes," I replied, surprised that he'd made that connection—and surprised that I found it to be true.

"So let's see what we are working with now," said Kisselstine. "You've had two long term relationships—with David and then with Renny—that practically from the beginning led you to think that they might not lead to marriage and yet you stayed with these partners. If I understand you correctly, you were thinking that someday, things might change, although you had meaningful clues that they would not." He paused to let this words sink in and then he continued in a kindly manner. "Sophie, it appears you were comfortable with the status quo." He paused again. "Something to think about."

What was definitely *not* comfortable was that he waited for a response and I just sat there, unsure of myself. This therapy session had me bewildered.

"Sophie, today I learned a great deal about you. Is it too soon to ask you what you learned in today's session?"

"Is this a test?" I felt cornered.

"No, of course not, Sophie, I didn't mean to rush you." He closed his notebook, the signal that my session was over, and he offered a conciliatory smile.

I wouldn't give him the satisfaction of a smile in return, but as I walked home, I did find myself thinking about what had transpired in that office. Why did I stay with David when I realized he was in no position to get married...for years? Why was I satisfied with that? As for Renny Chapman, I have to admit that he did have virtues that appealed to me, beyond his intellect and his wit: his emotional independence and total self-reliance. Kisselstine was right. Renny required no maintenance on my part—except for the home-cooked meals which he enjoyed and which made me pleased because…well, because I liked to cook and I guess I was happy that I made him happy.

So, was I using "someday" to mask my real feelings? Could it be that I, myself, didn't want to make a commitment? Well, I'm not buying into that theory just yet. Perhaps I was waiting for the right moment; perhaps I was confident that things would change; or, perhaps I'm just a dreamer, after all. Honestly, I'd like to believe that I'm as normal as the next single girl who's thirty-three and hears the clock ticking. Damn, I wish Dr. K hadn't put those ideas into my head. He must be wrong—because if he's right—then I'm deliberately involving myself with men who are not marriage material. This is an unexpected development.

Damn, I went to Kisselstine for grief counseling—for help in dealing with loss—and now, *he's* the one giving *me* grief.

# August 3ʳᵈ

*I*t's probably of no importance whatsoever but today Kisselstine wore a white shirt instead of his usual beige. That certainly perked him up. It made me wonder if his wife laid out his clothing every night, deciding whether it would be the taupe or the beige shirt that would be paired with the brown tweed or beige khaki pants—as if there were much of a discernible difference. There aren't too many options when your clothing style is *medium*. Why was I so fixated on that damn shirt? Probably because I was going to tell him details about Sarah/Sherri for the first time and I wanted to have the comfort of Dr. K looking exactly like Dr. K. No substitutions.

After two weeks of avoiding Sarah/Sherri on the telephone, just carrying on a casual email correspondence—I really had to take her call. Make that Sherri with an "i," I'd said to Kisselstine. "Actually her real name is Sarah, which worked for her for about fifty-two years. Oh, Dr. K, also write down that she's my mother."

I told him that my parents were married for thirty years and had operated an upholstery shop in Brooklyn. Dad passed a little more than three years ago, I said—and I actually did so without getting weepy. Recently, I had turned a corner when it came to talking about my father. I had gone from full-scale sobbing when he first died to simply tearing up (it took quite a while to get to that point) and lately just having a catch in my voice when I talk about him. God, I missed that man. But my mother had moved on. Moved on at a gallop.

Kisselstine seemed to lean forward slightly, indicating heightened interest. Good move, Dr. K, because this one's for you. I told him that after my father died, Sarah, my mother, sold the store, let her hair grow longer and dyed it Marilyn Monroe blonde, lost about twenty pounds, dressed provocatively and changed her name to Sherri with an "i." "Frankly," I confessed, "in these last three years, I often had to remind myself that she was the same woman who'd brought me up."

I told Kisselstine that Sarah/Sherri went trolling on the internet and met various prospects, but about a year ago, she found Edgardo, an émigré from Cuba—sort of a poor man's Antonio Banderas: a little heavier and a little older, but still a sexy dude with enough Latin charm to flutter my mother's heart. Yes, Sherri is, shall I say, *satisfied,* but it is probably costing her.

"So, do you object to her using the internet to find partners or do you just object to Edgardo?"

I thought for a while. "Well, a little bit of both. I mean, anyone can turn up without being properly vetted. If you were getting a puppy and you went to a breeder, you'd know more about the dog's provenance than any random inter-net guy—like Edgardo."

"Tell me about him."

"Ah, the pseudo Antonio clone. He's a bit smooth and I think he's a taker. He moved in with my mother and plans weekend getaways, gets theater tick-ets and makes dinner reservations and I'm afraid that all that might come out of her pocketbook. Dr. K, my parents lived in a lovely apartment in Brooklyn Heights that they'd owned for years. When they went into the city—you know, that's what outer borough people say when they're going into Manhattan—they always took the train. Not Edgardo. I don't think he's touched a Metro card since he's moved in with her. What would my father think if he knew what his Sarah was doing?"

I felt upset just talking about it. "Oh, by the way, I have to call her *Sherri* now that she's reinvented herself. She probably thinks that makes her look even younger than the Victoria's Secret push-up bra she's wearing for Edgardo." I know, I know—I sounded mean-spirited, even bitter, but the words just tumbled out.

Kisselstine leaned forward. "Perhaps, for some reason, you're feeling some-what... jealous?

He spoke gently but his words stung. Whatever happened to psychologists who just sat there and nodded their heads thoughtfully while scribbling their notes? Haven't I heard that tired old joke that they're probably writing their grocery lists while the patient prattles on? But in my heart, I know he was actively listening to me as he hunched over his notepad.

"I don't think I'm resentful," I replied slowly, weighing that possibility seriously. "Just worried. She wasn't this...this sexpot with my father."

"So," said Kisselstine, "you feel this is somewhat of an affront to your father?"

"I guess so. Yes. Everything's turned upside down and that makes me really upset."

"Sophie, let's consider this: if one partner passes away, does the surviving spouse have a right to find happiness with a new partner?"

Of course, I was supposed to say *yes*. It was a leading question and that was the obvious answer. However, I chose to remain silent. But Dr. K didn't push me any further. Instead, he said, "Let's talk about your mother's financial situation." I told him that all those years when she had been Sarah, she had been careful with money. Actually, my father had seen to that. They both were very watchful spenders, saving money for my college education and my wedding. Well, there's money to burn right there, considering I'm thirty-three and no closer to a wedding gown than when I was in kindergarten.

"I can see why you're troubled because money is a major concern. But, I also see that your mother is enjoying a rebirth of sorts. That must be exhilarating at—remind me of her age."

"Fifty-five."

"She's still young, Sophie and she has the same needs that you have: finding someone to love, making a life-long connection and experiencing intimacy. Sometimes that's hard for a daughter to accept because it seems like a betrayal of her parents' marriage. You might not like your mother's choices, but you need to find a way to accept the fact that she's happy."

"I'll tell you what's making her happy right now. She and Edgardo are taking tango lessons and they are very serious about it. I went to one recital and I can't believe what I saw. Believe me, dancing the tango is like making love on wheels. Dr. K, maybe this passionate affair has overwhelmed her and she doesn't realize that she's spending her money foolishly." I did want my mother to be happy, but she and my father had worked so hard for their money and I didn't want this whirlwind affair to ruin her financially.

"I see you have two concerns," said Kisselstine. "One is that your mother is involved in a relationship that makes you uncomfortable. Secondly, you're worried about her finances. Let's deal with that one first."

We sat in silence for a few minutes. I wasn't sure about what I could do, but I wasn't worried because I was fairly certain that Kisselstine had a proposal in mind. I was correct.

"Instead of directly confronting your mother about financial issues, why not take a more neutral position. Ask her if she's made financial plans for the future; perhaps ask her about long-term health care. Show your honest concern and then suggest a certified financial planner. He or she could examine your mother's finances and recommend any changes that would be beneficial. A planner may even work with her to develop a budget to help her conserve resources. This would take you out of the equation and would rein in Edgardo, if that were necessary. I can make some recommendations if you can't find someone on your own."

That sounded like a proposal that might work.

"Sophie," he continued, "We don't know the exact situation with your mother and Edgardo. It's entirely possible he'd come with her to the meeting with the financial planner. But, I'm certain a professional would not let him sit in on such a conference because the advisor has a fiduciary responsibility to his client that would not include her boyfriend. That would protect your mother."

No doubt Kisselstine was right. A third party, someone impartial, could lead Sarah/Sherri in the right direction.

Dr. K moved on. "Sophie, have you told your mother about the miscarriage?"

I told him that I got as far as telling her that Renny and I were no longer a couple. I didn't say anything about a baby. Not yet. Probably never. And she was predictable.

"So, Mr. Wall Street bailed out on you. I always told you he would disappear... whenever! Why? Because he's selfish!" She shook her head. "It was all about him."

I'd assumed, correctly, that sooner or later in the conversation "I told you so" would show up. "Mom/Sherri, we had three good years together," I protested, all the while knowing that my shrink had managed to suggest flaws in that assessment.

"Sweetie, not so good. You always were on pins and needles with that man. Let's see, you were never sure if you were going to meet after work or when a conference out of town would turn up and he'd have to change his plans. On for the weekend and then off. It's a wonder you weren't dizzy all the time." She nodded her head, sagely. "A mother knows."

Of course, I have to admit that this wise woman had told me from the beginning that he'd never marry me. So did Carla. Natalie had also weighed in: "He's a player, kiddo. There's no future with him, although he's lasted longer than I ever thought he would."

My mother threw up her hands in frustration. "Because, Sophie, he had it all. The money, for sure, the nice looks, definitely the ambition and what else did he have? He had *you*, a patient girlfriend who never set him straight. So, tell me, did you ever let him know *you* wanted to get married?"

"Not exactly." A few seconds later, I admitted, "Well, no, actually. I didn't bring up the subject of marriage. I guess I was waiting for the time to be right." I didn't tell her that according to my shrink, I was actually content with the present and was drifting into the future, comfortable that my arrangement with Renny did not include marriage. Imagine if I shared Kisselstine's disturbing theory with her.

When I told Sarah/Sherri that I'd never talked about marriage to Renny, she shook her head, clearly frustrated. "I couldn't believe how satisfied you were with your arrangement. And I know, for sure, that man never wanted children. The few times we were all together for a holiday and Natalie and the kids were there, he ignored them. No, he *disliked* them." She couldn't hold back—not where *her* future unborn grandchildren were concerned.

"Well, I always thought that someday...." I trailed off. I could hardly explain what was going on. I'm just barely getting a grip on it myself.

My mother softened. "It's probably for the best, sweetie. He wouldn't have made a very good husband and maybe this is a good thing." She patted my hand and thought for a moment and then her anger got the best of her. "He wasn't such a friendly person, you should know. Did he care about family? No! Your friends? No! Always busy with the hiking, the kayaking, the traipsing in the woods, whatever. But being with your people? No! Money, he had, but did he take you out for a nice dinner? Not if he could get you to cook for him." She stopped to catch her breath and regroup. Then she surprised me with a smile and a totally new train of thought. "Well, now, you have a chance to meet some-one who'll be Mr. Right. So, it's a good thing."

I told Kisselstine that when she kissed me good-bye she'd exclaimed, "Don't worry, your mother is on the case!" That gave me my first good laugh in a long time. "Dr. K, when she said that, I had a mental picture of Sarah/Sherri in a Sherlock Holmes' stalker hat, wielding an oversized magnifying glass, on the prowl for an eligible Manhattan man who desperately wanted a wife, who adored kids and had enough money for a down payment on a two-bedroom condo."

"That's a very amusing picture," he responded. "You have an interesting mother."

"Dr. K, how come she could see it and I couldn't? And why was it also so obvious to Natalie and Carla—and not me? Renny would never have wanted a child."

Kisselstine said very quietly, "You didn't want to see it, Sophie." He closed his notebook. Session over. I walked out of the office into the bright August sunshine wondering why I was in the dark about so many things.

# August 8ᵗʰ

*I* was feeling terrible about not being honest with Sarah/Sherri and telling her the truth about my pregnancy and miscarriage. But, I couldn't risk the possibility of more worldly wisdom from Sherri with an "i" that highlighted my limitations in choosing proper boyfriends. So, I'd gradually come to the conclusion that I'd never tell her about the baby I'd miscarried. Even if she didn't reproach me about Renny, even if she were sympathetic and understanding, which she probably would be when she realized how miserable *I* was, there was no point in having her feel as unhappy as I did.

Weeks after I'd lost the baby, Renny checked in on me with a call instead of the few vague texts he'd sent my way. "I feel bad about all this," he murmured into the phone. I surmised that *all this* was a generality that relieved him of specifics. Was he sorry I lost the baby? Sorry I had an emotional and medical ordeal? Sorry he was not supportive in any way? Unfortunately, he was offering a noncommittal statement that didn't mean much at all. Probably he was most sorry that he had to make the call.

As far as I was concerned, he had chosen the path of avoidance, and in doing so, made everything worse. The bottom line was that I had been his *good-time* girlfriend. But *not so good* when I became an obligation. I knew he couldn't wait to close our awkward phone conversation.

He ended our brief conversation saying, "Take care of yourself, Sophie. I'll be in Chicago for a week with the Telfax merger and then I'll give you a call when I get back to see how you're doing." I was certain those were polite but parting words. I doubted he would get in touch; I had penetrated his safety zone and he was definitely in the process of repair and retreat.

I didn't need Sarah/Sherri to tell me this was it, over and out. I was alone. On my own. I felt so downhearted that I called Kisselstine for an appointment. I showed him the message that Renny had texted me after our telephone conversation. "Sophie, you're a wonderful woman. I'm just not the right person for you, as you probably have figured out by now. I'll always care for you. Renny."

Dr. K scanned it and then looked up at me. "He does express affection for you and it sounds sincere. However, texting you, but not speaking to you directly and basically avoiding you for weeks…" Kisselstine didn't need to finish the sentence. I got the idea. "So, what do you think?" Kisselstine asked in his most neutral voice.

"Are you implying I'm lucky to be rid of him?"

"Well, that's for you to decide. I'm saying that he behaved badly at a time when you needed him. He scores very low in the marriage and children department. And, he's responsible for a great deal of pain."

We sat in silence for a few minutes. I was kind of relieved that Kisselstine acknowledged my distress and didn't try to minimize it. Carla and Natalie have avoided talking about my loss. Instead, they've touted the positive: how lucky I was to be free to find someone who would be right for me.

Kisselstine inquired, with a hint of a smile on his face, "I was wondering if you have given any thought to what Renny might have presumed from your "Custer's Last Stand" proposal? I believe that's what you called your offer to bring up the baby with or without his input as a parent. You told him he didn't even have to be on the birth certificate and that you would be willing to bring up the baby on your own and basically, not see him anymore. Correct?"

"Correct." I wondered where was this going.

"Well," said Kisselstine, "I think that your offer sent an implicit message: you wanted the child more than you wanted *him*. Think about it, Sophie. Although he handled the situation quite badly, he, too, had to deal with rejection issues. You were telling him he was expendable."

"Oh! Should I blame myself for Renny abandoning me?"

"Not at all," he said calmly. "No blame here—just awareness on your part. I'm asking you to consider the possibility that he realized you were willing to abandon *him* in order to have a child. That indicated what was most important to you. It doesn't excuse his behavior, but it can add a new depth to your thinking because it also says something about *you*."

Sometimes Kisselstine made my head spin. Fortunately, at that point, he changed the subject. "I know you're unhappy right now, so we should talk about what you can do to feel better. This is a good time to consider something new. Perhaps a painting class? Ceramics? Volunteer work? I think you've been through a lot and need a distraction." He saw the sour expression on my face and stopped.

"Okay, scratch that. Well, what about dating? If your friends can't fix you up, perhaps you can go online and test it out." He smiled encouragingly. "It worked for your mother."

"I'm more particular," I said acidly.

He took a deep breath and frowned. "I'm sorry, Sophie, I shouldn't have made those suggestions. I apologize. I mean, I shouldn't be telling you to take painting or ceramics or start dating again. Those are good outlets, of course, but that's not what should be happening in this office. I'd rather say to you that I understand how you feel and I know that your unhappy feelings will persist for a while, but I also know that you are a grounded person and you'll find yourself feeling better as we sort things out. And time is the great healer that works side by side with therapy."

I couldn't contain my surprise. "Are you telling me *you* just made a therapy mistake— talking about ceramics and dating, things like that?"

He nodded his head. "Yes, yes I am."

He paused and then spoke in a casual voice, as if we were having an ordinary conversation and he wasn't my shrink. "I had a mentor in Chicago, a Dr. Allen Wilkerson, who said that the major difference between the psychologist and the patient is that *we* have the key to the room. It means we're only human, after all, and we should recognize when we're heading in the wrong direction."

Actually, his telling me to get back in the dating game was exactly what Carla had said last night when we met for dinner at the trendy Standard Hotel. She, too, wanted me to get back into the game and go online because she thought it would be therapeutic. Then she said, "Look around. There's plenty of material right here."

Had I gone to the Standard because it's such a happening place and there were definitely single men in arm's reach? Was I was subconsciously looking for a man? I don't think so. I'm just so angry with the species: they're unreliable and emotionally unavailable. Especially men in finance.

I had scanned the various specimens of manhood at the bar and I'd wondered which one of these perfect strangers could be the potential father of my children. I came up empty.

Dr. K surprised me with a question. "Would you take Renny back if he said he was sorry?"

"Absolutely not!" I said firmly.

But in my heart I wondered if I would weaken when I became tired of being on my own. After all, I hadn't been alone in a long time. Three years. Then I remembered that I wasn't exactly alone; I had Kisselstine now. Although he had the capacity to both help me and upset me—all in one session—I truly believe that ultimately, I will benefit from his therapeutic approach. The man made me reflect; the journal made me evaluate.

I believe Kisselstine will put me on the right track and will fortify me in a few more sessions. Then, I will re-enter the dating arena as one tough chick. So, look out, single males of Manhattan, because the new and improved Sophie Marks will soon be coming to a neighborhood near you!

As Kisselstine closed his notebook, I smiled at him, my first smile of the session. "Thanks, Dr. K. See you soon." I guess I made him happy, because he brightened considerably and allowed a small smile in return.

I'm sure he had no idea of what was going on in my mind. I was thinking that he was in the rescue business and sooner or I'd catch his lifeline.

# August 10th

Writing a journal definitely has a positive effect. I feel as if I'm putting the pieces of a puzzle together. I might not know how everything fits, at first, but I have hope that they will fall into place, eventually. As Dr. K suggested, I'm writing without over-thinking and I'm sending him my entries with fewer edits. He's a big boy; he can take it.

It's a strange phenomenon: when I'm sitting in his office, I talk to Kisselstine directly. When I'm sitting at the computer, I talk *about* him as if he's someone who will never read the journal entry. It appears that if I acknowledge him in the journal as *you*, I just can't write openly and honestly. So the *you* becomes a *he* and I am liberated. Clearly, the act of baring my innermost thoughts, both good and bad, requires some deft literary calisthenics and I have perfected certain verbal cartwheels in my journal.

That explains this entry. Tonight, Carla and I met at Charlie T's after work; it's a downtown bar where the drinks are reasonable, the burgers are great and the music's not too loud. What's more, it draws a crowd of Manhattanites who are upwardly mobile and mature enough not to be carded.

Carla was planning a birthday celebration dinner for Jake who, amazingly, had not yet gone back to his wife. He was staying with his married brother in the Bronx, but was planning to move into Carla's place within the month. She was in the process of dedicating *one* of her four closets to Jake and was making frequent trips to Goodwill in order to purge her wardrobe of items she was willing to part with—a true sign of devotion I'd told her. "Don't give me too much credit, Sophie," she said, rolling her eyes. "I'm not exactly ridding myself of great stuff in order to accommodate the man I love. Truth is, I'm getting rid of my size twelves because I'll never fit into them again."

"Well, you still deserve praise because you're not forcing him to live out of a suitcase, which was another possibility. Anyway, tell me about the birthday extravaganza."

"I'm having you, my friend Diane from the office—you'll love her—and Natalie and Warren. That's six of us. It will be just right for conversation while I'm messing in the kitchen."

"Oh, you're actually cooking?" Carla, whose collection of take-out menus filled an entire drawer, customarily avoided the trappings of the kitchen. That would be the oven, pots and pans, measuring spoons, whatever.

She shot me a look. "I'll be in the kitchen doing what I do best—unwrapping and reheating."

I had to laugh. Carla loved to eat but had no interest in cooking. "Let's get serious," I insisted. "Jake doesn't know any of us. Face it, Carla, I've only been with him a few times because we both know he didn't care for Renny, so we're virtually strangers. Why are you subjecting him to a dinner with people he doesn't know? And none of us have met Diane."

"Oh, everyone will like her," Carla said confidently. "You know, I used to think it was her long blonde hair and glamorous vibe that got her all the listings, but I have to admit she's a very good realtor—and I've learned a lot from her. She'll be good at keeping the conversation going."

"I'm still mystified. Why not have an intimate dinner for just you and Jake?"

"Sophie, I need to integrate him into my life after all this time and this is a good excuse. He needs to make connections with my people. Natalie and Warren have been married for nine years and they kind of represent the ideal— you know, a happy couple who both had bad first marriages, so they're kind of role models for Jake."

"I do hope that's not too subliminal for Jake to get the message."

Carla ignored me. "Diane is in real estate—and Jake works with mortgages— so that'll be a conversation starter. Sophie, you're my best friend and you need to know him and he needs to know you."

What could I say? I had a feeling this dinner would not be a good idea because Jake might want to be with *his* friends when he celebrated his birthday, but Carla was so enthusiastic about the plan that I had to put aside my doubts.

I ate my burger while she went over the details. When I looked up, maybe four tables away, sitting at an angle to me so I could just barely see his profile, I suddenly thought I recognized Kisselstine. Or some stranger who mysteriously looked *almost* like my shrink.

"Don't move. I'll be right back."

Yes. It was him. I don't know why I lost it, but I went to his table and stood right in front of him and blurted out, "I can't believe you're wearing a black shirt." I took a sharp breath. "And black slacks." If I'd seen him in a wife-beater, I couldn't have been more surprised. Even his hair looked different— still parted on the side but softer, unplastered, wavy—and no glasses. He had blue eyes. It was unnerving: Kisselstine in real life.

"What are you doing here?" I demanded. Kisselstine, my "medium" shrink who had no distinguishing characteristics and who was supposed to be dressed in beige and taupe and who wore thick-lensed black-framed glasses. In a bar?

"I'm waiting for a friend."

I sat down, unbidden. "What about your wife?"

He was surprised. "There is no wife." Concerned, he wrinkled his fore-head. "I never suggested I had a wife, did I?"

I ignored the question because I had no answer. I'd just assumed.

"Well, I can't believe you go to a bar. I mean, I just can't believe it." I sounded foolish, I know, but I couldn't help it. Regular persons go to bars—not shrinks.

But he was kind. "Look, Sophie, I understand your confusion. After all, when we see each other in the office, I learn a great deal about you and your life, but you really don't know anything about me." He paused to gauge my reaction. "I sometimes meet my clients outside the office and when I do, they're often disconcerted."

"Are you here looking for women? Because I am not, repeat not, looking for a man. I'm here with Carla, just talking." Holy crap, if only somebody had a hook to pull me offstage. But Kisselstine was unperturbed.

"Same as you, Sophie. I'll be catching up with one of my colleagues. Now, tell me—the problem with the black shirt?"

Just then a good-looking man walked over to our table. "Sorry I'm late, Rob." He turned to me with a smile. "And with whom do I have the pleasure?" he said, extending his hand. Before I could speak, Kisselstine said, "James, this is Sophie."

I appreciated the fact that he didn't say I was a client. Good Hipaa behavior, Dr. K. You have protected my privacy in accordance with the regulations of the United States government.

James was still holding my outstretched hand. "Delighted to meet you," he said enthusiastically. "I hope you'll be joining us for a drink? I see my friend here," he gestured toward Kisselstine, "has started without me."

Before I had a chance to reply, Kisselstine spoke up. "Actually, James, Sophie was just leaving. She's with a friend." He motioned in Carla's direction. So, he had seen me. I gave him credit for not slipping away unnoticed, for standing his ground even though it was awkward. What am I thinking? It was just awkward for *me*. Kisselstine was cool and composed, as usual. I managed a tight smile as I waved goodbye in what I hoped was a blasé manner.

At the table, I told Carla, "That's my shrink."

"Uh oh. Not quite what you described."

"What do you mean?"

"Well, he's good-looking, for one thing."

"For heaven's sake, Carla, he's my shrink." I wanted to tell her that he *really* didn't look like that—but I knew that would've sounded absurd.

My beer had gone flat and so had the evening. I wondered how I could face Dr. K in the office, now that he was not just Dr. K. It was as if your gynecologist turned into an actual person, a *man*. He wears a starched white lab coat with his name embroidered on the patch pocket and he has a stethoscope around his neck that automatically gives him credibility and helps to neuter him—meaning his MD credentials override his masculine gender. And when he slides that chilly speculum inside you, you remind yourself that he's a doctor and what he is seeing is simply a body part, no different than an eye or an ear and his interest is totally clinical. That's what you want to believe. Footnote: any sane woman who believes her vagina has no more significance than an eye or an ear is actually *not* any sane woman.

Anyway, what I've come to expect of Dr. K is this: a totally professional, gender-neutral and non-masculine health care provider. Frankly, the best way to share your fears and admit your foolishness in a therapy situation is to have a totally neutered person seated opposite you.

Screw it, then he shows up in a bar wearing a black shirt and blows his cover.

# August 14th

After Carla's dinner for six, I really needed a therapy session. Although it was August and psychologists were supposed to be on vacation, my shrink blazed a trail of individualism. Okay, so I exaggerate. The point is that he had taken his vacation the first two weeks in July, so he was available to take care of any client meltdowns that happened to occur in August. *Like mine.*

I had to tell Dr. K about Carla's dinner—the dinner that was supposed to introduce Jake to the pleasures of her friends and the joys of marriage. Second marriage, that is, and not the unhappy first one that led to his five-year affair with my love-struck friend.

I told Kisselstine that for a couple of hours it had actually been a pleasant dinner party with easy conversation, punctuated by Natalie's ability to make her kids' antics seem like a *Saturday Night Live* sketch and by Warren's storehouse of off-color jokes. Then, later in the evening, we were sitting around the table nursing cappuccinos from Carla's fancy new machine, her two hundred dollar investment that she believed was going to be repaid with a walk down the aisle.

Natalie had just finished the comical tale of her little Alice's toilet training odyssey, which involved her setting her potty right in front of Natalie—and using it enthusiastically, not only clapping her hands with gusto but also insisting that her mother join in the applause. And then, the hilarious part: the child would burst into tears and have a major tantrum, screaming "mine, mine" when it's contents disappeared as Natalie flushed the toilet. "Evidently," Natalie observed, "my youngest has the makings of a hoarder."

We all laughed. I privately wondered if Jake was enjoying this chitchat, considering his own daughter was now eighteen and way past toilet training. But Jake chuckled and seemed comfortable, so I assumed Carla's plan was working.

Natalie's story encouraged Diane (who really was as glamorous as Carla had indicated) to talk about her five year-old niece who was quite a grown-up. Little Emma insisted on choosing her clothes every day, mixing polka dots, stripes, plaids and jungle prints, even non-matching socks, with abandon. Diane was proud of her amazing sister who went along with her daughter's outrageous choices in order to nurture her independence. All the women present agreed that our more old-fashioned mothers would never have put up with this creativity.

Then, something Diane said caught my attention. "My sister has a new boy-friend who's just crazy about her little one. You wouldn't think a Type A Wall Street guy who's a big shot at Headley Capital would turn into jelly over a little kid, but it's true. When Maya finalized her divorce two years ago, I thought she'd struggle, you know, having a child and dating, but she got lucky. This guy's a keeper."

Carla looked at me and shook her head, almost imperceptibly. I got the message. She wanted to handle this, probably because she knew I had stopped breathing. Don't be ridiculous, Sophie, I scolded myself; Headley Capital is overrun with Type A guys. It couldn't possibly be my Renny she was talking about.

But it was Natalie who rushed in with a warm smile and a question. "He must have children himself, right? That would make him appreciate your sister's little one." Very smooth, that Natalie.

"Oh no, not at all." said Diane, "He's quite the bachelor. Renny's thirty-six and doesn't have children. He had an early disastrous marriage fresh out of col-lege and I understand he's just gone through a very unpleasant break-up. From what Maya has told me, she thinks he's ready for marriage and the icing on the cake is that he just adores little Emma." Diane laughed. "Of course, he adores my sister, too."

I felt reckless. "Does she look like you? Your sister, I mean."

Diane wasn't fazed by my inappropriate question. "Well, we've been mis-taken for twins at times, but Maya's slightly taller and somewhat thinner than I am. Our brother always teased me by saying that she was the prettier one."

Since Diane was clearly model material, that would make her sister a shoo-in for the cover of the next *Sports Illustrated* swimsuit edition. I felt a rush of emotions—jealousy, disappointment, anger—all in the mix. Then, I had to remind myself that I didn't want Renny back in my life. But I did want him to want *our* baby and his rejection of our child was heartbreaking. And wouldn't it make me feel a little better if Renny was desperate to win me back?

Carla chimed in. "Is Maya in real estate as well?" Good to know, Carla, in case I want to check out a new high rise condo, I'll identify which agent to shove down the elevator shaft.

"Oh no, she's director of marketing for the Lincoln Hotel group."

At this point in the session, Kisselstine handed me a tissue box. He let me sniffle for a while because I found it difficult to continue. It was so painful to recount this because there was no easy way to understand a man who would turn away from his own flesh and blood, discard its future with a platinum American Express card, and then fall in love with another man's child.

"I know this is hard for you. Sophie, I'm so sorry." Dr. K spoke with such concern in his voice that I felt we really had a connection. I had to disregard the incident at Charlie T's because the man in the black shirt wasn't the *real* Kisselstine. I realized just then that this man in this office was the only person who knew what was really going on in my life and that's all that mattered.

"Sophie, Renny was with you for three years. That tells me he cared for you. You must know that. He'd never have been with you if you were not important to him."

"I guess."

Kisselstine continued, "But, when it was crunch time and he had to face the fact that you were expecting his child, he turned away. What does that tell you?"

"I'm not sure." Certainly, that was a better answer than "it told me I was road kill."

"Here's what I think. He was a successful, smart and attractive man and he fit your ideal of what a partner should be like. And you were his counterpart—also an attractive, successful woman who was very independent; a woman who didn't press for a long-term commitment, which seems to be exactly what made him happy. I'm convinced Renny did care for you. It was only when you wanted to raise the child that he terminated your relationship. He just couldn't handle that."

"Then why is he enamored with this woman's child?"

Kisselstine shrugged. "Perhaps he regrets his decision to encourage you to have an abortion. Perhaps he's trying fatherhood on for size. Perhaps he could connect to a flesh and blood child, rather than a shadow in the womb. Perhaps he'll turn away from this little girl; maybe it's only a matter of time before he admits to himself that he doesn't want to raise a child. Look, there could be any number of reasons for his behavior. Whatever they are, we may never know."

He paused and then said gently, "I know how painful this has been for you, Sophie.

And to be honest, I don't think either of us is in a position to understand Renny at this point. But, I am very sorry for your loss."

I don't know why, but his empathy made me feel better. I was grateful he'd acknowledged my hurt, that he didn't try to diminish it, that he didn't tell me to "snap out of it."

Carla and Natalie carefully avoid references to my miscarriage. I suppose they feel that not talking about it is best; perhaps they even believe that I am better off not being a single mother. So, it was a relief to hear Kisselstine validate my feelings.

After a few quiet moments, he continued. "At this point, we can't know what's in Renny's heart. But, do know something about your heart." He paused for a few seconds to let that thought sink in. "In our sessions, I've been trying to figure out why you were so patient, so undemanding with this man. You're now thirty-three years-old, so one would think you'd want to marry at this point, but according to you, you never pursued the issue. Why? Why was there no talk of marriage on your part? Three years is a long time for a woman your age."

*A woman of my age?* I suddenly had a mental image of a satisfying response to his nasty *age* comment: me striking him repeatedly with my trusty cane; or me careering into him with my walker on wheels. Then I felt bad; after all, he was just trying to help. Luckily, he couldn't read my mind. And luckily, I always edit my journal entries for him.

Kisselstine continued. "Sophie, we touched on this issue last session. Let me repeat: it seems to me that you—like Renny—wanted the comfort and the convenience of the relationship without the constraints of marriage. You wanted him in your life, but you really didn't want to get married to him." He paused. "I've given you time to think about it. Tell me, am I on the right track here?"

"Well, I have been thinking about your theory—and it just doesn't feel right. I'm sorry."

Kisselstine shook his head. "Three years, Sophie. That's a long time when you're thirty-three years-old. And from everything you've told me, it could have gone on even longer, if not for..." he paused, looking for the right words, "if not for the pregnancy."

Yes, *pregnancy* sounded less hurtful, less personal, than "baby." Once again, Kisselstine was harping on that unpleasant subject. "You're telling me that I subconsciously didn't want to marry him? Really, I've given it a lot of thought and I believe that I wanted a relationship that would lead to marriage."

He shook his head. "I think you were both content with each other and didn't have marriage as an objective. Sophie, I can't help thinking you were fine with things just as they were." He looked at me, anticipating a response but I was too uneasy to speak; I hoped that the woman he was describing wasn't me. He took my silence to indicate uncertainty, I guess, so he said very soothingly, "Don't worry, Sophie. I think we are going to figure this out, together."

I couldn't answer him; my emotions were like a pendulum that was shifting from confusion to frustration. In seconds, Kisselstine had altered the mood. I'd had to listen to his theory for two sessions now and I wanted to tell him that he was mistaken. I wanted to tell him that he had no right to repeat his unproven assumption. That's just not the way therapy is supposed to go. At least, my idea of therapy.

"Well," said Kisselstine, closing his notebook, "that's something to think about until our next session."

I walked out of the office with my head spinning. What thirty-three year-old female doesn't want to get married? Is he saying there's something wrong with me? No, there's nothing wrong with me! Of course, I'm normal and I want to get married. I was just dealing with a man who'd been burned, so I was biding my time. I admit that Kisselstine had me doubting myself for a while—but I've thought about it and now I'm damn sure he's absolutely wrong,

I should set him straight. Why does he always get the last word?

# *August 21ˢᵗ*

*I* didn't make another appointment with Kisselstine because I was too wounded after that last session. I really wanted to tell him he was way off base; I didn't think he could back up his unscientific views about my intentions regarding marriage. The more I thought about it, the angrier I became. What kind of shrink actually forms an opinion based on such flimsy evidence?

I couldn't confront him in the office because, let's face it, he has all the power and I am weak. He is the one who calmly makes notes in his little notebook and I am the one who is subject to tearing up and to bouts of uncertainty. And—I could never get in the last word. In therapy, we are separate *and* unequal.

So, I decided I'd see him on neutral territory. I'm not ashamed to say that for five evenings in a row I went back to Charlie T's in hopes of *accidentally* meeting him there. I didn't drink my way through this tracking adventure; I nursed one or two Chardonnays with a capacity for patience that I didn't know I possessed. I brought Carla along for the first two nights and my iPad for the next three because Carla gave up on the project. She had little tolerance for my scheme. "Sophie, just make an appointment and get whatever it is off your chest," she'd advised.

"Do you think I'm going to allow myself to be billed for therapy just to express my frustration? Screw it. I'm taking him down right here, in this bar, if he ever shows up."

He showed up on day five.

Once again, he had that off-duty look. It was more than the striped shirt with the RL logo, the wavy hair, and the absent eyeglasses. It was also about not assuming that buttoned-up posture that he had in the office. The man practically telescoped into his stiff therapist chair. But now, there he was, sitting up straight with his shoulders squared and his legs crossed and a casual lock of hair grazing his forehead and looking like…like what? Like a man I could find attractive if he weren't my shrink. WTF, I'm certainly going to edit that sentence. I don't know which one of us would be more embarrassed if he actually read that.

I had fantasized that our confrontation would look like a movie scene. Since I was the *auteur* of my own film, I decided I'd be actress Jennifer Lawrence, cool and steely, not likely to be intimidated by man or beast, let alone therapist. I'd walk over to his table and toss my wine in his face. He'd be shocked, speechless, as some of the guys at the bar spurred me on. I'd tell him exactly what I thought: "Your theory that I don't want to get married is garbage. Bottom line—you don't know me at all!" And then as I turned on my six-inch heels and made my dramatic exit, I'd hear the cheers of the bystanders. The only thing that was wrong with this picture (other than my non-resemblance to Jennifer Lawrence) was the six-inch heel part: four inches and I walked like a model; five inches and my ankles lost their will to live. And six inches! Only the real housewives of New Jersey could handle that.

Back to the wine tossing: it didn't happen; I'd already drained the second Chardonnay, so no dramatic Hollywood scene. And when he saw me, he came right to my table and sat down. "I was hoping you'd make another appointment because we have a lot to talk about. But, we can't do it here."

"Really? I feel much more comfortable right here. I have a lot to say to you!" Would Jennifer Lawrence have sounded as shrill? I was losing it.

"That would be very unprofessional and you know it. You're angry because I hit upon something you didn't like, but it may very well be true. Sophie, you came to me for help. Give me a chance to work things out with you."

"How could you suggest that subconsciously I didn't want to marry Renny? How could you?" I could see people at the next table turning their heads, surprised and curious. Regrettably, unlike my fantasy, nobody cheered me on.

He hesitated, took a deep breath and then said very softly and urgently so only I could hear, "Sophie, you asked Renny for help with the baby, right? Financial help. Don't you see what's missing? You never said anything to him about sharing a life together. That's what committed couples do when they're expecting a child together; the baby is often the catalyst for the marriage. True, some couples don't plan a wedding, but they do move in together to parent their child. Others, when they find out they're expecting, get engaged, leaving the wedding date up in the air. But, the point is: these couples get together to bring up the child. It's clear to me, if not to you, that regardless of Renny's intentions, *you* didn't suggest any of these alternatives. Not one."

He paused to let his words sink in and this time there was a bolt of lightning and I took the hit. He was right. I'd never even considered marriage with Renny. Never. Somehow what didn't make sense to me in the office seemed perfectly true at Charley T's.

Kisselstine sat there, waiting for a response, but I was too shaken to reply. Then he continued. "Look, I know *he* acted like a deer in the headlights—and took off for parts unknown because he clearly did not want a child—or a wife. But consider *your* response, Sophie. " He paused to see if I would reply, but I was silent. Then he recapped. "You didn't suggest *any* of those long term alternatives I just described. Your primary goal was to have that baby. In fact, you showed what I think is a surprising willingness to give him up entirely in exchange for financial support." Again, he waited for my reaction, but I held back. I sensed he was right but I hated to agree with him..

I think my silence encouraged him to speak with an intensity I'd never heard before. "Sophie, can't you see you were both safe with each other? Neither of you wanted to get married."

Who knew my "medium" shrink was capable of such emotion? He must have realized that he had lost his office cool, because he abruptly stood up and said in a neutral tone, "It's unprofessional for me to talk to you here. Please call my office and make an appointment." And with that, he walked away, leaving me with that last word—still unspoken. And now I don't know what the hell my last word should have been.

If Sarah/Sherri heard him say that I was *deliberately* avoiding marriage, she'd faint! But first, she'd take care of business, firing him for putting such vile, loathsome thoughts in my head. And now it was too late. Those thoughts were percolating in my brain, bubbling up to the surface, chiding me for not appreciating what was patently true.

I didn't want to be married.

# August 23rd

$\mathcal{I}$'m conceding that Dr. K is correct. This new insight—that I am reluctant to get married—is not particularly pleasant, but I'm not fighting it any longer. I don't know where this will lead, but I'm sure Kisselstine will point the way. He is the concertmaster; I'm just learning to play the melody and I have to admit it's a somewhat mournful tune. How that would distress Carla, for whom wedding bells are the only music worth playing

I never kept a diary as a youngster—not my style. But here I am, at thirty-three, propped up in bed against the pillows at the end of the day, balancing my laptop and writing whatever comes to mind. Writing about today.

Sarah/Sherri and I had lunch together. I had every intention of following through on Dr. K's suggestion and hooking her up with a financial counselor. Things went *almost* according to plan.

My mother: first of all, she shows up in a leather skirt, stilettos and a scoop-necked, clinging sweater. I was impressed. "Mom//Sherri, you look wonderful." Actually, she did. If she weren't my mother, I'd have been captivated by this fifty-five year old siren.

"Thank you, sweetie." She leaned across the table, bouncing cleavage in my direction. I averted my eyes. "Sophie, I've lost five pounds since Edgardo and I started taking tango lessons. Let me tell you, the weight just melts off." She looked at me shrewdly. "It seems to me that you've lost weight yourself. And you didn't have enough meat on your bones to begin with."

I've had some stresses, obviously, so I might have lost a few pounds. Or was she comparing our relative endowments? True confession here: I am a shallow C cup while Sarah/Sherri, with her Victoria's Secret push-up bra and her own God-given voluptuousness is definitely a double D. Is this too much information for Kisselstine? Will this be awkward for him? Of course not: he's a doctor. Well, not a *doctor doctor* as Grandma used to say, drawing a distinction between the physician who had the desirable *M.D.* after his name and the practitioner who had the *Ph.D.* after his. The first one was a Jewish prince and the second? Well...he was surely worthy, but if he didn't wear a stethoscope around his neck, he could never be in line for the throne.

After commenting on my weight loss, Sarah/Sherri brightened. "But, my little girl, you've got your father's good curly hair and you take after him with your height. That tall gene, you got it from him, thank God."

That made me smile. My mother is a diminutive five feet and since I've been thirteen years-old, I've been taller than she is. My growth spurt that led me to be 5'6" in my freshman year of high school also ended in my freshman year—so I remain 5'6". And my father, who passed on that so-called *tall gene* to me, was 5'7."

"So tell me, what's new in your life?"

I knew what that meant. "Mom/Sherri, I'm not seeing anyone. Look, I'm all right with that. I think I need a dating time-out for a while. Seriously." I meant it.

"So listen up. Edgardo has a nephew who's single," she said eagerly, as if I'd never mentioned the dating freeze. "He moved here from Miami, about sixteen months ago and he's just opened a little restaurant and it's doing very well. Believe me, I've eaten there and it's to die for. Edgardo and I want you to meet him."

"Mom/ Sherri, fish tacos are not my thing."

"Don't be such a smarty-pants." She thought for a minute. "You know, I don't even think fish tacos are on the menu. Should I mention it? Tacos are so big now. Anyway, he's a nice boy and you'll like him. He's smart."

I couldn't help myself. I had to ask. "How old is this *boy*?"

"Oh, he just turned thirty-five. In fact, Edgardo and I bought him the nicest cashmere scarf for his birthday from a fancy, fancy shop with chandeliers, you should know," she said proudly.

I ignored the expensive present and the issue of which wallet produced the money for it and I also decided not to question the likelihood that a thirty-five year-old man was still a boy, wrestling with puberty issues, no doubt.

"Look, I appreciate what you're trying to do. But I'm just not ready. And, I have to say, right now I like being unattached."

My mother took my hands in hers and rubbed them gently. She used to do that when I was growing up and had a problem and it always made me feel better. Now it made me want to cry. This woman, no matter what color her hair and no matter how low cut her sweater, was still my mother. I had to hold on to that or I would lose her, too.

"Humor me. Meet him somewhere for a drink. Or meet him at the restaurant and enjoy a good meal."

Suddenly, it came to me. "I'll do it if you do something for me."

"Of course, darling. For you, I'll do whatever."

"I have someone I want *you* to meet. His name is Kevin Flanagan and he's a financial advisor. He helped me with my investments and some pension issues and I thought it would be a good idea for you to meet him. You know, to make sure you're covered for...for long term care insurance and...other good stuff. For the future."

She looked at me for a few seconds, calculating the proposition, still holding my hands. Then she smiled. "Good. That's settled. I meet this Flanagan fellow and you'll meet Enrique. Oh, I already gave him your number."

To fatten up for Enrique, I ate a BLT slathered with mayo and even ordered apple pie for dessert.

# August 25th

*T*he *boy nephew* called. We didn't speak for long, but just long enough for me to appreciate his mellifluous Spanish accent which sounded quite captivating. He asked me to meet him tonight for a drink at 7 o'clock at the bar of the trendy W Hotel downtown. I would recognize him because he would be wearing a yellow rose boutonnière in his lapel. He would know *me* because Sarah/Sherri had shown him my picture. I wouldn't be surprised if she'd had it photoshopped.

This date required a consultation with Carla. "So, what outfit do you think works with fish tacos? Oh wait—my mother says that's not on the menu."

"You're a food snob, Sophie."

"Only kidding. It's me being ornery because I really don't want to go out with this man. It's actually comical, Carla. Mother and daughter dating uncle and nephew! Pretty ridiculous, right? You know, Sarah/Sherri really manipulated me in the nicest way. Now I have to meet this Enrique Barranco and when I don't go on a second date, assuming he even asks me, I'll just hurt Edgardo's feelings and cause trouble for my mother."

Carla was practical. "Give it up, Sophie, because now you have no choice." She got down to business. "What will you wear?" Carla scrunched her face as she usually does when heavy thinking about fashion is involved. She knew the entire contents of my closet. "No boots. Although I can't believe how many young women walk around this town in boots—and it's still August! I can never remember when autumn starts, but I know it has to be September something. Anyway, wear your blue short-sleeved cashmere and your black pencil skirt with the black high-heeled gladiator sandals you bought at that pop-up sale in Brooklyn. Oh, and your silver hoop earrings. But no other jewelry because you don't want to look as if you're trying too hard." Carla is the *doyenne* of the fashion world. She knows about every sale, every pop-up store and every new off-price shop that opens in all five boroughs of New York. She's responsible for most of the pieces in my wardrobe.

It didn't occur to me until this very moment, writing my journal entry, that when I met Enrique I was wearing an outfit that practically duplicated Sarah/Sherri's—the one I'd mentally critiqued when we had lunch. Except for the cleavage—my neckline was more modest—we were sartorial twins. What would Kisselstine say? I know: "Something to think about." I thanked Carla for her advice. "But the bottom line is I really am not ready to meet anybody right now."

"You never know. The important thing is that you're looking ahead—not in the rear-view mirror." Yes, the rearview mirror, where I'd see my ex-boyfriend running a four-minute mile—in the opposite direction.

I arrived at the bar early because the W Hotel was walking distance from my apartment and I guess I was a little unsure of myself and it seemed right to be ensconced on a bar stool and have Enrique find *me*. It was hot outside, perfect weather for a beer, but I ordered a Pinot Grigio instead (a classier beverage) and paid for it immediately because I didn't want to have the boy nephew pick up the check. If this turned out to be a walkaway it would be best if I made a clean break. Probably Enrique felt the same way, considering his uncle Edgardo must have leaned on him to meet the daughter of his sexy girlfriend.

Cut to the chase. Enrique found me and greeted me with a very continental kiss on both cheeks. He was tall, wearing a black European cut suit that had the requisite V look, broad in the shoulders and tapering at the waist and hips— with a jacket that seemed just a shade too body-hugging on his slim frame. Actually, the correct description would be *sexy*. His longish dark hair was parted in the center and a tiny diamond flashed in his ear. I've never been a fan of earrings for men, but I have to admit, Enrique carried it well.

"At last we meet. Your mother has told me so much about you and I see for myself it's all true."

It was a fantasy first date. We sat in a booth and had an easy conversation, although I must admit that he did most of the talking. He called me Sophia,

Latinizing my name, making it sound far more intriguing than Sophie and he gave me his biography, which also sounded much more fascinating than mine. Edgardo had gotten him out of Cuba when Enrique was eighteen. At that point, his mother and father had died and he was quite poor, desperate to make a life for himself.

"I took everything America had to offer," Enrique said with pride. "I went to the community college in Miami with very little English on my tongue and in two years..." he waved his hand in an expansive gesture, "and in two years, I speak the language. I speak well enough to go to the Florida University in Tampa and get my business degree." Enrique took out his wallet and showed me his college graduation picture. The much younger Enrique was adorable; the mature Enrique was gorgeous.

"I carry this with me always because this is what America did for me."

"That's wonderful, Enrique. You're a true success story." I meant it; I'd never met anyone like him before.

He continued, speaking with a pride that seemed justified, rather than boastful, perhaps because he was felt so positive about his adopted country. "I opened up a restaurant in Miami with mi amigo and we did very, very well. For nine years, that was my baby. But I always knew I would go to New York and open the restaurant here. This is the big time, right? So, when we made enough money, my partner bought me out and I came to New York. This is where it counts, Sophia. And by this time, I have the investors to help me with my American dream."

Maybe there was something to be said for fish tacos and I'd be more respectful of them in the future.

"That was my plan—my own restaurant in Manhattan." He took my hand and kissed it, just as a Latin lover would do in the movies. "I am a man with many plans, Sophia."

I was surprised that he was so open, so intense. I'd never met anyone like him before. And I was charmed with the continental kiss on my hand. I'm a pushover for the romantic gesture, I guess. I have to admit that was not in Renny Chapman's playbook.

"Perhaps you are hungry," Enrique said as he looked at his watch. It was almost eight o'clock and we had each eaten only a shrimp cocktail. Enrique had ordered it, even though it was pricey. I'd tried to order sliders instead, but he'd insisted. "Let me feed you in my restaurant," he said urgently. "It will be my pleasure." Mine, too. I was starving; at this point, I'd even eat a fish taco, if necessary.

Our taxi took us to uptown Madison Avenue and then there we were at Cascada, of all places. Cascada! Of course, I'd read about this new, exceptionally fashionable restaurant on Page Six, the celebrity gossip site of the *New York Post*. Whenever I admit that I read the *Post*, I always make it my business to add that I also read *The New York Times* and the *Wall Street Journal*, because I hate to come off as an intellectual lightweight. The tabloid *Post* is my private vice. In fact, that's where I read that Leonardo had just taken one of his model girlfriends to Cascada.

This was no taco joint. The interior had a sophisticated design with dark blue and silver fabric on the walls and elegant lighting fixtures shedding a subtle, rosy light that made everyone look younger and healthier. A towering cascade of water plunged into a stone enclosure that was set in the center of the room so that most guests had a water view. The gently rushing sound of falling water and the soft lighting lowered the decibel level considerably. People seemed to be conversing in hushed tones as if dining at Cascada were akin to a religious experience.

Enrique led me to a table for two near the back wall, nodding to various patrons on the way, sometimes shaking hands, other times patting a shoulder in a show of camaraderie. He whispered to the maître d', Luca, who had materialized almost instantly as we sat down. Enrique gave Luca a thumbs-up signal.

"I have taken the liberty of ordering for you," said Enrique with a big smile.

I feel compelled to write down what I consumed because years from now, I want to look back at this and remember that I tasted my first pork belly with quail eggs at this time, followed by monkfish cloaked in béchamel in a baby lettuce wrap. Heavenly.

It's strange, but Renny and I rarely shared a gourmet experience like this. He was basically a steak and potato eater and he avoided upscale restaurants because he didn't find the collaborative ballet of self-important maître d's, over-attentive waiters and all-knowing wine sommeliers to his liking. That was his account, not mine. He also had little tolerance for expensive restaurants that attracted hedge funders, bankers, CEOs and other corporate types. He used to say that he needed to limit them to his working day because after hours, he had little tolerance for bullshit. So, Renny and I ate in diners or Irish bars or local family-run restaurants. Whenever it was convenient, I'd cook dinner at my place.

And, it wasn't about money either—because Renny could definitely afford a Cascada dinner. It was about simple food and speedy service and getting on with his life: watching the Knicks or the Rangers, sweating it out at the gym, reading the *Wall Street Journal*, escaping the city for a hike in upstate New York or enthusiastically playing poker for money at his once a week card game and generally wiping out his fellow players. I'm proud to say that I wasn't a push-over; I beat him at cards often enough and I think he actually enjoyed it. I believe my poker victories, instead of injuring his pride, actually justified his choice of Sophie Marks as his girlfriend.

Yes, it was rare for Renny and me to dine in an upscale restaurant. On the flip side, he liked my cooking, eaten in the comfort and quiet of my apartment with its wide screen television and my overstuffed couch and my apple strudel cooling on the counter. When I cooked a dinner for him, it was the only time that I felt as if *I* were pulling the strings in our relationship. If I were not writing this journal, I don't think I would have had this insight. Yes, I've certainly become more introspective, now that I have a shrink in my life.

Enrique Barranco is charming, social, interesting and attentive. This is what Dr. K had wanted for me: a new man to erase the heartache of losing Renny and the baby. It could be a new beginning for me with someone special. Someone, by the way, who could legitimately be described as eye candy.

I'm mailing this journal entry to Kisselstine to show him that I am open to a new relationship that—who knows? —could lead to love and *marriage*. It's not that I am some teenager engaging in an adolescent fantasy about matrimony on the very first date; it's just that I am well aware of the possibilities. Perhaps Enrique Barranco will liberate my subconscious reluctance to get married. I do want to see him again.

And I definitely want another crack at that monkfish.

# *October 21ˢᵗ*

*T*hese past weeks have been a whirlwind. Enrique and I caught a couple of Broadway shows, regularly dined on Cascada's incredible food and attended a charity benefit that was heavy on glamour. Enrique was in his element, enjoying whatever attention came his way, always charming the crowd and appreciating the new contacts who, he hoped, would eventually make reservations at Cascada. He is very social; so different from Renny.

Unfortunately, we are accompanied at all times with a torrent of texts, phone calls and emails that seemed to require immediate attention. He's involved with a group of investors in an apparently hush-hush deal to open another Cascada in Los Angeles. He's also working with an agent to get him to appear on a cooking show and he's writing a comfort food cookbook that's in the early stages of development and is actually being collated by his former partner in Miami.

The downside of this relationship, for me, is his cell phone. While the texts and calls are an irritating distraction, I'd have to say that the food, the glorious food, more than compensated. Poached salmon filet with juniper berry salsa served with a spinach and wild mushroom risotto. Dover sole topped with cauliflower flan on a bed of eggplant and red pepper hash. Pecan crusted duck breast burnished with a fig and balsamic vinegar reduction accompanied by a puree of champagne roasted beets. I had found gastronomic heaven on the island of Manhattan. Viva Enrique!

I asked Enrique how he came up with all these exotic dishes that were not traditional Cuban fare. His answer reflected a great deal about his business acumen. "I am always the curious one. So, I have my people at work in Los Angeles, in Houston and in Miami. They're from the old country and all of them have found a place for themselves in America. They are my—how do you say—lookovers?

No, lookouts! They report to me about the restaurants' menus, they take the pictures and they ask questions. Luca is the genius who recreates the recipes."

I was puzzled. "Do your friends own restaurants?"

"No, no, no. They have nothing to do with the business. Diego owns a shoe store, Javier is a lawyer and Emilio runs a limousine service. But they all can afford to eat at fine restaurants and then they give me the information. My Chicago amigos, Luis and Tomás, they cannot pay so much money, so I give them an expense account to go to the finest restaurants... maybe two or three times a year. Sophia, I know that it is possible to read the restaurant menu online. But my people, they talk to the chef, himself, about the dish. Even the waiters give them the information that is so important."

I had to laugh. "Enrique, you're running a regular detective agency—but with a twist. Your stalking recipes instead of unfaithful husbands!"

"I also have the secret ingredient," he said with a satisfied smile.

"And that is...?"

"Manolo, my main man in the kitchen. He has the sixth sense when he is told about the recipe combinations. If Luca cannot find the correct proportions or the secret ingredients, Manolo can figure out what will work. And his genius is to change the recipe just enough so that we look like we are the inventors. Manolo has the feel for it. To him—it's a game.

To me—to me, it's the money."

To me, it was the dish in front of me: a lamb curry with a saffron yogurt sauce studded with pistachios over coconut and pomegranate rice. Paradise on a plate.

Often, when Enrique was doing paperwork and the restaurant was quiet late at night, Luca would sit down with me and keep me company, telling me stories about growing up in a small Cuban fishing village with his best friend Enrique. Long before school started in the morning, they would go fishing and bring home their catch which would later show up on their plates at suppertime. Luca said, "Miss Sophia, I have to say that when I came to this country, I did not eat fish for a very long time. And Enrique...he, as well, couldn't eat it for maybe two years. That's how it was for us when we had so little." He looked around the restaurant with pride. "Now we have so much." No wonder Enrique's drive to succeed was so consuming.

Luca had that same lean and hungry appearance that mirrored Enrique's. In addition to exotic good looks, both men generated charm and charisma, which I'm certain added to the restaurant's appeal. Whether models, matrons or moneymen walked through Cascada's door, both Enrique and Luca projected a warm welcome with a suggestion of simmering sex appeal. The women loved it and the men seemed to savor it as well. Perhaps these patrons felt that Enrique's and Luca's frisson of sexuality would somehow attach to them and they would reap the benefits—later that night in their bedrooms. Food and sex—an unbeatable combination—that was Cascada's trademark.

My dinner indulgences were not to be taken lightly. When I went to spin class in the early morning after my first few Cascada dinners, I felt as if I had to make the effort to cycle the equivalent of New York to Chicago in order to atone for the richness of the cuisine. Then, I self-regulated and ate less, because that was more in keeping with my appetite. Actually, after I'd been served several lunches and dinners, I realized that Luca saw to it that I received smaller portions. Even then, I often couldn't finish what was on my plate. But, I relished Cascada's amazing bread; it was a crusty miracle of flour, yeast, butter and secret seasoning that shamed other bread baskets. I was always amused when I spotted obviously affluent female patrons surreptitiously wrapping their bread in napkins and depositing it in their handbags.

Often, Enrique would bring out delicacies for me to sample. "These snails, these little beauties, they have been married to garlic and shallots and parsley and I, myself, performed the ceremony in the kitchen. I present them to you, my Sophia," said Enrique, napkin over his arm, as if he were the headwaiter. Or he would carry out a steaming clay pot and lift the lid with a flourish. "For sweet Sophia, I give you this artichoke that offers a surprise." Indeed, it had Iberico ham and roasted clams tucked inside, an exquisite combination that I'd never been exposed to and found enormously indulgent. Enrique would watch me eat with a thoroughly self-satisfied smile—just as Natalie would take pleasure in observing her little Alice eagerly reaching with chubby fingers for the Cheerios on her plate and stuffing them into her mouth with gusto.

Who knew a grown-up—me!— could make someone deliriously happy just by eating?

Natalie asked me if this whirlwind adventure was the real thing. What could I say? I found my time with Enrique exciting but I had no idea if I wanted it to lead to something serious. I didn't dare tell her we'd never slept together. Not that I minded that. If I couldn't stick to the dating moratorium, at least I was taking a break from sex.

"Not head over heels?" Natalie mused. "Then you're definitely a food whore."

After I'd been seeing Enrique for weeks, I invited him to my apartment for dinner. He was very pleased because he said all of the women he'd met either didn't cook at all or were intimidated and refused to cook for him. I think he chiefly has dated take-out queens or models who dined on carrot sticks.

I admit I changed the sheets the morning of the dinner and I wore new lacy underwear—just in case. Enrique hadn't hurried me but I figured that sooner or later we would end up in bed together. By New York City standards, we were waiting for some time before we became intimate. But, that was good, because I needed to know that I cared for him before I could even think about having sex. And I do care for him. Tonight, he would be at my apartment and we would be alone for the first time with a bedroom nearby.

The evening progressed like this: a few kisses, white wine, more kisses, two texts, then what the kids used to call first base, followed by a sit down for Polynesian chicken (thank you, James Beard) one phone call, a meringue torte (thank you, Food Network), more wine, and finally, my queen size bed.

He was gentle but quick and I did something I've never done before. I faked it. I don't have a long list of lovers to compare to Enrique, but I knew enough to realize that we weren't passionate; something was missing. I felt strangely detached when we were intimate. However, Enrique seemed quite pleased with himself.

And that pretty much established the pattern: either no sex most of the time (which was fine) or occasional, unsatisfying sex (not so fine). When he left my apartment one night and I was restoring order to the kitchen after another home-cooked meal and a less than fulfilling sexual encounter, I decided I had to restore order to my thoughts as well.

I'm not happy about it, but I think I need Kisselstine to help me out, even if it means talking openly about sex. I'll just have to deal with it. It's ridiculous to be embarrassed because he's no doubt heard it all in the course of his practice.

My problem is that now he has to hear it from *me*.

# October 24th

So back I went. I settled into my cozy patient's chair and Dr. K sat in his more austere therapist's chair and we faced each other.

He smiled. "I'm really glad you came back."

"Well, I need to talk to someone." Damn, that sounded so flippant. I softened. "Actually, I really needed to talk to you."

"So, let's begin," he said as he telescoped himself into his chair—a study in beige and taupe, wearing his thick eyeglasses like a mask, looking nothing like the confident, good-looking man I'd met at Charlie T's. Frankly, I preferred *office* Kisselstine. There was something very comforting about my *medium* shrink. It was foolish of me to avoid him; it was better to hash things out and learn from his point of view or at least agree to disagree.

I reminded him about the deal with my mother that meant in exchange for her seeing the financial planner, I had to meet Edgardo's nephew. I told him the easy part first: Enrique's success in America, the excitement of Cascada, the amazing dinners I've had (here I might have gone a little overboard in describing the menu, but I admit the cuisine has definitely made Enrique even more attractive). Finally, I told him about that first less than successful bedroom encounter.

"I understand it wasn't a fulfilling sexual experience, but that's only one time."

"Well, no, not just that one time. But, a few times...um...not that often, actually, but...the same." This conversation was just as embarrassing as I'd expected.

He was silent for a while. Then, "If this relationship is important to you, we can enlist the help of a sex therapist. The problem might turn out to be easily rectified."

A low, moaning sound emerged from my throat. "Dr. K, can you imagine what would happen to this macho Cuban if I suggested such a thing?"

"Well, I do know there are sex therapists that can help. I've made a number of referrals and my patients have had good results."

I shook my head.

"Look Sophie, I don't have to tell you that if you are not satisfied sexually, that's a problem. This may not be the right relationship for you." He paused and then said, completely out of character, "There's all that good food going to waste."

Aha, psychiatric humor! "Not wasted," I countered, "just eaten by another lucky woman."

"I must say your descriptions of Cascada's food in your journal is ..." He searched for the right word. "Captivating."

It was so rare for him to break out of therapist mold and talk to me as a person. "I'm curious," I asked, wondering what went on in Kisselstine's medium world, "Does all that complicated food appeal to you?"

"Well, I'm not used to eating that rarefied fare. But you describe the food so lovingly that you make me want to try it. I can see why you're successful in advertising." He shook his head and frowned slightly, as if he were suddenly annoyed with himself for stepping outside of his therapist persona. He wrote a few notes in his notepad, which I believe were intended to conceal his uneasiness. Then he looked up at me. "Seriously, I'd hate to see you throw away a worthwhile relationship without trying to fix things."

"Dr. K, is that the only way to fix things? Going to a sex therapist?"

"Well, you can try something else. You can open up a dialogue with Enrique when you are together but not intimate. Just talk to him and make a few suggestions about what would give you pleasure. He needs to know what would make you happy when you have relations. Of course, it goes both ways: ask him what he would like as well."

"I can't imagine telling him I'm not satisfied. We could never have that conversation, Dr. K. He's a very confident, assertive man and if I brought that up, he'd be devastated. Emasculated." I sighed. "And truthfully, I would be very, very embarrassed."

"I know. That's why I suggested the sex therapist in the first place—an objective third party who would make it easier for you to talk about sex."

I shook my head. "That's not going to happen. Ever."

"Putting that aside for a minute, would you say that you and Enrique are a good match?"

"Well, the bedroom problem is not the only thing. I've kind of downplayed the phone calls and texts but they do add up. We're never really alone. Actually, we're a ménage à trois. We're Sophie, Enrique and an insistent iPhone. It can get very, very... tiresome." How to explain? I told Kisselstine that I wasn't resentful or jealous about the many claims on Enrique's time. I was simply finding the situation tedious and sometimes downright impolite. Enrique was being pulled in all directions and I think he welcomed it because it reflected his increasing success in his adopted country.

Kisselstine stepped in. "Sometimes I ask my patients to draw up a pro and con chart. It may sound simplistic, but it's actually an effective technique that will help you put your thoughts in order. As you're doing it, you'll actually find yourself weighing different aspects of the relationship and that's very helpful. Why don't you bring it in when you come for your next appointment." He made a few notes. "And let's put this intimacy issue on the back burner. Let me think about it for a while and see what I can come up with."

I agreed. It was a relief to stop talking about it for now.

Then, "Tell me how you're getting along with your mother these days."

"Well, I'm trying to do what you had suggested: practice seeing her as an independent woman and not just categorizing her as my mother. But it's hard. The tango lessons have now morphed into competitions. My mother wears a low cut ruffled blouse and a tiered black skirt with a bright red petticoat that flashes with every step and matches his red cummerbund and red bolo tie and would you believe it—his red socks. Matching clothes! They're not kids, you know. It's just too much."

Too much? Too much overt sexuality is what I meant. I know, I know, that petticoat/cummerbund "matchy matchy" reference was unkind. I wondered if Kisselstine would think less of me because I spoke so sharply. But, he did tell me to say whatever I was feeling and thinking.

"You're so upset about this," Kisselstine observed. "It seems almost out of proportion to the event. As far as I can tell, it's a good pastime, this tango dancing. You would think you'd be proud of their energy and initiative. Yet, you're so distressed."

"Shouldn't I be?" I felt defiant. "I've already gone to one competition and that's enough for me. Now they're participating in another one this Saturday and she wants me to attend. Dr. K, I'm actually embarrassed when I see them dancing. It's so...so erotic."

"Sophie, aren't all the other couples dancing the tango engaging in moves that could be called erotic? I'm thinking that they're doing just what the tango requires, just what every dancing couple does. But you seem to have tunnel vision on this. You're looking at a sensual dance and instead of appreciating it for what it is, you're fixating on the dancers' chemistry."

"Yes, Dr. K, I see their sexual chemistry because it's blatant."

Kisselstine was thoughtful for a while, longer than usual. Finally he said, "I'm beginning to think we have more to talk about when it comes to your parents. Let's go back to their relationship. I have a feeling that they were not quite the couple you described when we first met. Sophie, it's important that you tell me what they were really like, even if it hurts."

I had never spoken to anyone about their marriage before this. I knew I'd have to address the Sarah/Sherri and Edgardo relationship in therapy because that was something happening *now*—but my parents' marriage? That was history I'd rather forget, rather not talk about. And now, Kisselstine was making it topic number one.

"Well, I have to admit they weren't always the best of business partners. The upholstery business had a lot of stresses—fabrics could be cut incorrectly, mistakes made in sewing, patterns not matching, not to mention the older machines breaking down. Always deadlines. So, that was a given and it meant they were pretty stressed when they were working. And then they had different philosophies. For example, she wanted to invest each year in additional sample books of high-end material so people would have more choices and not buy the fabric somewhere else. That would give them the potential to make more money. My father was reluctant to make that investment—which was actually fairly costly. She also wanted to have many more in-stock bolts of inexpensive fabric in the store so that they would have a broader customer base, but again, he was cautious. It would mean a significant outlay of cash that might not generate a return. So they quarreled about that."

"And at home...what were they like?"

"Sort of okay."

"Sort of? Come on, Sophie, just tell me whatever comes into your head."

"Well, they did have their ups and downs. When I lived in the house, I saw my father sleeping on the couch more than once. They argued over foolish things—like whether or not the milk was spoiled. Small stuff like that. He ran a tight ship, I guess. On the other hand, years ago they bought their exceptional condo, a three-bedroom, two-and-a-half bath apartment in Brooklyn Heights with water views. It's amazing real estate, thanks to my father's financial vigilance."

"Hmm, I can't help but think that your mother might have minded this "financial vigilance" a lot more than you realize. Could that have been a factor in making them "sort of" okay?"

"Dr. K, my father was a good man and a good father. Kind of a workaholic, but he always found time for me. He would come home and have me search his coat pockets until I found the toy or candy bar he'd hidden. He'd take me to the park and we'd go on long walks and we'd identify trees and flowers. He talked about history and made it exciting because in his spare time, that's what he read. He taught me how to ride a bike—which is somewhat amazing because he, himself, couldn't pedal down the block. I was his little girl even as a grownup. God, I miss him."

Kisselstine handed me a tissue. "Everything you just said is a tribute to the wonderful bond you had with your father. But Sophie, that's not what I was asking you about," he said gently. "I was talking about your parents' relationship. Are you avoiding the question?"

"Am I? I suppose you're right. I was just thinking about my father and me. That was the good part," I conceded. "I guess I don't like discussing the relationship because in my heart I know it was flawed. My father's thriftiness probably was more of a problem for my mother than I've wanted to admit."

"Would it be accurate to say that he was the easier parent while your mother was more of the disciplinarian?"

I nodded affirmatively. "Yes, I was daddy's little girl—and I loved it. My mother was often angry with him, especially when I was young, and her pent-up emotions could suddenly spill over at times into an explosion. When that happened, my father would back off and retreat. I felt so bad for him."

"Perhaps you're so upset with your mother because she failed to make the father you loved so much—happy."

That had never occurred to me. "Perhaps that *is* true," I reluctantly agreed.

"And you resent Edgardo because he has done what your father could not do—make *her* happy."

I had never admitted it to myself, but I think I was often troubled because my parents didn't seem happy enough. When I went to Carla's house, I'd sometimes see her father give her mother a pat on her fanny and she would slap his hand away, but she was laughing while she did it. I was always surprised because that didn't happen in my house. But, then I remembered Edgardo. I threw my hands up in disgust. "How about Edgardo being happy because he gets to spend the widow's money?"

"Are you certain of that?"

"Well, I haven't exactly caught him taking cash out of her handbag." In spite of my dismissive remark, Kisselstine remained impassive. Suddenly, I wished I were nicer. Nevertheless, I appreciated the fact that I was in a judgment-free zone.

"Tell me, what did Edgardo do before he retired?"

"I'm a little hazy about that. He told me he was into exporting but he never elaborated. I guess that's why I mistrust him. Exporting what? Drugs? I mean it was so vague that he made me suspicious."

"Sophie, any proof?"

I shrugged my shoulders. "No, just my overactive imagination."

Dr. K shook his head somewhat reproachfully and I sensed he thought I was overreaching, but he didn't admonish me. Instead, he gave me a kindly smile. "Let's put that aside for now. The financial planner may be a great help sorting things out."

Fair enough, I thought. I had to stop jumping to conclusions about Edgardo. The only thing I was certain about was that he was attentive to my mother, that he was kind to me and that he had become a fairly good tango dancer. Was that enough?

Kisselstine looked at me for a while, before he spoke. "I believe that the unhappy nature of your parents' relationship would be a factor in making you very mistrustful of marriage. What do you think?"

I could sense that he was going to tell me exactly that—*what to think*—in his own, non-judgmental fashion, leading me along, slowly but surely.

Kisselstine continued. "Let's recap. One—you had a long-term relationship with Renny but you never actually explored the issue of marriage. Two—you say you wanted a family, but you never told Renny that was important to you. And three—you cared for Renny, obviously, but in my view, you were comfortable with the status quo—until you got pregnant and actually needed his financial help to raise the child." He paused for a minute, letting his words sink in. "Notice, I said a financial commitment. You didn't ask for marriage. Correct?"

I was silent. He already knew the answer.

"As I've told you in past sessions, I believe that's because *you* didn't want to get married. And now, we're talking about your parents' strained marriage. I see a connection there."

"Well, Dr. K, I've been thinking about that and I agree that I really wasn't ready to get married. Or at least, ready to marry Renny." Dr. K nodded in approval, letting a small smile escape, but then he reverted to neutral. No "I told you so"—and I was grateful.

Kisselstine continued. "Sophie, here we are, talking about your parents' unhappy union and that gives us an important clue as to why you feel the way you do...why you didn't press Renny for marriage." He paused. "I believe you were afraid to repeat your parents' mistake."

I stared at him, unable to reply. Was this another nail in the uncomfortable box I was metaphorically toting?—the box which contained my complicated views on marriage.

"Time is up, Sophie. Think about it and write in your journal. That will help."

I went to this therapist because I had an unplanned pregnancy, a miscarriage and a sudden break-up and I needed some support. Fast-forward a few months and now this psychologist is telling me that my parents' unhappiness seriously affected me in a negative way. First, Dr. K convinces me that I'm distrustful of marriage. Okay, I'm buying that. But now, he's blaming my parents for my issues.

I left the office, troubled, because Kisselstine had dragged my my father and mother into the equation to strengthen his case. That certainly didn't make me feel better. How could I blame my father, who did everything he could to make me happy? How could I blame my mother, who tried her best under difficult circumstances? What kind of daughter would I be if I went that route?

Once again, I decided to take the easy way out—that is—take a break from therapy. I needed time to think. I had expected Kisselstine to work things out for me so that I'd deal with loss. Well, yes, I do feel that I'm coping with the loss of the baby and with Renny's rejection. I'm in a much better place than I was in July when I first met Kisselstine. But now, he's exploring my subconscious and I'm uneasy about his assessment. I'm sending him this journal entry so he'll know exactly what I'm thinking.

There should be a sign in every therapist's waiting room that says, "Enter at your own risk, because there's a minefield of explosives littering the office. You are guaranteed to step in it." Ouch.

# November 12th

Carla and I were supposed to get together after work at the new hipster central hangout, Cavey's Tavern in Brooklyn. As soon as I entered, I spied Kisselstine in the back at a table with four men and three women. Really, New York is such a small town when it comes to trendy places to meet and drink. We're like lemmings, migrating in a pack, looking for the newest scene, so naturally, we were in Brooklyn—at Cavey's.

Four men and only three women at his table. I wondered idly what were the chances of my Dr. K getting lucky? Bottom line, without those creepy glasses he wears in the office, his odds were decent. Better than decent; he was looking good. I had a sudden feeling that I found him attractive; or more precisely, that I was attracted to him. But, I shook it off. Chalk it up to a moment of transference—when the patient gets erotic ideas about the therapist. I had no intentions of being a textbook case.

Of course, I kept my back to him because I wasn't in the mood to trade small talk between therapist and client in a bar, especially since I'd intentionally hadn't made an office appointment these last few weeks. If I weren't waiting for Carla, who was probably in a taxi stuck in traffic, I would've left immediately. It was her idea to go over the bridge to Brooklyn and now I might have to pay for it.

He spotted me. He came over with his beer in hand and sat down.

"You didn't make another appointment after our last session. I was thinking that perhaps I was too hard on you. How are you doing?"

*Too hard?* Because he thought I should accept the sensual nature of the tango instead of finding it lustful and embarrassing when performed by my mother and her boyfriend? *Too hard?* Because he thought my parents were directly responsible for my anxiety about marriage.

*Yes* to both questions.

But, in response to his query, "How are you doing?" I blurted out, "I had sex with Renny, yesterday!" There it was—on the table, exactly what I was supposed to confide to Carla. I'd confessed it without even managing a *hello*. Damn, Kisselstine's effect on me was like truth serum.

Slight raise of an eyebrow. "How did that happen?"

There was no turning back. "Renny called me at nine in the morning yesterday and told me he was in a bind. His friend," I hissed the word again, *friend*. "His friend had an important conference and her nanny didn't show up and she was desperate, so she asked Renny to watch her little girl. He said yes, but then he got a call from some honchos at the office and he had to come in even though it was Saturday. Something about the Libor interest rates in London that might have been manipulated and could lead to a possible financial meltdown." I halted my story to say to Kisselstine, "I'm wondering—would giving me that information add up to insider trading? Was I consorting with a criminal?" I allowed myself a rueful laugh. "Only kidding, Dr. K, although wouldn't that be just the icing on the cake? Renny's final offense?"

Kisselstine didn't change his expression; I can never tell what he's thinking as he let my semi-serious question pass. So, I continued. "I guess that's not the point, is it? Anyway, bottom line—Renny wanted me to watch little Emma. He actually begged."

Kisselstine sipped his beer. Nothing surprised him. "Go on."

"What could I do? The child needed to be cared for, so I said yes and he hailed a taxi and was at my apartment in forty minutes with Maya's daughter, Emma, and a box of crayons."

"How did that work out?"

"Well, when Renny left she started to cry. But I eventually won her over with games on my iPad and some chocolate ice cream I had in the freezer. That was around 10:30 in the morning and I wondered how we'd make it through the day. But actually, Emma was very sweet. We took a walk to the park and she played with other nannied kids and on the way home we had hamburgers and fries for lunch. And, ice cream again. "Hey," I said, somewhat defensively, "I was a substitute nanny—not a nutritionist."

I suddenly realized that I was marking time, giving Kisselstine a superfluous description of my outing with little Emma, when I actually was expected to give him the details about my sexual encounter with the man who'd walked out on me. Kisselstine waited patiently for the rest of the story—and finally said, "And then?"

"When Renny showed up at my door in the afternoon, Emma was exhausted and fast asleep on the couch in my living room." I told Kisselstine that Renny hugged me and told me how grateful he was and how wonderful I was. Then the hug turned into kissing and then the next thing I knew we were in my bedroom and he was tugging at my leggings. "Honestly, if a woman is uncertain about having sex, leggings can enforce abstinence." I stopped. I'm certain I make jokes about sex because I'm uncomfortable talking about it. The next part was harder to share. Kisselstine waited me out.

"Should I be telling you this," I waved my hand to encompass the bar. "Here?"

"Probably not. Definitely not. But go on."

"Well, it wasn't the same as it was before. Maybe it's more accurate to say that *I* wasn't the same. I didn't feel right about it; it just felt wrong." Kisselstine wore an impassive expression and he clearly wasn't going to comment until I divulged everything that was on my mind. So, I began again. "When Renny and I were a couple, I guess I responded to him differently. But yesterday it felt like gratuitous sex and when it was over, I didn't feel good about myself. In fact, I felt terrible."

"Perhaps you feel differently because you see Renny differently now."

"Yes, that's what I was trying to say. But, I'm also feel something's wrong when Enrique and I have... relations, although it's not that often so it's less of a problem for me." I could feel myself getting flushed and embarrassed, made worse because we were sitting in a bar and not his antiseptic beige office. "I do care for Enrique, so I go along with it, but something's not right. Dr. K, is there something wrong with *me*?"

"Sophie, there's nothing wrong with you. Nothing." He leaned over and spoke softly to avoid having anyone overhear his comments. "I think what you're feeling is that intimacy is best for you in a relationship that's caring and committed. That's a very healthy outlook. You no longer have that with Renny, so sexual relations were unsatisfactory. And as far as I can tell, you're not sure about your relationship with Enrique. Maybe that's part of the problem."

I could see a woman at the table next to us, leaning back in her chair, trying to overhear our conversation. I assumed she'd heard some of it and was hoping for more. "Are we really allowed to have this conversation in a bar?"

"Look, Sophie, I just wanted to check in with you because I want to help and let's face it, you do come to my office somewhat erratically, so we can't always work things through."

My phone pinged and I glanced at Carla's text. She was running late. And if you were on time, I thought to myself, I would be telling *you* about Renny, as I intended.

Kisselstine seemed unconcerned about our surroundings. "So, you seem to have re-connected with Renny. Would you consider seeing him again?"

"No. That would be a mistake." I turned my head to see if our eavesdropper was still on the case. No, she was now engaged in conversation with her table-mate, so I continued. "I'll never forget that Renny abandoned me when I needed him. Dr. K, I've come to terms with his decision not to support a child *he* didn't want. But I think he went about it in a manner that was insensitive and cruel." There was one more thing to tally. "And don't forget, I should take into account the fact that he just cheated on his girlfriend Maya—with me."

Kisselstine pursed his lips, an expression that I'd come to recognize as the beginning of a gentle difference of opinion. "You don't think *you* cheated on Enrique?" This time he sounded more forceful than than gentle.

"Well, no, not exactly," I replied, defensively. How could I explain it to him when I could hardly explain it to myself? "Enrique and I are not a couple. I mean, I like him, but we have no…no formal understanding. Anyway, didn't you just point out to me that we really haven't made a commitment to each other? So it's not cheating, is it? Although," I admitted, "I shouldn't have had sex with Renny. It happened so quickly, it was so impulsive, and for a moment I thought it was okay, but you know…it wasn't right. When it was over I regretted it—but I think that had nothing to do with Enrique." There I was, tying myself into knots.

I guess Kisselstine appreciated my confusion, because he responded in his most soothing therapist's voice. "Of course, Sophie, I understand."

"Actually," I confessed, "Carla and Natalie think this thing with Enrique is a food fling."

He laughed. "Food fling? I'll see that gets written up in the diagnostic manual."

Just then, Kisselstine noticed that his tablemates were standing up, putting on coats. "My group has dinner reservation at Amici's next door. Here's the irony: we're the ethics committee for the Interactive Psychology Confederation and if I stay here any longer talking to you, my principles will be down the drain. Perhaps they are, already." He stood up and spoke formally. "Please feel free to find another therapist, Miss Marks. I'll understand."

"Of course not, Dr. Kisselstine," I said in an equally formal tone. "I'll call tomorrow and make an appointment. And might I add, I've dined at Amici's and I recommend the osso buco." There, there, Dr. K—professionalism restored and reputation intact.

He turned away and headed for his group, but not before I noticed that his face had reddened. I'd never before seen a crack in his therapist demeanor and I couldn't have been more surprised. I think he was embarrassed about the inappropriateness of our little meeting. We were supposed to be in our assigned psychologist/patient chairs in his beige on beige office and he was expected to be attired in regulation camouflage of beige with taupe flourishes. He had broken the rules and I could see he was unnerved. I suddenly felt sorry for him.

Naturally, Carla arrived a few minutes after Kisselstine left. "Damn, the traffic was miserable. I think all of New York City is heading to Brooklyn because this place is beyond hip. Now, tell me, what's so important?"

"Too late, missy. I've already spilled my guts."

Carla looked around. "I don't see anyone here who could replace my sympathetic ear."

"Actually, it's a long story," I said, "and I need a rain check. Agreed?"

"Sure, that gives me a chance to make this all about *me*. Jake's daughter has threatened to stop talking to him if he doesn't go back to Audrey. The whole situation is ridiculous, because Jake told me Audrey's actually been dating someone for the last three months and she's crazy about the new guy. Believe me, that's a modern day miracle."

"That's a good sign," I agreed. "If she's happy with the new man, she'll probably influence the daughter to finally accept the divorce/"

"You'd think," Carla said sadly, "but his daughter still blames Jake and has threatened to cut him off. He's a mess, as you can imagine."

"Do you think she'll go through with that threat if Jake marries you?"

Carla looked as if she'd just swallowed a bitter pill—which I guess is metaphoric but true. "Who knows?"

I tried a little interactive psychology. "Carla, this has gone on so long that we both can see a pattern here. He cares for you, but not enough to take any risks with his daughter. She seems to be first, you seem to be second. It's up to you to decide if you want to be second for the foreseeable future."

"Damn straight. It's up to me. This calls for a drink." We downed a few and then I put her in a cab and walked home.

We're in our thirties, Carla and I. Weren't we supposed to be settled by now?

# November 17<sup>th</sup>

When I made my next appointment with Kisselstine, I wondered if he'd mention our chance meeting at Cavey's Tavern. I think it was awkward for him; it certainly was for me. I'm convinced he regretted talking to me outside the office. But, when I saw him this afternoon, I was relieved that he didn't mention it. Maybe our exchange wasn't as inappropriate as I'd first thought. Perhaps no cardinal rules were broken—just a mild hit on the ethics code.

I had a lot to tell him. Saturday afternoon Enrique and I, Sherri and Edgardo had a "double date". I wonder if today's young people still use old-fashioned terms like that? Double date? No, today it's all about hook-ups and booty calls.

Anyway, Enrique arranged it. He had said to me in a mock scolding voice, "This I cannot believe. We have not gotten together with my favorite uncle and your darling mother. We are family, so I will arrange lunch at Cascada this weekend, *querida*."

It was no ordinary lunch, although it started that way.

My mother was glowing. "I'm so happy we're all together."

Edgardo went on a charm offensive with me, telling me how pretty I looked and how elegant my outfit was. I happened to be dressed in standard New York City black from head to toe. My clothing was replicated all over town. The only stab at individualism I'd made was to add long silver earrings. Carla called them my "screw me" earrings because they were strikingly long and glittering with crystals. I insisted, somewhat disingenuously, that my goals were honorable and I just wore long earrings simply because my dark hair was long and I needed statement earrings if they were to be seen at all. Of course, like all women, I appreciated the fact that long, shimmering earrings had a suggestive component. But then so did the black belt worn over my sweater that hugged my hips and so did the high-heeled boots. But, isn't this a standard New York City uniform?

As I'm writing this, I have an unexpected insight: my mother is playing the exact same game that I am—with her sexy sweaters, her newly svelte figure and her blonde hair. Okay, I concede that her choice of sweaters is far racier than mine. But, do I really have the right to judge her? In our own way, aren't we both promoting our femininity and desirability? That's what Kisselstine has been alluding to all along. Although I couldn't accede to it in his office, I'm finally coming around to acknowledging he was right. And he was right about putting my thoughts on paper. Okay, technically, on the computer. The path of comprehension seems to wind its way from his office to my journal.

Sarah/Sherri had cut a page out of *Vogue* magazine to show off the advertisement my team and I had created for a new product, Celesta shampoo. The ad had been running since last December and she was proudly showing it to Enrique. A beautiful, golden-tressed model wearing a gauzy, golden dress is pictured on the deck of a luxury yacht. Even the sky is streaked with gold. Her hair and dress are ruffled by an unseen wind and a handsome man stands behind her, his face in close proximity to that long, wavy, golden hair. A caption above the picture reads:

*Celesta Liquid Gold. For blondes only.*
*No others need apply.*

Below that is a sensuously curved bottle suggesting a voluptuous nude and it's crowned with a gold-colored bottle top featuring a sculpted female head with windblown hair. The clear liquid inside has iridescent gold flecks that help to justify the upscale charge of $39 for a ten-ounce bottle. And a tag line completes the ad:

*Celesta Liquid Gold. When only the best will do.*

I had worked with the project crew redesigning that bottle and it had been a very rewarding experience. My end of the year bonus went toward the down payment on my exceptional one bedroom with an office loft, one-and-a half baths and two walk-in closets in a doorman building. What's more, three months ago, the board installed a rooftop deck which I never use but which adds value should I ever sell. Bless you, golden Celesta girl.

My mother was beaming. "You know, I read your ad and then went out and bought Celesta shampoo. And I love it."

Edgardo agreed. "I smell your hair and it makes me happy."

I am constantly amazed when I hear Edgardo speak. He has the nicest things to say about my mother and even about me. I initially thought he was too smooth, too slick—but I'm beginning to think there's a chance he might be for real.

'Mom/Sherri, don't buy any more because I have a case of it in my office. And it's for blondes only, so not for me." Why didn't I think of giving her the shampoo until that very minute? Perhaps I was conflicted and wanted to think of her as the matronly brunette I'd known all my life. No doubt that's what Kisselstine would say.

Enrique was puzzled. "Does that not hurt some women's feelings? 'No others need apply' is, how shall I say, exclusive...no, exclusionary." Enrique is a people pleaser, so he had difficulty understanding the ad. I guess that comes with his job description: a restaurateur whose mission it is to make everyone completely physically satiated and emotionally contented.

"Exactly," I replied. "It *is* exclusionary. The idea is to market it to an elite group, the blondes, who have a special place in the hair spectrum. Blondes have always garnered more attention, so we gave them a product formulated just for them, which reinforces their sense of elitism. Of course," I conceded, "Celesta is not the only product geared specifically for blondes, but it is the only one with expensive gold flecks and an ad campaign that works the blonde theme with a vengeance. Anyway, there are enough blondes in this country to make the product a huge success."

"And I'm one of them," my mother beamed. "A blonde for life." Edgardo patted her hair, seconding her opinion.

Enrique asked me what project I was working on now. My mother leaned forward expectantly. I could sense her pride. "Well, the company that makes Celesta also has a line of men's grooming products called Renegade which has had lagging sales for the last two years. So my print team is going to work with a television team at the agency to craft a joint print and television project."

Sarah/Sherri smiled. "Actually, Edgardo and I have a joint project." She took his hand in hers. "We're engaged to be married! We're planning a wedding!"

Enrique was so delighted that only his native language would do. "*Un proyecto muy importante! Este es maravilloso. Felicidades,* Sherri and Edgardo!"

Let it be noted that I did not lose my composure and I do think Dr. K was responsible for my calm demeanor. But, honestly, perhaps there's something wrong with me, but I did not see this wedding coming.

"Mom/Sherri, I'm so happy for you both." And I got up from the table and embraced her. Edgardo bounded up and suddenly we were locked in a group hug.

Enrique ordered Veuve Clicquot for the table. Luca uncorked champagne for us and for himself as well, and we all toasted the bride and groom to be. After two glasses I was smiling away; it doesn't take much to make me a little loopy. Plans went flying back and forth at the table. Have a destination wedding in Aruba? Or do a George Clooney and tie the knot in Venice? Christmas Day or New Year's Day? Vera Wang or 'Say yes to the dress' at Kleinfeld's?"

I can't remember all the ideas that were floated, but I do remember my mother's face: she was radiant. And I have to admit, I'd never seen her like this. Edgardo is a genuine happiness tonic. My mother couldn't stop smiling.

They were going ring shopping the next day. Enrique knew a jeweler in the diamond district. Of course he did. He seemed to have made connections all over town. During lunch, with all the excitement going on, he managed to answer three texts, left the table once to take an important phone call for which he clearly wanted privacy and he checked his email four times. I kept track. What can I say? He meant well even if he didn't always behave well. However, I told Kisselstine, the cilantro and cumin brined veal chops with mango lime salsa were divine.

"So, tell me," Kisselstine asked, "are you ready for this?"

"I have to admit that the woman formerly known as Sarah has truly become the *Sherri* she wants to be. She's not the mother I grew up with but she's definitely a happier woman. I'm really pleased for her." I looked at Kisselstine with appreciation. He had brought me to this place. "I guess I should thank you for that."

"Well, Sophie, thanks for giving me the credit, but it's you who deserves the recognition. You've brought new perspective to your thinking and that has also helped you to be more connected to your mother. I also think that makes you happier."

Yes, Kisselstine was right. I've really tried to open my mind and embrace my new, upgraded mother. No, as I write that, it sounds glib. I really mean it— I'm glad she has found someone who has given her the gift of happiness. And I've come to appreciate Edgardo.

Kisselstine asked, "Do you still believe he's spending her money?"

"Oh, I don't know. I'll *never* know, I guess. The financial planner told me not to worry. He made some adjustments to the portfolio, adding more bonds, but basically, he said her financial situation was excellent. He told me he reviewed everything with her, including her yearly expenses and he gave her a budget framework. I didn't get specific details and I just accepted his explanation without question. Now that she has an advisor, I don't want to intrude."

"Good. We all have to recognize that there is a zone of privacy that our parents are entitled to. Sophie, I have to do the same with my mother."

Dr. K has a mother! How sweet. I love it when he occasionally divulges something about himself that is totally unexpected.

He continued. "Sophie, were you ever led to believe you were promised a legacy? Did your father intimate that was possible?"

"I have no specific knowledge about my parents' finances and I've never expected an inheritance. But after all their years of long hours and hard work, it would be a shame for my mother to be poor in her old age. Flanagan assured me that's not something I should worry about, so I'm backing off. Honestly, Dr. K, I'm pleased to see that my mother and Edgardo make each other very happy."

"Sophie, I'm glad to hear you say that. You're accepting your mother as she is and that's a very big accomplishment. And it looks as if you've come to terms with your parents' relationship, which was compromised in ways *you* wouldn't accept—but *they* obviously did. I know that in the past, you took your father's side because you were closer to him and you were more aware of his....shall I say, melancholy? What I see in you now is a woman open to the prospect that her mother has a right to find happiness at this stage of her life."

"So, I'm through with therapy? I'm cured?" I teased.

He laughed. "There are no "cures" in this office. What we want is insight and understanding and hopefully acceptance. Let's just say you've worked out several issues that troubled you. And that, I have to say, is a victory."

"Well, thank you, Dr. K. I mean it. Thanks for everything."

He closed his notebook, signaling the session was over. Since he was obviously satisfied with the way things were going, I decided to take the plunge and ask him a question he might not be too pleased about. "I have to ask you something. Are those prescription glasses, Dr. K?"

He frowned and countered with, "Why do you ask?"

"Oh, come on, please tell me. I tell you everything."

He looked down, avoiding eye contact. "No." He looked so uncomfortable that I was immediately sorry I'd asked. And what did that signify, actually? I didn't know, but my intuition was right: he wouldn't lie to me.

# November 22nd

$\mathcal{E}$nrique and I were together in my apartment tonight, having dinner, and his cell phone had not rung even once. There were three texts, but he merely glanced at them and didn't reply. So we were truly alone. I'd made a stir-fry of beef and bok choy in oyster sauce with jasmine rice—items that were definitely not on Cascada's menu, so no comparisons could be made. Of course, I realize there's no way I could cook Cascada's complicated items, but I did enjoy sharing my domestic skills.

Enrique sat back, contentedly. "Sophia, you are a one of a kind woman."

"Because I dare to cook for you, the noted restaurateur, Enrique Barranco?"

"Exactly. I love the fact that you will cook for me and not be intimidated. It's my pleasure when you give me this gift. And I must say, I love the way you eat."

What did that mean? No man had ever said that to me. "Really, why?"

He leaned forward, quite serious. "The other women I've known, they eat like the little birds. A bit here and there, just tasting. You eat with love even if you don't finish what's on your plate. And I like that you eat the bread. Bread is the balance for the sauces and the seasonings; it gives the harmony, like when you hear music that is beautiful."

"Enrique, that's so poetic. I've never thought of bread like that."

"One woman I was with, she would eat the bread, fast, fast, fast—and then go to the rest room and she would throw up. Throw up good Cascada food!" He rolled his eyes in disgust. "I know this because the staff told me."

He took my hand in his. "Some women just want to be pampered and never go out of their way, but you do all this for me." He waved his other hand, encompassing the table set with china and cloth napkins and the requisite candles and flowers.

"Enrique, I enjoy doing it because I love to cook. And when I set the table with my grandmother's china and candlesticks, it reminds me of her and that's wonderful. Of course, I'm pleased my dinner makes *you* happy. After all, you're always treating me to amazing dinners at Cascada."

"What makes me happy is that you are kind and beautiful and perhaps you don't know it, so I value your modesty. Of course, now that I've told you that you are beautiful, you'll leave me for someone with more success," he said in mock despair.

"Well, I'm not leaving you tonight, so you're quite safe," I said lightly. Truthfully, although Enrique always says such flattering things to me, I have to admit that he is vague about a future for us. It's not that I want him to make a commitment—I don't—but I do find it curious that his extreme compliments and romantic declarations never reach a tipping point bringing him closer to… what? A declaration of love? A suggestion of permanency? A hint of commitment? "Don't leave me" is not the same thing as "stay with me forever." Just saying.

"You are more than a beautiful woman, my treasure, *mi tesoro*. You would be a good wife and a good mother. This I know."

Uh oh, had I just heard the man start to tip? Would I even want Enrique to get serious? No, definitely not. Yes, I'm appreciating the ride, but I reserve the right to get off the train when the time is right. Can't a girl just enjoy the moment? This isn't about me being afraid of marriage; it's about me not being in love. And truthfully, with all of Enrique's compliments and gallantry, he's never intimated that he's in it for the long term either. We're just a couple of hedonists eating our way into a semi-platonic relationship.

To change the subject, I brought out the flourless chocolate cake that my mother always made for my birthday which I've adopted as my own. Enrique praised it most enthusiastically. I think he did so because he, himself, realized that by mentioning my *wife and mother* potential, he'd gone too far. Maybe I'm reading too much into this, but that's the way I interpret his over-the-top reaction to a chocolate dessert.

I'm emailing this entry to Kisselstine so he can appreciate how insightful I am about my feelings and how well I know myself. Sophie Marks: amateur shrink.

Bottom line: the dinner was delicious, my partner was unusually romantic—but the sex was middling.

# November 24th

aybe everyone should keep a journal and have a safe place to vent. It's extremely therapeutic; I can allow the mean girls' streak to escape. It's just that my mother—or should I say the new version of my mother—sometimes baffles me and I react badly.

Like today, when my mother and I went to Saks Fifth Avenue to shop for my dress for her wedding. Yes indeed, I am her thirty-three year-old over the hill maid of honor.

"My dress is a surprise," she said, "and you'll see it at the wedding. All I can say is that it's champagne color." She sighed. "In the upholstery business, we called it beige. But at Vera Wang it's champagne. Fancy, fancy."

I felt a sudden twinge. She'd bought her wedding dress without me! She must have sensed my disappointment, because she turned to me as she was riffling through the rack and said, "I wanted you to look forward to the big moment and be surprised." She shrugged her shoulders. "Maybe going to your own mother's wedding is surprise enough. But what can I say? I thought it was a good idea when I did it." She paused. I could see the worry on her face and then she brightened. "Anyway, the Vera Wang people were so nice and they helped me and now I'm helping you."

"I'm pleased you found a dress you love." Okay, not that pleased, since I was really disappointed, but there was no point in expressing it now and hurting her feelings.

"Sophie, now it's your turn. So buy whatever you want," she said. "It's my treat."

I told her that everything I was looking at was very expensive and I'd be happy to leave and shop at a more moderate dress department, but she was insistent.

"You're my beautiful maid of honor and you deserve the most beautiful dress." She zeroed in on an exquisite gown, a strapless, body hugging number dotted with cobalt blue sequins with a black net overlay. I have to admit it was beautiful; it was also two thousand dollars and it was ridiculous to spend that amount of money on a dress that I'd never wear again.

"Mom," I said, but she cut me off with a negative wave of her hands. "Okay, *Sherri,* please tell me how you can afford this—or I won't even try it on. In fact, I will stop this dress hunt right now." All that was missing was me stamping my feet in frustration and anyone watching would have thought I was acting like a six year old. Bitchy, bitchy me. Why couldn't I take her word for it and make her happy?

She considered this for a moment. "Look, darling, I can afford it. Trust me, I wouldn't do it if I had to watch every penny. Ask your Mr. Flanagan," she challenged. And then she added, very deliberately, "Who even knows if this dress will fit? With all those meals at Cascada, maybe you're not a size four anymore."

Come on, Sophie, did you fall for that ploy? Your mother baiting you so that you'd try on the dress. It was a classic provocation and totally obvious. Naturally, I grabbed the dress from her and marched into the dressing room. She followed me, probably with a triumphant smirk on her face that, luckily, I didn't have to see.

It zipped up without any difficulty and I'd never felt so glamorous in my life. The sequined gown literally blended with every curve of my body, flaunting my cleavage, yet managing to stay within the boundaries of propriety; the net overlay, fitted at the top, flared out gently below the waist, floating around me just like the gauzy dress on the Celesta model. But much sexier.

"You wear this dress to the wedding and Enrique is sure to propose." Obviously, for my mother, this wasn't merely a dress; it was a solicitation for a lifetime partnership.

I turned to my mother and placed both my hands on her shoulders. "Mom/ Sherri, you should know that Enrique has never said that he loves me. As for me, I do care for him, but...but I'm not *in love*. I appreciate the fact that he's charming and gallant and very good to me—but that's just not love."

"You don't love him?" She was shocked.

"I like him—I don't love him. Anyway, I don't think he's the "settling down" type. That seems to be the men whom I attract." I rambled on. "You know he's incredibly busy with the phone, the texts and the emails. So, if I did love him, I'd have to put up with all that. And he travels to Los Angeles every four or five weeks and that lifestyle is not for me. And, I don't know how to explain it, but he's never read one book that I've read and I think that's important." That last reason probably didn't make sense to her. It barely made sense to me, but somehow I felt it was significant.

My mother was silent for a bit. Then, "So, maybe the sex is not so good."

I was incredulous. I had no idea she was so intuitive. "How did you come to that conclusion?"

"Look, my darling, I know what it's like to have a, how shall I say, a not so good time in the bedroom."

"Oh God, please don't talk about sex and my father in the same sentence!"

"So how can you learn?" she countered. "If the bedroom is good, you might be able to work things out." She added sharply, "Maybe find a nice book to read in bed together."

It was clear to me that we had to stop talking at that point. How many women can talk openly about their sex life—with their own mothers? And how easy was it for the saleswoman to overhear our conversation? She was three racks away, staring off into the distance, but possibly in earshot. I fully expected her to turn around and weigh in with an opinion, perhaps urging me to consider counseling before I gave up on this successful young man. I could see her linking arms with my mother, both nodding in agreement, as they cautioned that I was not getting any younger.

I had to decide what to do about the dress. I was torn, wanting to have it and wanting to give it up at the same time—but my mother was insistent that it was meant for me. Finally, she paid for it and handed me the box and we silently walked toward the train station. She took the four to Brooklyn Heights and I caught the six to Greenwich Village.

I sat on the train, feeling remorse, knowing I should have apologized to her. Hadn't I told Kisselstine that I would not get involved with her finances? Wasn't I supposed to be trusting her? And, why did I let my concern prevent me from making this shopping trip a pleasurable experience? I guess I let my worry about her finances get the better of me. I'll call her this evening and apologize; I'll tell her how delighted I am about the dress. And, I'll even mail this journal entry to Kisselstine, just so he can see I've had a relapse. And I won't edit the bitchy part to make me look nicer.

Damn, I have to admit that I would have much more integrity if I'd said *no* to the dress.

# *December 3rd*

Carla was euphoric. Jake's divorce, which was five years in the making—a longer time than it takes to build a space station!—was now a reality. Jake's on and off, down and dirty divorce had suddenly become almost cordial because of the miracle of love. It seems that Mrs. Jake, the formidable Audrey, was certifiably in love with a new man (or just certifiable, as Carla claimed) and was no longer the rebuffed, angry wife. Equally important, Jake's daughter had finally come around now that her mother was happily getting married again.

Carla reported that Audrey's new man was quite well off. He owned a series of car dealerships in New Jersey and had bought up practically every billboard along I-95 to prove it. Travel south in New Jersey from the George Washington Bridge, she explained, and you'd be inundated with offers from Tom Daddario, otherwise known as *Mr. Easy*, the man who was open to any deal, any offer. Evidently, Carla observed, Audrey's proposition for a lifetime of parts, labor and maintenance had been agreeable to Mr. Easy. Her prior contract with Jake was now subject to termination without penalty; both parties accepted divorce mediation, the non-confrontational way to divest oneself of a spouse. And because Mr. Easy had an overstuffed wallet, Audrey did not squeeze Jake's last penny from him. That made Jake euphoric.

Carla and I were sprawled on my sofa, feet up on the coffee table—both sporting Comfies. The Comfies Slipper Company was my first major successful account early on and I had them to thank for my big promotion. In addition to a bonus, I was given ten pairs in my size seven that will undoubtedly outlive me. The slippers were a nice touch, but it was the bonus that convinced me to stay in the advertising business.

Carla and I were celebrating her upcoming marriage by smoking some weed that she'd scored. I'd like to think it was medicinal since I was nursing a sore calf from spinning class and I'd taken a week off from the gym to rest, ice and dose with painkillers.

"What's with the wedding plans," I asked, blowing a perfect smoke ring. I have to admit that was an achievement I'd perfected in high school when I smoked cigarettes for a while, until my father found out and shamed me into quitting. The exquisite irony is that he, who never smoked, died of lung cancer. I placed that occurrence in my "No Justice" mental file.

Carla giggled and popped some M&M's into her mouth. "I'm going to do it up right with a strapless, virginal white wedding dress, of course, and an open bar, a three-course dinner and a band—the works. I'm thinking the Chelsea Piers in the spring. It would be a great venue because it's right on the Hudson River and that will be beautiful, don't you think?"

"Mmmmm," I replied, "beautiful." I was really happy for Carla. She deserved the big wedding and all the trimmings although at age thirty-four she might have gone for something a little more understated. But, I was feeling no pain and I'd go along with anything she wanted.

"You'll be my maid of honor, of course. Natalie will be the matron." With that, we burst out laughing because the last thing you'd call sexy Natalie was a matron.

"You know, Carla, yours will be my third maid of honor gig this year. I have my mother's wedding this New Year's Day. And, remember, last March, I flew down to Aruba for a destination wedding when I was maid of honor for my college room-mate? I had to go alone because Renny had a conference in Denver which, to this day, I believe he didn't have to attend, but went because he wanted to ski out west."

The pot was getting to me; I went to the freezer to get some ice cream, remembering my Aruba trip, dancing on the beach, the sand between my toes, and the fifty-year old divorcée who was my dancing partner by default. We were the only two singles in attendance—the only two women willing to spend money for airfare, hotel, suitable beach dress and, of course, the gift. "And now I have my mother's wedding on New year's Day. It's getting to be a habit."

"And, unlike some of the other weddings we've gone to in the past," said Carla, "this time we both have partners for your mother's wedding. You've got Enrique and I've got Jake. It's great to be a couple, isn't it? No sitting at an empty table all by yourself with a fake smile on your face while the couples get up to dance." She thought for a moment and said soberly, "We've both gone to way too many weddings alone, haven't we?"

I raised my joint in salute. "God bless Jake and Enrique, our saviors!"

Carla did the same. "Amen to that!" And then she chanted a series of *amens* as she clapped her hands above her head and swayed side to side, as if she were in a church choir. I couldn't help myself; I jumped up and danced around the living room with her, chanting our lyrical *amens* with spiritual fervor.

There's nothing like having a date for a wedding to make two grown women find religion.

# December 12th

"That's quite a story," Kisselstine marveled.

Yes, even a shrink is occasionally surprised by information revealed in his office. Today I told him about my mother's visit. She'd called and insisted she come to my apartment to talk; as it turned out, she did all the talking.

"I have to tell you something...something about your father and me. It just seems the right time that I should be telling." She shook her head and threw up her hands in a gesture of helplessness. "So, now I'm telling."

My mother revealed that before she married my father, she had seen him in the neighborhood and had a crush on him although they'd never met. She knew he was engaged to a beautiful woman, the daughter of a prosperous dentist, named Rita. Rita Orloff. My mother knew this Rita, also from afar, and was dazzled by her beauty and sophistication. She said to me, "I was no Rita Orloff in the looks department and I was always a little chunky."

I felt so sorry for her. "Mom, you *are* pretty. Even before the blonde hair... and all."

My mother shook her head, "I know what I am now and what I was then." She went on with her story. Rita's father was against the marriage because, in his opinion, my father didn't earn enough money as a high school history teacher. So, Dr. Orloff sabotaged the engagement by introducing his daughter to a successful accountant and after three months they eloped and moved to New Jersey.

My mother said my father was devastated. One day, soon after he was jilted, she tracked him down. He was alone, sitting in a diner having his customary breakfast. She slid into the booth, across from him, and told him she was Sarah Becker from the neighborhood and she was single, a good cook and could mend his broken heart.

Kisselstine shook his head in surprise. "I must say that's a new one for me."

I nodded in agreement. "Well, she told me that they started going together and a few months later, she got pregnant, so her father and his mother—that's my wonderful grandmother I've told you about—hastily arranged a wedding. That summer he worked in the upholstery shop and he turned out to be a quick learner, quite gifted, my mother said. At the end of August, two things occurred. My mother's father died suddenly and my mother couldn't run the shop alone, so my father gave up his teaching career in order to keep the business afloat. And then my mother lost the baby." I paused. "Just like me."

Kisselstine held his hand up to stop me. "Let's remember that later on your mother carried a child to term and named her Sophie," he said reassuringly. "You know, many people I treat have reason to worry about something unpleasant that *may or may not happen* in the future. So, I often remind clients that it's helpful to concentrate on what's going right in their lives in the present. That kind of thinking requires resourcefulness; you have to purposefully concentrate on the aspects of your life that are working well. I think you can do that, Sophie."

True, I had to remember that I could still become a mother and feeling sorry for myself about *possible* future miscarriages was a definite barrier to a happy outlook in the present. "You're right, Dr. K. I shouldn't perseverate about my miscarriage. I should just hope for the best and not think the worst." I hesitated. "Now, where was I? I'm lost."

Kisselstine frowned, obviously annoyed with himself. "You have something important to day and I've sidelined you. I guess I was taking advantage of a teachable moment. Sorry."

I'm always surprised about his honesty, his willingness to admit he made a misstep. I admire him for that. "Oh yes. My mother lost the baby—the child that was the catalyst for their hasty marriage. Ironic, isn't it? My mother told me that after about six months, Rita returned to the neighborhood. It seems her husband was abusive and she'd left him and came back to Brooklyn looking for my father—her "true love," my mother said bitterly. Some months after Rita's return, my father begged my mother for a divorce, but at that point my mother was six weeks pregnant with me. She hadn't said anything to him because she wanted to make sure the pregnancy would take. At that point, he couldn't leave my mother with a child on the way."

"That's the story," my mother had said firmly, and she stood up and gathered her coat and handbag and looked at me with narrowed eyes, clearly indicating that she was not to be questioned. "Look, I never want to hurt you but, what can I say? This is something you should know." I was about to speak, but she shook her head and said, "End of story."

I'd felt incredibly sad and I could feel my face crumpling. "Oh, I'm so sorry!"

"Sophie, don't cry and don't be sorry. Just be a grownup and understand. That's all." And she quickly put on her coat and left, just like that. No hug. No goodbye.

"Your mother is one tough lady," Kisselstine said. "So, almost from the beginning of the marriage, things weren't going well."

"No. And I'm sure she wanted me to know this before she started her new life with Edgardo."

Kisselstine agreed. "Yes, your mother wants you to understand that she didn't have much of a chance to have a happy marriage once Rita came back and your father couldn't have her. I believe she also wants you to realize that she wasn't completely responsible for your father's unhappiness. Perhaps she wants you to recognize that she always carried the burden of not being loved or loved enough. I believe that telling you this story surely is her way of helping you to accept Edgardo."

'Yes. I'm certain you're right, Dr. K."

"Are you surprised that she revealed a side of your father that was less than honorable?"

"Wait a minute! My father didn't leave her. He did the right thing."

"He was having an affair while he was married, " Kisselstine countered. "And perhaps he could be faulted for marrying a woman that he didn't love."

"For heaven's sake, Dr. K, he got her pregnant!"

"Given their history, we can't be sure who was responsible for that pregnancy," he said quietly. "I think we also have to consider the fact that your mother took a risk in marrying a man who was still longing for another woman; a man who was probably not in love with her."

I protested, my voice rising. "The idea that she got pregnant on purpose— that's just speculation on your part."

Kisselstine said, "You're right; it's just a supposition on my part. But the circumstances do suggest the possibility. What is certain is that your father was having an affair with Rita Orloff when she came back. And for how long? That we don't know. Sophie, do you appreciate that? The way I see it, both your parents have something to answer for as far as their relationship is concerned."

I sighed, defeated. He was right.

"Now, let's look at the positive side," Kisselstine said encouragingly. "They stayed together and obviously worked out some sort of accommodation with each other."

"Not an affectionate, loving marriage," I countered.

"Not everyone gets the prize, Sophie. This is what I've learned as a therapist: if they're lucky, many people are happy most of the time. Unfortunately, some people are marginalized in the "happiness" department. I believe there's a happiness spectrum and sometimes we move forward on it and sometime we slide back. One of the objectives in this office is to gently nudge people toward the better part of the spectrum, if I can."

"I guess that's what you're doing for me."

"Sophie, remember, we can only know so much about the lives of people who are close to us. That means we should try not to be judgmental. Let's agree that your father suffered because he lost the woman he loved and your mother suffered knowing he might never love her as much as he loved the other woman in his life." He paused. "Or, he might not love her at all."

"Honestly, Dr. K, when I heard my mother's story I had a strange feeling that I'd seen this Rita Orloff woman in our house. I know it's trivial, but somehow I feel that I know what she looks like; I mean, I think she was in our kitchen. I'm so certain she had beautiful red hair."

"Really? You think you've seen her?" He leaned forward, suddenly animated. "Perhaps we should see if there is something to that feeling of yours. Look, I don't do it often, but occasionally I'll hypnotize a client and we sometimes get a recovered memory that's very important. Shall we try that next session?"

Hypnotism? To me, that's getting a dozen people on a stage and having them pretend to take their clothes off or having them flap their arms like birds in flight.

He recognized my hesitancy. "Don't worry, Sophie. All I'll do, once you're under hypnosis, is ask you some questions as I guide you to the past and give you the opportunity to retrieve a memory that might be worth bringing out in the open. I promise there's no theatrics and no embarrassment."

Kisselstine had already helped me in so many ways. Of course I trusted him. "All right. I'll try it if you promise me I won't make a fool of myself."

"I promise."

I agreed to hypnosis as if it weren't a big deal because at this point in our therapist/client relationship, trust wasn't an issue for me. But when I left his office, I wondered if I could trust *myself.* Who knows what painful or embarrassing memory would be unearthed that should have been left untouched? The best I could hope for was that if the repressed memory from the past was damaging, Kisselstine would be sensitive enough to conceal the details from me in the present.

Okay—one other thing I could hope for: when I'm put to sleep, I don't get all sloppy, snoring with my mouth wide open and slumping in the chair with my legs splayed. Not a pretty picture.

# *December 15th*

hree days later I had a momentous therapy session with Kisselstine. Normally I considered the words said in that office to be private, but I could hardly contain my emotions, so I asked Carla to come by after work. We settled in on my sofa with a great wine that Enrique had given to me and with the ruffled potato chips that were Carla's contribution.

"Why can't I stop eating these? I'm supposed to be starving myself for my wedding gown so that I'm at the the thinnest point in my life—which would mean what I weighed in eighth grade, "Carla moaned. "I'm eating ten chips to your every one. Not that I'm counting."

"Well, I hope you can eat and concentrate at the same time," I replied. "I want to tell you about yesterday's therapy session. I can't stop thinking about it."

Carla straightened up at once, clearly engaged, because I usually didn't discuss what went on in therapy.

I finished the remains of my wine. "Okay, here goes. Kisselstine's theory is that I'm actually afraid of marriage. He thinks I was safe with Renny because he, too, didn't want to get married so we balanced each other."

"What? Why wouldn't you want to get married?" This revelation didn't sit well with Carla, a woman who had been waiting for years for her married lover to finally make a permanent break with his wife and give her a ring. And now that she and Jake were living together, she still had to wait for the divorce process to run its course.

"Well, when I first told Dr. K about my family, I initially downplayed my parents' marital problems. I thought I was in his office only because of Renny and the baby and the break-up. After a while, Kisselstine encouraged me to be more open about my parents. Then, a few days ago, my mother sat down with me and gave me some upsetting history. She told me that my father had been jilted by the love of his life, a woman named Rita Orloff. I don't think he ever loved my mother."

"How terribly sad for her. But I have to tell you, now that we're having this conversation," Carla confessed, "I never thought your parents were a great love match."

"I know, I know. I told Kisselstine about that conversation with my mother and he had a feeling that there was more to it than I realized and he wanted to hypnotize me. He assured me that it might unlock some lost memory that might be helpful."

I'd gone this far and now there was no stopping. I told Carla that under hypnosis, I revealed an incident that happened when I was seven years old. I know I was seven because it was the day of my birthday party and I distinctly remember the cake with a big number seven candle. My father was sent out in the morning to buy some balloons but he didn't come back in time for the party or even when it was time for me to go to bed. I was so upset about that. I mean, I remember in real life that he missed my birthday; I didn't need to be hypnotized to recall that.

Nevertheless, I told Carla, under hypnosis, I revealed the complete incident to Kisselstine. My father showed up very late and I was already asleep. However, a loud argument woke me up. As I came around the hall from my bedroom toward the kitchen, I heard my parents and an unfamiliar voice. I held back out of sight, somehow sensing that I didn't belong in that angry space. It was Rita Orloff's voice I heard, the woman who'd jilted my father and run away with another man.

I had to fill Carla in on the backstory. I explained that my mother had just told me that this Rita Orloff woman had returned to Brooklyn months after she'd eloped and by that time, my father had already married my mother. Rita had left her abusive husband and she begged my father to take her back. But when they confronted my mother, she revealed that she was about six weeks pregnant with me. My father couldn't leave her with a baby on the way and a struggling business.

"Carla, I think my mother told me all this because it was time I knew more about their history. I'm certain she was looking for forgiveness from me. In the past, I've been kind of hard on her at times about the way she treated my father. And I'm sure she told me this dreadful story so that I'd accept Edgardo."

Carla put her arms around me and held me tight, as if her hug could crush my sadness into tiny particles that would float away and release the burden that weighed on me. "Oh, Sophie, I'm sorry you had to go through all this," she commiserated.

"Carla, my mother never told me the whole story. The part that was buried in my memory came out under hypnosis. Kisselstine told me what I'd repressed. My father had been having an affair with Rita ever since she had returned to Brooklyn and she was with him the day of my birthday. That's why he missed my party. They both arrived at the apartment very late and the three of them were having a blazing argument which awakened me. I could hear my mother saying that she *hated* their marriage. Over and over again, she said it was a mistake. And then my father said, "Sarah, it *was* a mistake and I'm sorry. You're a good woman and you deserve someone better."

I poured some more wine to help me along. "Then I heard my mother speak very quietly, so quietly that I could barely hear. "This marriage was a mistake. A terrible mistake. But it would be a worse mistake if we ended it. We have a child. We have a business. You have responsibility here. Damn you, you have to live with your mistake."

She spoke so softly that I edged around the doorway to see them. And while I stood rooted there, I saw my mother grab a kitchen knife and bring it down on the wooden counter with such force that the sound of the knife biting into the wood unlocked my frozen body and I ran into the kitchen, screaming."

"Poor Sophie, poor Sophie," Carla soothed.

"Poor everybody," I murmured.

"What happened after that?"

"Well, under hypnosis, I told Kisselstine that my father sat down and put his head on the kitchen table and started to cry. Do you know how terrible it is to see your own father cry? Rita Orloff backed away toward the door. She waited there for a while, no one spoke, and then she ran out. My mother picked me up and carried me to my bed and lay down with me. The next morning, nobody talked about it—*as if it never happened!* And that's my terrible recovered memory."

"I don't know what to say," said Carla. "It's so sad. And you were only seven years old! You must have been so frightened."

"Probably, but I honestly don't remember. This all came out while I was under hypnosis."

"What did your shrink say about all this?"

"Basically, he said that explains why I'm fearful of marriage and why I never allowed myself to get close to anyone I've ever dated. It helps to explain why I've had only one other long-term relationship. That is, until Renny came along and I sensed he was a kindred spirit and not likely to propose marriage, so I was safe with him."

"Does it help to have that recovered memory?" asked Carla, sounding doubtful.

"Well, Kisselstine says it does. He said that even an unhappy memory helps to fill in the blanks about why we do what we do and why we think as we do. He says that this memory will help me understand my parents and appreciate the tensions they had to deal with. And it will help me understand myself."

Carla thought for a minute. "But even if you don't want to get married, you do want to have a baby, don't you?"

"Yes, I really do. Maybe someday I'll want to get married. At least, that's what Kisselstine says."

Carla rolled her eyes. "That's my girl—*Someday Sophie.*"

"I'm working on that *Someday Sophie* thing, Carla. In fact, Dr. K says this memory will help me move forward."

Carla popped some chips into her mouth. "You're lucky to have that Kisselstine shrink. He's going to pull you through." She nibbled on the chips for a while as I sat there, emotionally drained. Then she said plaintively, "You really didn't want to get married? Unbelievable!"

I couldn't believe it either, at first, but now I know it's true. I need a handsome prince to break the spell and rescue me.

# December 16th

*J*ust when you think there are no surprises left, what happens? Renny's girlfriend, Maya, called *me*! My first thought was—how did she get my number? Well, she told me that when Renny had me watch little Emma, he'd left a message on Maya's cell phone, indicating his plans so that she would know where her little girl was. And now, Maya was suggesting we meet for coffee. I couldn't imagine what she wanted, but it really didn't matter, because I was extremely curious about the woman Renny had chosen as my replacement.

Tonight, we met at the diner near my condo. And, no surprise, she was even more beautiful than Diane, the sister I had met at Carla's apartment. She was also taller, just as described. I tried to sit as upright as possible so that my 5'6" wouldn't be crushed by her 5'11" physique and killer heels.

Most of the early December snowfall had vanished, but some icy patches were still shimmering in the dark, so I was wearing sensible wedge boots in order to navigate the sidewalk with dignity and remain upright. And here was Maya in her strappy Christian Louboutins—as if she were going to a spring dance.

After we were served our coffee and muffins, she got down to business. "When Renny told me he'd asked you to watch Emma, he also was very honest and admitted he had dated you. Well, I asked to meet with you because... because he just broke up with me." She sniffled a bit and I handed her a tissue and felt like Kisselstine, who was always at the ready.

"Sophie, you dated him for years," Maya said. "I had him for only four months. So, obviously, you know him much better than I do. Please tell me why he can't commit because I thought we were good together."

I hesitated. "Well, you must have some idea."

"He said he didn't want children but I know he cared for Emma."

"Maya, I'm not a shrink, although Renny helped to send me to one. All I can say is that he doesn't want the whole package—the wife, the child, the shared apartment, the shared life. It's him, not you. I realize that's a cliché, but it fits."

She sighed. "You know, this time I thought I'd won the boyfriend lottery. Renny's more than arm candy. He's interesting and he's smart and financially, well, let's just say he's a keeper. I even went on all those goddamned hikes!" She shook her head, regretfully. "I'm just sick of dating and I really thought he was the one."

"But you're so beautiful, you could have anyone." I admit, sometimes my feminist ideology loses steam; of course I know that beauty is not the gold standard by which we should measure our worth, but I have to admit, I was very impressed with this stunning woman.

Maya looked at me quizzically. "You're beautiful—and you're still single." She sighed and then she gently lectured me. "It's not all about looks you know, despite what some of the magazines say. There's intelligence, humor, values and so forth—and let's not forget chemistry."

"Yes, of course," I agreed, thoroughly chastened.

"Anyway, I also wanted to thank you for taking care of Emma. Believe it or not, she wants to visit you again. And I wanted to meet you because I know you meant more to him than I did, so, I thought you'd have some answers. Look, I'm not jealous; I'm just exhausted. Right now I feel as if I don't want to date another man ever again. I want to learn to be happy on my own." She paused for a few seconds. "And I don't know how."

"I'm working on that myself," I replied. "Well, officially I'm dating a very fascinating man, but I know we're not meant for each other long term." I stopped to gather my thoughts because I wanted to say this right. "Maya, please don't think I'm out of line, but you might find it useful to see a therapist to help you get it together. I mean, I've found it very valuable."

Maya rolled her eyes. "I was prom queen and voted most likely to succeed. This wasn't supposed to happen: divorced and a single mother at forty."

"Forty? You look like you're in your twenties. Early twenties!"

She dotted a manicured index finger under her eyes. "Well, I've had work done around here," she said. "Who hasn't? And there's the miracle of Botox," she added without any hesitation.

Botox? That's definitely risky business. I'm afraid that if I ever went that route, I'd have both eyebrows hitched to my hairline. And if I did have the courage to actually go through with it, I'd probably treat it like the atomic bomb Manhattan Project. Top secret.

"So tell me, who's your shrink?" she asked.

Not a chance. I couldn't share Kisselstine with Renny's ex. "I'll tell you what I can do. I'll ask my therapist for a referral and get back to you."

"Thanks, I appreciate that. Now, please, can you shed some light on the subject. Why can't he commit to a relationship? I thought he cared for me and, frankly, the sex was terrific."

Honestly, I know this woman for about twenty minutes and she's talking about her sex life! Obviously, she'll have no trouble speaking openly with a therapist. "Well, I'm certain he doesn't want children to complicate his life," I replied. "While he might care for Emma, I don't think he wants to bring her up. What's more, I believe he really doesn't want to be married, so if you suggested a long-range commitment, that would have been the catalyst to scare him off."

"Well, in a way, I guess I did; I talked about a future for us. Yes, I rushed him. Big mistake, right?"

"Maybe not," I countered. "At least you found out, sooner rather than later, that Renny is not the marrying kind. Perhaps this is for the best."

Maya crumpled her napkin, threw it on the table and pointed at it. "Just like me— disposable."

"I'll get you that referral," I promised.

We exchanged emails and split the bill. Just as we parted on the street, I confessed. "You know, Emma really liked me because I plied her with ice cream, twice in one day actually, and then a hamburger and fries for lunch and I bought her a Slinky and a cupcake. So, I pretty much bribed her into submission."

"Ditto," Maya replied with a sheepish grin. We gave each other a goodbye hug and walked in opposite directions. When I was about halfway down the block, I turned to see how she navigated the icy patches in her stilettos.

She was as sure-footed as a mountain goat.

# *December 17th*

*R*enny called. He told me he had stopped seeing Maya. I didn't admit that I already had that information from her.

"Really?" I said. "Have you become a serial womanizer?"

"That's not fair, Sophie. You and I were together for three years. That's not the action of a serial womanizer. Besides, I've only been with Maya a few months and, of course, we've never lived together."

Of course.

I asked Renny, trying to be casual, "So, why did you break up with her? In what department did she fail to meet your high standards?" At that moment, I realized that I shouldn't have asked that leading question. I was subtly asking him to compare Maya to me and that was foolish. If I allowed myself to be threatened by other women's achievements or attractiveness, I would be consigning myself to a lifetime of insecurity. Better to sign a non-compete clause with my own sex, especially the glamorous Mayas of the world. I had an inclination to share my epiphany with Dr K. He would approve. Well, he'll have his chance when he reads this journal entry.

Renny was a gentleman; he did not compare us. "Sophie, she wants the picket fence, the the SUV and the dog. I couldn't lead her on because...well... because that's not what I want. And the child was a problem. Not that I didn't get to care for her. It's just...just not what I wanted."

I was silent, thinking of the child I could have had. Then he surprised me. "Let's start over."

Amazing, I thought to myself; he's confident that I still want him and that, unlike Maya,

I'm not angling for a wedding band now or in the future; and it appears that he's also willing to overlook my desire for a child. Perhaps he believes my desire to have the child I was carrying was merely a momentary lapse on my part. "Renny, that's not going to happen. I can't go back."

"We were good together, Soph."

"It was good for the old Sophie, but I'm not that person anymore."

It was so easy for me to say goodbye to him because I'm in a much better place now. If Renny's entreaty had come months ago, before Kisselstine, I might have relented.

When I told Natalie about this conversation, she said now was the time to go on the internet to find my perfect match. "Really?" I replied, laughing. "Have you forgotten about my Cuban lothario who nourishes my stomach—if not my heart?" I reminded her that just last night Enrique and I had dined at Cascada on pomegranate dusted short ribs sauced with a porcini mushroom puree accompanied by banana and chive fritters. Pure bliss. And he had regaled me with stories about his early days in Cuba when he and Luca and some friends had a rock band that they hoped would make them famous.

He had said to me with pretend sadness, "Poor me. I once thought the drums would give me the celebrity. Now, I have the fame and the fortune that depend on these very tiny ribs. What do you think, Sophia?"

I confessed to him that I'd always found drummers to be sexy, but given the choice,

I'd go for the ribs. Hearing this, Natalie said, "You slut. You're just using him for the food."

There was some truth to that. The food, the charm, the excitement—I was enjoying it. Anyway, I had to be practical. My mother's wedding would be on New Year's Day, an intimate affair with about twenty-five guests. Enrique had become a Universal Life Minister and would marry them at Cascada. This was hardly the time for me to start dating other men. After the wedding, I'd probably make the break.

My mother had invited several relatives from upstate New York and had included my best friends, Natalie and Warren and Carla and Jake. She also had two couples from the neighborhood that she kept up with, the Rosenfelds and the Vitanzas. Edgardo had his closest friend, Juan, from the old country, as he phrased it, with his wife, Jessica, and several other Cuban expats and their wives flying in from Miami, Chicago and Texas. Of course, Enrique had invited Luca the maître' d, his confidante as well as his employee. Cascada would be closed New Year's Day and we would convene at five p.m. for the ceremony followed by a dinner prepared by a small crew of cooks who would come in about two in the afternoon. Tables would be put in the basement so there'd be room for dancing. Everything was planned and expected to go smoothly.

I have to say I was at peace with this marriage. Sarah/Sherri and Edgardo were so blissful that I couldn't help being pleased for them. I should thank Kisselstine again for my serenity, and I will, at some point, but right now I didn't feel the need for a therapy session. I'll send him this journal entry to keep him up to date and let him know I'm in a good place. Now, all I have to do is show up on New Year's Day at Cascada and take pleasure in my mother's happiness as I'm wearing the most beautiful dress I've ever owned.

My glorious princess dress! If I truly want to impress the crowd, I should leave the price tag on.

# *December 18th*

*I* was an AnnaLisa virgin until today. Natalie drove us to New Jersey to an AnnaLisa Bridal Salon. I sat up front with Nat and Carla sat in the back, spreading out the torn pages from various bridal magazines so she could study the wedding dress possibilities up to the very last minute. The pages were wrinkled and dog-eared, clearly showing wear. Carla was agonizing over every aspect of her wedding with the dress taking first place honors.

Wherever there's a major mall, there's usually an AnnaLisa, dressing brides of all shapes and sizes at all price points. Our mission: to find the most absolutely perfect wedding dress—*ever*—and that's an exact quote from the bride. Or should I say Bridezilla—for that is what Carla had transitioned into. She wanted a shower (check)) and a strapless dress (check) and a wedding with all the trimmings (check)—just like a twenty-two year-old.

The dress. There were so many beautiful dresses that would have looked good on Carla: especially those that gently flared at the waist to flatter any hint of generous hips; and those with straps so that the bride's substantial endowments would be supported. Carla rejected all of them. Instead, she chose a strapless lace mermaid gown that hugged her body from chest to waist to hips and then flared out generously at the knees. Even as she examined herself in the mirror, Natalie and I could see that she frequently tugged at the bodice to hold its contents in place.

I felt it was my duty as maid of honor to speak up. "Carla, I see that you keep pulling up the dress at your bust line. Maybe it will be uncomfortable at the wedding, like when you're dancing. You might prefer something that keeps you in place—something with straps, perhaps. Or how about a nice scooped neck? And sleeves would look very pretty."

Carla replied very firmly, "Sophie, I always imagined myself in a strapless dress." And she twirled around, beaming, seeing something in the mirror that Natalie and I failed to observe.

Natalie turned to me and said in a whisper, "And she probably always imagined herself twenty pounds thinner."

"Now *you* say something," I hissed at Natalie. "But be nice."

Natalie walked over to Carla and pointed to her chest. "You might want to put those puppies back in the crate, kiddo."

Carla gasped. "I want a strapless dress. I've dreamed of this since I was in the eighth grade. And by the way, these boobs were made for strapless!"

Even Natalie knew when to quit.

So, Carla bought her dream dress and Natalie and I hosted a shower at my apartment. In addition to pasta salad and quiche and copious bottles of wine, we spent quality time opening twenty presents from Carla's bridal registry. She could barely contain her surprise or enthusiasm as she opened each gift, even though she'd personally spent five hours at Crate & Barrel selecting every item. I was there for four of those hours and felt I had paid my dues as her maid of honor.

The pièce de résistance at the shower was the toilet paper event: the bride was creatively festooned in toilet paper to fabricate a headpiece and a gown using three whole rolls of white toilet paper, plenty of Scotch tape and two yards of white ribbon—plus a great deal of ingenuity. I must say, our little group did a fine job and I was well aware that our toilet tissue creation was more flattering to Carla's figure than the mermaid one she'd selected at Annalisa's.

After group portraits and mix and match selfies, we sat down to a cake that I'd ordered: a perfect baby blue square with a white ribbon and bow made of fondant that looked exactly like a Tiffany gift box. It had made a sizable dent in my paycheck, but it was worth it. Carla, truly amazed and very excited, came perilously close to hyperventilating. I made a mental note that if I ever got married, I'd be the reasonable one. Cupcakes.

After the shower, when Natalie and I were cleaning up, we both agreed that an alien from a planet far, far away, had replaced our wisecracking, sensible, feet-on-the-ground friend. For Jake's sake, I hoped that when the wedding was over, the real Carla would show up for the honeymoon.

Speaking of the honeymoon—wouldn't that be the more appropriate time for Carla's boobs to tumble out of her strapless wedding dress?

# December 19th

*I* was a jet setter this weekend. How will they keep me down in coach—now that I've sat in first class? On Friday night, Enrique and I took the red eye to Los Angeles where he'd set up a series of meetings for the new restaurant. I felt like Hollywood royalty when we checked into our luxury hotel. Enrique said it was worth the expense because he had to present himself as a successful businessman. And it was tax deductible.

We were welcomed at a desk in a private room off the lobby, were given flutes of champagne and wonderful cream-filled macarons, those delicate confections that melt in your mouth so quickly you barely have time to wonder if you should have paid $4.50 apiece for the experience. I've submitted to their temptations many times in New York. And now, I had a box of them—eight macarons that were about to disappear as soon as we checked into our suite. And best of all, my gluttony would be reasonably private. I could see the flash of amusement on Enrique's face; he had no taste for them, but he knew I was on the cusp of bingeing.

I wasn't really tuned in to Enrique's business in LA and most of what I'd gleaned about his operations were from the one-sided telephone conversations I'd occasionally overheard. But this morning, he was unusually expansive. When we were settled into our suite, I asked him what he expected to accomplish here.

"This operation requires a great deal of money, as you can imagine," Enrique responded. "For New York Cascada, my share was twenty-five per cent and Edgardo was my principal backer at forty per cent and then he sold shares to three of his business partners. This has worked out very well for me."

Edgardo? Edgardo a money man? I nearly fell off the chaise. We were sitting in the elegant living room of the suite. I'd kicked off my heels and was basking in the unexpected luxury. Why didn't my mother tell me about Edgardo? Or did she not realize I was terribly worried that he would spend her money recklessly? Perhaps I should have sat down with her a while ago and had an open, honest conversation instead of harboring my foolish speculations.

I had another question. "And the money for the Los Angeles Cascada?"

Surprisingly, Enrique was forthcoming with the answer. "Sophia, I have so much excitement. This time I will have a forty per cent share because Cascada New York has been a success from the very beginning and I now can afford to invest more dollars. And I make the assurance, if this works out, and I have none of the doubts, then I will surely have a fifty-one percent share three years from now when we do Cascada Las Vegas."

"Enrique, how can you run all three restaurants and make it work?"

He gave me a proud smile. "All the big name chefs do it, so why not Enrique Barranco? I know it can be done. Luca will be stationed here in LA. And you know, Luca is the charming one. I can count on him to infatuate both the men and the women, yes? Of course, I will be taking the red eye flight perhaps two or three times a month to make my presence known. And when I open Cascada Las Vegas, I will be there most of the time at the very beginning. Very important, I'll find a manager who will be just like my Luca."

He took my hand and kissed it. "Surely Luca and I cannot be the only two handsome and so charming Cubans in America!" he teased.

"Trust me," I assured him, "I'll make it my business to be on the lookout for any stray, absolutely fascinating Cuban who could do the job for you."

"Ah, I can't take any chances that I'd lose you to someone else, so I, myself, will conduct the research. To be serious," he continued, "you see it is all working so well at Cascada New York and I'm sure it will be the same here in Los Angeles. We give the manager a percentage of profits in addition to salary, and so he has the incentive to grow the business, as we say in America."

"I feel like I'm in the presence of an empire builder." He kissed my hand again in appreciation of my compliment. And then, the empire builder sent me out to sightsee while he met with his potential investors. I went to the Getty Museum and wandered about blissfully until my feet got tired and then I settled in front of Renoir's *La Promenade*. A man and a woman were enveloped in a leafy green garden and he was ahead of her with an outstretched hand holding hers, as if to guide her. She had a modest demeanor, with her eyes downcast, but you could sense that she had given herself to him. The artist made it clear that they were in love.

I'm certain that I am not in love, thank goodness, because if I were, I'd be dealing with a lifestyle that has no attraction for me. I can't see myself sitting home while Enrique captivated the rich and famous thousands of miles away in Los Angeles. What's more, I couldn't picture myself in Las Vegas with the high rollers. That was certainly not a lifestyle for someone who wanted some semblance of stability. And the bottom line is: I don't love him.

But, what if Enrique is my *last chance,* my only opportunity for marriage because no one else who's suitable will come along? Was I destined to check off *single* on my 1040 for the rest of my life?

Of course, Enrique has never actually asked me to marry him, so I'm way ahead of myself. Nevertheless, I do occasionally wonder if I would want Enrique to be the father of my children. That speculation came with the territory, I suppose. A young woman in her twenties might want an active social scene with a good looking guy who had all his hair and who would squire her around, taking care of drinks and dinner and general all around good times. And if she's trying to work her way up the corporate ladder, marriage is not necessarily her immediate concern.

But, in her thirties and forties, I think that same woman changes her expectations and makes some compromises. She's looking for that good provider who likes kids and seems stable enough to happily forfeit rounds of "frat boy" shots with the guys in favor of a two bedroom condo near a decent pre-school. And at that point, thinning hair is not a deal breaker and love doesn't have to be all-consuming or passionate. What am I thinking? Enrique sports a full head of hair; what is missing is the stable life-style. Oh, and one more thing, of course: I'm not in love with him.

Could I evolve into that second woman—the somewhat desperate compromiser? No. I'm not going to commit to a man who isn't right for me. I know I'm just marking time with Enrique. He's fun and he's charming—but I know I don't love him. I'm going to let this food fling run its course; after the New Year's

Day wedding, I'll gather my courage and end the relationship because I have no right to lead him on. Hopefully, I'll meet someone and fall in love. Someday. I believe I'm being very sensible in assessing my situation with Enrique, so I'm forwarding this journal entry to Kisselstine—just to let him know that I'm doing well and I'm in control of my life.

However, I have to admit, Enrique Barranco would definitely breed beautiful babies who, in no time at all, would not only become epicureans, but also ambitious corporate types. Imagine little baby boy Barranco adjusting his bib and then digging into his peanut butter and foie gras sandwich on an artisanal brioche with a side of carrot foam. Yum.

# December 25th

Christmas morning. Ho ho ho-ly shit. I really screwed up.

This is not turning out to be a Merry Christmas. I woke up over- champagned and under—rested, because last night nine of us singles from the office, both male and female, partied at Cavey's Tavern until two a.m. I had one champagne glass too many and I was not the sharpest tack in the toolbox as I began my day. That's my excuse for not thinking clearly when I was on the computer this morning, writing a journal entry.

I hadn't joined Enrique at Cascada for Christmas Eve because the restaurant was incredibly busy and I'd decided I'd be too lonely watching him work. And, he didn't want me to help because, as he put it, I'm a civilian. My mother and Edgardo were sunning in Florida, resting up for their New Year's Day wedding. Natalie and crew were in New Jersey at her Mom's house and Carla and Jake had decamped to Connecticut to be with Jake's sister and her family.

Usually, on Christmas Eve, I'm the lucky Jewish girl who spends the evening with Carla's spirited, extended family, enjoying the Feast of the Seven Fishes—an amazing mix of kinfolk and seafood that involves laughter, bickering, hugs, songs and stories that make for a memorable evening. And every year, Grandma DeLuca would share a treasured family recipe with me, pleased to pass it on, but dismayed that her namesake—my friend Carla—had no interest in cooking. But, when Carla would sweep her nonna into a loving embrace, all was forgiven.

Last night, with not a cod or a mussel in sight, I joined an assortment of singles, separateds and divorceds who earned their living at Dean Hathaway Chung. Actually, some of my co-workers were like family in a way, because we'd been through a number of ad campaigns together—although this would be the first time I'd linked up with them for a holiday celebration. Maybe it was the champagne at work, but we really had a lot of laughs.

I slept late this morning, unfortunately not late enough, made coffee and opened my computer and wrote about last night's champagne extravaganza and then I absent-mindedly forwarded everything—everything!—to Kisselstine. Clearly, I was overtired and dysfunctional because I sent him the wrong file— the entire *unedited* file! The "for my eyes only" file.

Actually, I'd never even intended to send this morning's entry to Dr. K. Did he really need to know that tipsy Paul from accounting had backed me against the wall while I was waiting to get into the ladies room and had tried to touch my breasts? I waved him away and he just laughed and later made out with Sandra from IT. And did Dr. K need to know that newly divorced Steve, our soft-spoken, shy art director, had arrived with a sprig of mistletoe and had positioned it in my cleavage and all evening he'd come up to me and crouch, insisting we were under the mistletoe together and he wanted a kiss—which I never gave him—but it was good for a running joke. Silly stuff, I know, but this entry and all the other unedited entries, were *not* meant for Dr. Robert Kisselstine. I was like the tax cheat who did double bookkeeping—one for herself and one for the IRS, except I'd foolishly handed my real stuff over to the agent.

Now everything I've ever thought, both good and bad, about Kisselstine was at his fingertips. Christ, when I described him folding into his therapist's chair, I remember I practically labeled him a munchkin. Munchkin! What the hell else did I write about him? Good God, I remember that I once wrote that I found him attractive when he wasn't suited up for our beige on beige therapy sessions. Attractive! That is so wrong, so unnatural and so embarrassing. I mean, I know there's a transference issue that women in therapy can experience, but I'd be awfully embarrassed if he thought that was going on—especially since I'm dating Enrique. Anyway, I am *not* attracted to Kisselstine. I just wrote that *he* was attractive. Surely that's a significant distinction. Or did I actually write that I *was* attracted to him? Damn, I'm too upset to re-read my journal and find out. At this point, I don't need to gather more evidence to increase my humiliation.

Can I ever face him again? No, I just can't. Thank God, I have no future appointments scheduled. It would be so mortifying to sit across from him in that office knowing that he has a full record of my innermost thoughts—the kind you might share with a girlfriend, if you're desperate to get them out there—but you'd never tell a man, even if he is a licensed shrink. I have no choice; I'm finished with therapy.

Merry Christmas to one and all. Me excluded. Damn, I'm going to miss that man.

# January 2ⁿᵈ

*S*herri and Edgardo's wedding went according to the plan; ceremony, food, music dancing and toasts—all executed perfectly. As for me, everything went awry. The day after the wedding, I called Kisselstine's office and left a message that I had an emergency. At that point, I couldn't give a damn about what he'd read in my journal.

Kisselstine called back almost immediately. "Sophie, what's going on?"

"I'm miserable and I'm desperate. I must see you."

He said nothing about my unedited journal and I was grateful for the reprieve. Maybe he'd bring it up when I was in his office. Well, I had more urgent issues to deal with. Kisselstine squeezed me in for an end of the day appointment. I'd never asked him for an emergency visit before, and I could see the look of concern on his face. "Tell me what's happening."

I took a deep breath and started from the beginning. I told him that Enrique and I had a quiet New Year's Eve dinner downtown, in a small Thai restaurant where he wasn't known and then we went back to my place. He made love to me more slowly and with more passion than I'd come to expect from him. We didn't have sex often—a situation that was perfectly acceptable—so I was surprised when he initiated the encounter with an urgency that was unusual. He left early because he had to be prepared to conduct the wedding and he needed to fine-tune the marriage vows.

The invitations called for a five o'clock ceremony on New Year's Day. A sign on Cascada's entrance would indicate a private party in progress and just to make sure, one of the waiters would man the door, admitting only the wedding guests. I left my apartment early, figuring the holiday would render taxis scarce, but—Manhattan surprise—I caught a cab immediately for the trip uptown and with traffic eerily absent, I arrived at Cascada at 4:30. The restaurant was locked. Even if I pounded on the door, I wouldn't be heard because there was a small entry lobby and then another door to the restaurant itself. So, I went around the corner, because I knew that the kitchen entrance was often left slightly ajar to counter the heat.

I felt as if my heart stood still; I could barely breathe. There were Enrique and Luca in an embrace, *kissing*. Not a continental left cheek/right cheek maneuver, but a passionate kiss. I gasped and they both turned around and gasped as well. Luca bolted for the office while Enrique rushed to me.

"*Querida*, it's all right, all right," he murmured as he drew me close.

I struggled out of his arms. "No, it's not all right. It's…it's unbelievable!" He reached out to me but I backed away.

"I am in love with you, Sophia, and that's all that matters." He saw the response on my face; I was in shock. Then he quickly added, "What you saw means nothing, *querida*. Luca means nothing." He reached out to to me and gripped my shoulders. "It is of no importance."

"Enrique, you were kissing him, like a lover." My voice rose. "He's your lover!"

He dropped his arms to his side and said so softly that I could hardly hear him, "Only Luca. Only sometimes." As if that made it better. Then he drew me to him again. "You are the one, *querida*," he kept repeating. "*Querida, querida*."

When I halted my story to blow my nose, Kisselstine, once again showing no surprise, said very calmly, "That must have been so hard for you, especially because it was the night of the wedding."

I was just stunned, I admitted. "I immediately questioned in my mind whether he had exposed me to…to, you know, a disease." I turned away from Kisselstine, too self-conscious to face him. "How could he do this to me? And I was processing all this just minutes before everyone would gather. I didn't know how I could deal with…with what I'd seen." I was too upset to continue and I took a few deep breaths to steady myself. Kisselstine waited patiently.

"My first instinct was to run. But how could I? This was my mother's wedding and I couldn't ruin her day. So I went to the ladies room to pull myself together." Did I really need to tell Kisselstine how superficial I was that I felt it was imperative that I repair my make-up and paste a fixed smile on my face?

Seriously, I looked in the mirror and tried on various artificial smiles until I found one that appeared relatively sincere and I arranged my face accordingly.

No, it was not about me being shallow; it was more about me protecting my astute mother who would likely detect any cracks in my façade and would insist on knowing what was going on.

I told Kisselstine that all the guests assembled by five o'clock and were served champagne and hors d'oeuvres and then the ceremony began. Enrique had become a Universal Life Minister for the occasion and he handled his office with solemnity as he joined Sarah/Sherri and Edgardo in matrimony. No one would ever guess that he was upset about what had happened earlier. But I could tell he was hurting; his expression was strained and his energy was forced. I worked my fake smile all evening, even when Enrique draped his arm around me and told everyone I was enchanting. His words were tender, but they meant nothing to me.

Between courses, I went to the ladies room and Natalie followed. She didn't mince words. "What's wrong? Something's wrong."

"It's nothing, really, Nat. It's just a little overwhelming for me."

She shook her head, doubtful. "Do you want to talk about it?"

That's what happens when you know someone for years. She caught on quickly. Then, Carla showed up. "Sophie, I thought you were cool with this wedding, but maybe not. Do you need a hug?"

"Girls, no hugs or I might break down. I guess I'm just being emotional. My father, you know." That satisfied them. We all reapplied our lipstick and fluffed our hair, Carla gave her Spanx a final tug and we made our re-entry.

Sarah/Sherri was radiant. Her "champagne" dress was exquisite, a glamorous and sophisticated choice that was perfect for her. She and Edgardo exchanged kisses often because the Rosenfelds and the Vitanzas tapped on their wine glasses frequently, cueing the bride and groom to stop everything and kiss and then laugh, suddenly shy. It was sweet.

Edgardo had hired a violinist, a flautist and a cellist, and after dessert, the happy couple performed a tango that demonstrated their artistry; sinuous and sexy describes it best. I actually felt my distress fade, if only temporarily, as I watched them dance and I did savor the moment. I wished I could someday be as happy as my mother. I already knew that my own happiness was out of the question that night.

"It sounds as if you were very brave that evening," said Kisselstine.

"Why, yes, I think that's true. I danced with Enrique and I believe I maintained a pleasant appearance. When he gave the toast, I granted him that *First Lady look*—you know, eyes opened wide, face upturned and expression enraptured. An Academy Award performance," I said bitterly.

"So," Kisselstine responded, "you carried it off well. It's a gift you gave to your mother and Edgardo and I commend you."

"But I'm shaking now, Dr. K. I'm sure I need to be tested for …you know… for HIV. Because, how do I know he slept only with Luca? And even so, how do I know whom Luca has had sex with? I'm so frightened and it's all my fault. I should have suspected this, right?" He was about to speak when I waved him off. "Nothing you can say can make me feel better."

"You might not feel better right away, but I promise I'm going to help you get through this," said Kisselstine with an authority in his voice he rarely used. He added, "And this problem is not your fault."

"Look, I Googled it and I can take the AIDS test at home. Privately. I'm just afraid to be alone when I do it."

"I understand. Sophie,

I just want you to know that if it turns out to be positive, you'd have to repeat it in a physician's office, using a different test, the Western Blot test. I think it's best to get it done professionally the first time. I believe the rapid HIV antibody test will give a result in about twenty to thirty minutes. If it's negative, that's it. You're good to go. If it's positive…" He let those words hang in the air for a few seconds and then regrouped. "If it's positive, which is not likely, we'll handle it. Together, I promise. And you do want to see a physician just to make sure there's no STD involved."

I went from distress to embarrassment. Now I was talking to this man about the condition of my genitals; I could feel my face turning red. "I'm frightened and I'm ashamed," I confessed.

Kisselstine shook his head. "Shame isn't the issue here. And I can tell you for a fact that many people get tested when they begin a new relationship. You must know that. This would be seen as routine in a doctor's office."

"Just one time—just one time!—my diaphragm was AWOL and I had unprotected sex with Renny and you know how that turned out. And now, a different boyfriend, and I find out that he's bi-sexual or gay and I'm in trouble." On top of everything else, it was humiliating to discuss my vintage method of birth control with my shrink. Did I really need to tell him that I couldn't take the pill or use an IUD because I had suffered complications from both?

"Sophie, how can I help you?"

"Damned if I know." I curled up in the chair with my head in my hands. "You are supposed to know."

"Look, let's be practical. You'll get a blood test and then we'll deal with the results. Do you have a physician?"

"I have a gynecologist but I'll be damned if I'll go to him and get tested. When I get my check-up, he always asks me if I use protection, as if I were a child and needed reminders after all these years. I mean, that's not a bad thing, but he often sounds patronizing. I wouldn't put it past him to chastise me about why I couldn't figure out that the man I was dating was bi-sexual. And he'd be right."

"Sophie, you shouldn't have to go to that physician if he makes you uncomfortable. He doesn't sound like the right doctor for you, but that's an issue for another day. I can refer you to someone who's sensitive and compassionate. We can work this out and take care of this very quickly."

"Oh, Dr. K, what was Enrique thinking, putting me at risk and saying I was his *querida?*"

"We can't waste time on what *he* was thinking. Right now, we have to get you tested and then go from there. Let me recommend a doctor." Before I could speak, he added, "A female gynecologist that I've known since college."

"I just can't face it alone. Believe me, I can't tell my mother because God knows how she'd react. And Carla, Carla…she's so excitable these days; her upcoming wedding has made her a little crazy. And I can't tell Natalie because she'll probably be judgmental. She's just as likely to say I should have figured it out because, well, you know…Enrique and I weren't that compatible in the bedroom and we really didn't have relations that often. That was a clue and *I* ignored it. This is all my fault."

Kisselstine had an impassive face, as usual, as his listened to my rant. Then, he asked very gently, "Are you finished?"

"Maybe," I sniffled. Then I laughed, in spite of myself. "I'm a mess, aren't I?"

Kisselstine smiled. I think he was relieved that I could still laugh in spite of my predicament. "Sophie, I'll take you to my friend, Leah, who's a gynecologist practicing in New Jersey. She won't be judgmental, I assure you. And you won't know anybody in that office so you'll have your privacy. In fact, I'll ask her if we can come in after regular office hours, so it will be very private. I'll drive. That should make it a little easier for you."

"You're not allowed to do that. I mean, drive. You're my therapist."

"I think you need me more as a friend right now than as a therapist. Let me help you. Then I'll refer you to another psychologist, a colleague you'll be comfortable with."

I went on a tirade. "What are you saying? You'll drive me to Jersey and stand by me—and then you and I are finished in this office? After that, I'll have to spit out my family issues, my problems, to another doctor? Go through everything that I've already told you, again?" I eyed him suspiciously. "And that journal is private. I've gotten used to the idea of you reading it, but you can't remotely expect me to have someone else…some stranger…" I stopped, totally frustrated.

Kisselstine took off his glasses and rubbed his eyes. "Let me call her and see if we can get an appointment. Yes?"

I had to think. It would be comforting to lean on him for this, but starting over with a new shrink would be intolerable. "I do not, repeat *not*, want a new psychologist, Dr. K. The idea of that is nearly as frightening as getting tested for HIV. Can't I stay with you?"

"I could lose my license."

"Oh, would your Jersey doctor friend turn you in?"

"No, that won't be a problem. I'll escort you to her office and there's no need to tell her that you're a former patient. I can simply bring you in as a friend. But, then I have to do the right thing after that. Unfortunately, I just can't see you outside the office and then continue the therapist/client relationship."

I wanted to throw our little conversation at Cavey's Tavern in his face—where he sat down with me, beer in hand, to hear about my post break-up sexual encounter with Renny, but I refrained. He had somehow let that episode pass the shrink litmus test and if I reminded him, it just might thrust him over the edge and then he wouldn't even drive me to New Jersey. Honestly, when I did encounter him outside the office, it was always unintentional—accidental—except for that one time I stalked him. He shouldn't be blamed for that.

"All right," I relented. "Make the damn appointment. Of course, it would be better if I were going to a doctor in—I don't know—Katmandu? I'm sure I absolutely wouldn't run into anyone I know over there. And if a doctor in Katmandu reproached me about having sex with a man whom I should have figured out was bi-sexual, fine, fine—because who the hell understands Katmandese? Katmanduish? Whatever."

Kisselstine shook his head, waiting for my outburst to subside. "Good. We'll go together. And when things quiet down, I'll refer you to a colleague. One other thing: I work closely with a psychiatrist when I want to prescribe meds for a patient. I'm thinking that I'll get you a prescription for a low dose of Ativan just to take the edge off and help you sleep at night, if that turns out to be a problem."

I nodded my head, allowing him to take that as acquiescence. There was no more fight left in me. Perhaps, I could change his mind after the test. After all, I said to myself, tomorrow is another day. Note to self: when in distress, Sophie Marks turns to Scarlett O'Hara—a fictional character, rather than a real person—to deal with life's assortment of knockout punches.

Oh well, whatever works.

# January 5<sup>th</sup>

r. K picked me up at six o' clock for the drive to Cranbury, New Jersey. For some reason, I expected him to show up in a Prius, so it was a surprise to see him in a Lexus 350. It just demonstrates how many troubled souls are out there—me included—whose combined angst adds up to a luxury car.

He had that off-duty look. Wavy hair, no glasses, black sweater and tan chinos and his navy pea coat. It's still somewhat unsettling to see my shrink morph into a real person. Tonight, it would have been very comforting if good old *medium* Dr. K arrived in his neutral taupes and beige. Nevertheless, I was glad to have him in my corner.

I was no longer the semi-hysterical woman who'd shown up in his office three days earlier. I'd had more time to reflect and I realized I had no choice but to handle whatever came my way. Obviously, I came to this acceptance with Kisselstine's help, but I also believe the time interval had also given me more perspective. I had a lot to be afraid of but it would do more harm than good to give in to panic. I would simply have to deal with whatever options I would be given. I would be a grown-up.

But I did need a distraction. I decided I would take the opportunity to learn more about the enigmatic Dr. K who obviously had two identities: one for the office, one for after-hours. I figured if we talked the entire trip, I could tamp down the butterflies in my stomach and satisfy my curiosity as well.

"You look so different outside the office. I mean I understand that you strive to be neutral, but aren't you taking it to an extreme?" I was thinking particularly of those thick, black-framed glasses. They always reminded me of something you'd wear with a Halloween costume.

He just shrugged. "Oh, come on," I pleaded, "I'm tense about the test and I need a distraction. Talk to me." And he did. Just like a psychologist.

"Interactive Psychology tries to minimize transference by setting up a structure that downplays gender and offers as neutral a setting as possible. Stripping ourselves of "sartorial" personality means that our clients don't focus on us. It makes it easier for them to see the therapist as a facilitator. That's also why the office is so neutral: no pictures, no patterns, no distinctive touches."

Thankfully, he was watching the road and didn't see me blush. If he'd bothered to read the complete journal I'd accidentally emailed him, he would have noted that at some point I said he was nice-looking—outside the office, of course. Would he find that weird and be wary of my transference potential? I tamped down that embarrassing thought. One disaster at a time, Sophie.

He was silent for a while and then said in a conversational tone, "I once had a patient who had trouble focusing and finally, she told me that the geometric design area rug in my office was the exact same pattern she had in her dining room and every time she looked at it in my office, she was unnerved."

"Seriously?"

"Seriously. It just threw her off; she couldn't concentrate. I replaced it with a plain vanilla beige carpet that is virtually invisible. I don't even keep a clock in view because that, too, can be disturbing."

"I always wondered how you knew the time was up."

He glanced at me and smiled. "Did you think I had supernatural powers? Actually, I have a watch that vibrates five minutes before time is up and then again at two minutes."

"But deliberately wearing fake glasses, limiting your wardrobe to drab colors, plastering your hair down…" I stopped because I was getting perilously close to hurting his feelings; I may have already crossed that line. Nevertheless, I knew I had a point. "What I'm trying to say is that you're not presenting your authentic self."

"I know, I know. I don't want to be a caricature, but that's what works for me." He hesitated and I could sense he was deciding whether or not to continue. "Sophie, I had a terrible experience when I was just starting out in practice. I was about twenty-seven years old and I had a new patient, a very attractive woman about forty years old, who, after a few sessions, came on to me very aggressively. I terminated therapy immediately, as gently as I could, and she became very angry and quite out of control. Then, she brought charges against me, claiming that I forced her to have sex. I had to appear before the state licensing board. Basically, it was a he said/she said situation and I had no idea if I would come out of that meeting alive."

"How awful for you."

"Sophie, I still get chills thinking about it. Honestly, for the longest time, I had nightmares about her even after the issue was resolved. But, I had a lucky break at that hearing. One of the docs on the panel, a fellow of about fifty, had treated her for about ten years and he'd diagnosed her with Narcissistic Personality Disorder along with other issues. She had come to our meeting with her own lawyer and was ready to destroy me, but when she saw that psychologist, she panicked. She couldn't make a case for herself because her former therapist asked all the right questions and she ultimately broke down and admitted that I'd never touched her. That coincidence—having the psychologist there who'd treated her—saved me and saved my practice. But, that episode convinced me that I had to be neutral. I can't hide my gender but I can minimize my..."

I interrupted to finish the sentence for him. "Appeal?"

He laughed. "That's your word, not mine."

"Well" I teased, "now that I've discovered you're a person of the male persuasion, how will my therapy proceed?" That's right, Sophie, let him think you *just* figured out that he was a good-looking man with obvious sex appeal. Maybe he'll fall for that.

He frowned. "You're very persistent. But, let me remind you that you're no longer my client."

"So, if it turns out that I have a positive test, God forbid, I can't believe I'm even saying that, you'd abandon me in my hour of need? I'm not joking, Dr. K. That surely is a violation of the Hippocratic Oath."

"Sophie, let's take one step at a time. We'll deal with the test and then we'll go from there."

I figured if that's the case, I might as well dig deeper. "So tell me about yourself. We're friends now," I reminded him. I needed him to talk to keep my mind off the appointment.

He was silent. Then I coaxed, "Come on, speak to me as a *friend*," italicizing the word to remind him he was not a working therapist at this point in our relationship.

"Okay, my *friend*. I grew up in Brooklyn, your basic non-athletic, somewhat nerdy Jewish guy. Other kids were playing softball while I played the violin. I can't tell you how happy that made my father, who was a frustrated musician. I didn't discover tennis until I was well into my twenties, so I've compensated somewhat for my basically inert childhood."

"Were you teased about your last name?"

"Quite a bit. But it helped me learn how to defend myself. Now I wear it as a badge of honor."

"That's what I'd figured when I booked my first appointment. I assumed your last name had toughened you up and you'd have the skills do to the same for me." He nodded his head affirmatively and smiled. "Okay," I said, "please, continue."

"After Harvard, I went to the University of Chicago for graduate psychology work and then back to New York for a fellowship. I love what I do, Sophie. There's tremendous satisfaction when you can help people decode the events they deal with and give them the tools to address the roller coaster ride that is life." He paused. "Hey, I didn't mean to pontificate."

"As your patient, I know that you do love your work and I appreciate that. So, tell me, what's *your* roller coaster ride like now?"

He looked straight ahead at the road. I tried another tack. "I know you're not married, but have you ever been married?"

"Yes, I was married for a short time when I was doing graduate work in Chicago. My wife was a dermatology resident. She was very beautiful and blond, very smart and driven, and frankly, I couldn't believe my good fortune that she was interested in me. I'll tell you something, Sophie," he said with a sudden burst of recognition, "she was just like your Celesta Liquid Gold girl!"

"Your fantasy woman. I understand that."

Then he surprised me. "Do you have a fantasy man?"

"I think in some ways Enrique fit the bill because he's so gallant and chivalrous. I have to admit that his attentions made me feel special. And, I was seeing celebrities, politicians and theater people at Cascada and that added a sense of excitement to our relationship. I felt like a teenager, sometimes, thinking about getting an autograph. And remember we had that weekend trip to Los Angeles. There definitely were fantasy aspects during our time together."

"But you knew you wouldn't marry him. I made the mistake of marrying my fantasy." Kisselstine pointed out.

"You were young, so all is forgiven."

"Thank you, *Dr. Marks.*"

I urged him on. "I know there's more to your story."

He nodded. "When it came time to do my psychology fellowship, I planned to go back to New York. My wife knew that's what I always wanted and I thought she had agreed to that. However, she chose to settle in California. Not alone. She'd been having an affair with a fellow dermatology resident whom she married right after our divorce was finalized. I hear they're happy and filthy rich in California. I have a West Coast colleague who tells me that between the two of them, they've Botoxed half the female population of San Diego." He laughed without rancor. I admired him for that.

"So, did you have therapy because of the divorce?"

"As a psychology fellow, I had therapy because it was part of my training. I paid my dues in suffering just like any other guy who's been cheated on. Eventually, I came to the conclusion that my ex-wife and I were not right for each other and divorce would have been inevitable. Naturally, I would have preferred a more dignified parting that didn't include infidelity."

He sighed. "Even psychologists aren't exempt from making mistakes. I was infatuated with her. She was the unattainable girl whom I'd never dare ask out in high school or even college for that matter. And when she showed an interest in me, I just fell head over heels, as they say."

Evidently, he had no idea he was a "catch." But I didn't say that to him. Instead, I asked, "Don't many of us make mistakes when it comes to matters of the heart?"

"Sophie Marks, I commend you. Even in your hour of need, you have the capacity to help others."

Although he was mocking me, I think I detected a note of approval in his voice. His mistakes, my mistakes—weren't they the inevitable debris that churned up as we barreled through our good and bad experiences. I was dealing with the consequence of my mistake right now —and wasn't it best to just promise myself that no matter what happens, I would ride the wave and do my best to stay afloat? (I think I'm allowed to mix metaphors, even though NYU awarded me honors in English and expected verbal purity from me.)

We drove in silence for a while and then I asked a question which had been on my mind. "How do you deal with patients chattering on about the trivial things—the minor slings and arrows—that they talk about? I mean like my babbling about my mother's tango competitions or my expensive dress from Saks Fifth Avenue?"

"Actually, when you're sitting in a therapist's office, nothing's insignificant. Everything that's said is a piece of the puzzle and is important to help the therapist and client navigate the issues. The little things sometimes unlock the answers for the big things."

"Really? You don't get bored. Or annoyed with the nonsense?"

"Sophie, I'm never bored. But, you're right. Sometimes people do talk about seemingly unimportant things. But, when they do, they attain a certain comfort level in sharing their experiences with me. Ultimately, it makes it easier for them to dig deeply into the significant issues that brought them to the office in the first place."

Suddenly, I had to catch my breath. He was pulling into the parking lot of Cranbury Medical Associates. There were no distractions now. I had to face the reality that I was getting a test that would determine my future. I know that sounds dramatic— but that's what I felt at the moment. Kisselstine steadied me with his hand on my arm and we walked toward the office.

Just as he'd promised, his doctor friend, Leah, was supportive and gentle. She drew blood and told me there'd be about a thirty-minute wait. After my physical exam, she reassured me that I didn't have an STD and, a half hour later she gave me the best news. I'd tested negative. Honestly, I was so happy that I threw my arms around her and hugged her. For the record, I restrained myself with Kisselstine, but to my surprise, he gave me a hug and whispered in my ear, "I'm so relieved."

True to his word, Dr. K had introduced me as a friend. I felt so grateful to him for his friendship because it eased the way for the test and the exam. Nevertheless, I still believe that I will be back in his office, sitting in that plush patient's chair, sharing confidences about my life.

By the time we left the office it was nine o'clock and we were starved. Dr. K steered me to a nearby Italian restaurant. I think I was giddy with happiness. He suggested a celebratory drink. I quickly downed two cabernet sauvignons as if they were diet Cokes and was annihilating most of the third when he put a hand on mine. "Hold on there, cowgirl. Let's slow down." He'd never have ordered wine for me if he'd known I hadn't eaten all day.

"I'm celebrating," I replied, giggling.

"Let's party just a little more slowly, young lady."

"Right you are! I am young, thirty-three damn years young! And guess what? I already have a spot on our agency's Hall of Fame walkway. Every day as I go to my office, I see the framed posters lining the hallway that showcase Dean Hathaway Chung's greatest hits." I raised my glass and toasted, "To greatest hits." Then I drained the rest of the glass. He reached out and took the glass from me and placed it on the table upside down. I guess he figured if I didn't take the hint, at least the waiter would.

"I'm taking a chance here, Sophie. Tell me if Celesta Liquid Gold put you on the wall."

I shook my head. "Too soon to tell on that one, buddy. But, I am indeed on the wall. Hey, you know those colorful slippers that are lined with shearling, Comfies? I created their ad. *Slip into Comfies and you'll slip into comfortable.*" I distinctly recall giving Kisselstine a thumbs up at that point. "Hey, remember the picture that went with it—a daddy, a mommy and a little boy and girl wearing identical light blue flannel robes, snuggling on a couch with their feet up on the coffee table— and what are on those feet?' I demanded. He didn't answer. Damn, the man didn't know my ad! "Blue Comfies, you betcha!" I wagged a finger at him. "And what about the roaring fire in the fireplace. One thousand percent Americana!"

I stopped in order to burp without apology. Then, "Don't you know that the family that's comfortable is also loving and connected? Hey, Dr. K, if only my folks had Comfies, everything would have been different!" I noticed a few people in nearby tables tuning to look in my direction, but I was on a tipsy roll. "Do you realize how many people have warmed their toes in Comfies thinking they'd be like that totally fake magazine family? You know, I spent hours doing research to decide what was the best damn color for their robes and finally, I determined that baby blue is the color of comfort."

I looked at him through narrowed eyes. "I should have told you to wear baby blue tonight so I'd be comforted! Just in case."

"Had I known, I'd have done a wardrobe check with you."

At that point, we were served our dinners and we concentrated on eating because we were both famished. I think the meatballs and spaghetti neutralized my excessive wine intake on an empty stomach. When I was halfway through dinner, I became more sensible. "Dr. K, was I being so unreasonable before? I mean about not going for the test by myself. Please, please, answer me as a therapist."

He was silent for a while, gathering his thoughts. "Well, I think you conflated two issues and that's why you had so much anxiety. I mean it's obviously completely reasonable to be apprehensive about an HIV test. But for you, there was this self-mortification because your sexual experience with Enrique was not fulfilling and you blame yourself for not realizing he was bi-sexual. So, the normal anxiety you'd naturally experience was heightened because you were so angry with yourself." He paused. "By the way, I don't believe that you necessarily could have ascertained Enrique's sexual orientation."

"So, you don't think I was a fool because I didn't figure out...um, the bedroom problem?"

"Absolutely not. You're way too hard on yourself." We sat in silence for a while. I think he was letting me digest this information. In a way, he was trusting me to come around to his view and giving me the space to think. After a few minutes, I smiled at him. "Thank you."

Then he surprised me with a question. "Will you miss him?"

"Honestly, no. I think my fear, my worry, crushed any feelings I had about having a charming boyfriend. I might miss the idea of him," I conceded. "Women turned around to look at Enrique and that was...well, it was something unique for me. But, the bottom line is that we were never going to be permanent. Actually, I'd been thinking it would be best to end the relationship after my mother's wedding."

"Perhaps you'll miss the duck with cranberry glaze over a bed of farro studded with roasted oysters," he said with mock solemnity.

"You really did read my journal!" Then I winced, not knowing which journal he was referring to. Was it the original abridged one I'd faithfully sent to him or was it the Christmas Day unedited one that had too much information? Incredibly, he jut nodded his head affirmatively, maintained an impassive expression and didn't make any further comment. I began to appreciate that he was a consummate professional who—if he'd read the second version—accepted whatever I'd written because he was trained to understand the human condition. That would be mine.

We finished our dinner and headed back to the city. I promptly fell asleep in the car and cannot recall one minute on the New Jersey Turnpike—for which I am grateful. He parked near my building, woke me up and escorted me into the lobby.

"Thanks, Dr. K. Thanks for everything."

He put his hand on my shoulder. "My name is Rob."

I looked up at him in surprise. "Oh, I can't call you that! You're Dr. K."

He dropped his hand. "Of course. Goodnight, Sophie."

Dr. K. My one and only shrink.

# January 11ᵗʰ

*I* had decided to be tested for HIV before I told my friends that I was no longer dating Enrique. Now that I was certain I was healthy, I was ready for the next step. I planned to see Carla and Natalie in person to give them the news. Probably at lunch, perhaps sometime between the breadsticks and the salad, I'd just drop it into the conversation without fanfare to show how inconsequential the break-up was to me.

The other issue was Kisselstine. In a text to Carla and Natalie, I casually mentioned that I was finished with therapy. Since I rarely discussed details of my sessions with my shrink, that information didn't arouse much interest or suspicion.

I had been thinking about finding the right time to have the conversation about Enrique with Sarah/Sherri, but it turned out I had no control over that. When the honeymooners returned from London, Enrique told his uncle that we were no longer a couple and of course, Edgardo immediately passed that information onto my mother.

The first thing she said to me was, "You broke up with him? I can't believe it! Nobody sticks with you."

"We just weren't right for each other," I said. But she wasn't buying.

"At least tell me why. He seemed so romantic with you." Of course, I told her appearances were deceiving but she brushed that off. Finally, I decided that there had been enough secrets between us and I simply told her the truth. "Mom/Sherri, he's bisexual. He sleeps with men also."

Dead silence. Then, "That's not good." More silence. Then, "I'm so sorry, Sophie, dear. I shouldn't have figured it was just *you* being difficult. So, he told you this?"

"I discovered him kissing Luca the night of your wedding. Mom/Sherri, believe me, I didn't misinterpret anything because Enrique admitted the truth to me. It's a fact: he's bi-sexual. Or maybe he's homosexual, I don't know. I don't know if *he* even knows who he is."

"Bi-sexuals, homosexuals, lesbians, and those what do you call them?—transformers—they're just like everyone else, I'm sure, but we didn't have them in my day."

I decided it would be best to ignore that comment. "Mom/Sherri, I know you're disturbed about this, but please don't blame Edgardo for setting us up. I'm fairly certain Edgardo doesn't know, because Enrique is conflicted about his sexual orientation and I'm sure he's kept it secret from everyone. It's best not to say anything."

"No, I won't discuss. Why should I upset Edgardo if he doesn't know already?" She paused. "Look, I know Edgardo and I am certain that he has no idea. Silence would be best."

"Mom, Sherri, I don't want you to..." I sighed. What didn't I want? Finally, "I don't want you to be unhappy. Don't be disappointed." That's what I said, but I really meant that I was sorry *I* was disappointing her—once again.

"Sophie, don't worry about me, darling. I'll just have to find you someone else."

I was impressed with her practicality, not wasting time with anger or reproach as far as Enrique was concerned. Instead, she was looking forward to resolving my embarrassing single status. Dr. K would probably say the same thing. Onward.

"Sure, Mom/Sherri, you work on it." Why not? She had solved her own problem of loneliness and lack of love and here was another problem just waiting for her to attack and triumph over.

Let Sarah/Sherri do the hard work of finding the right man for me in Manhattan. I needed a break from men. Seriously.

# January 13<sup>th</sup>

*N*atalie, Carla and I squeezed in a lunch date today. Carla and I arrived in working girl uniform—tunic, leggings and boots while Natalie wore a sweat suit. Her toddler, Alice, was in daycare and Natalie had just one hour before she had to pick her up.

"You girls are so glamorous," Natalie sighed. "I'm straight from the gym and my only accessory is deodorant."

Carla pointed out Natalie rocked the sweat suit, having returned to her pre-baby figure in record time. Motherhood looked good on her. Carla, however, was always on a diet and could never lose those last sticky twenty pounds. However, she was pretty, vivacious and well-built and had attracted boyfriends all her life.

I decided to withhold my announcement about Enrique until we'd almost finished our salads. I figured since we wouldn't have dessert—God forbid at lunch!—my timing would be impeccable. Natalie would be on the run to pick up Alice and Carla and I would have to get back to work, which meant limited discussion time.

"My friends, we haven't much time so let's get right down to business. Enrique and I are over. Finished." I stopped. How to say it? Just say it. "It turns out he's bi-sexual…or perhaps just gay. I didn't wait around long enough to find out."

That certainly halted coffee cups in mid-air. They both expressed surprise and indignation. "Really, Sophie, how could you have missed that?" Natalie asked, puzzled. I had a feeling she'd say something like that.

"Honestly, I didn't have a clue." Of course, that wasn't quite accurate. I did feel that Enrique was often going through the motions when we had sex. And having sex was never a priority for him. But, I was never sure if it was his issue or my own. Most often, I took on the responsibility for our bedroom difficulties. Okay, I'd convinced myself that I needed much more stimulation or had developed organic trouble coming to orgasm; perhaps I was distracted, tired or undersexed; yes, all the excuses one could make when one is shouldering the blame instead of looking for answers. I had dealt with it briefly with Kisselstine and then dropped it because the solutions he proposed were definitely out of the question.

Carla was comforting. "Sophie, I'm so sorry. Don't worry, someone will come along who checks out in all the right categories." Then her anger bubbled up to the surface. "I can't believe Enrique put you through this crap!"

Natalie agreed. "It's like your whole relationship was a lie. Son of a bitch."

"Cool it, ladies. I'm really okay right now. But, I'm hereby announcing that I'm taking a time-out from men. Honestly, I cannot imagine getting involved with someone right now—after Renny and Enrique. I feel as if I should do a study of men and dating. What are they thinking? Why do they do the things they do? I should write an article for a women's magazine. There's a lot to say, you know. Unmask the bastards."

Natalie shook her head. "It's been done, Sophie. *Sex and the City* studied men for about six, seven years and guess what? As I remember, Carrie, Miranda, Samantha and Charlotte never quite figured them out. Anyway, the writers had them get lucky and by the end of the series, everyone was happily coupled up."

"Duly noted," I sighed. "Is there no way I could vent and earn money at the same time?"

Natalie was sympathetic. "Look, I had one lousy marriage before I struck gold and found Warren. Believe me, the right man is worth it. Sophie Marks, don't give up on men!"

"Well, look at me," said Carla. " I waited over five years for Jake to leave his wife. He was so utterly miserable and yet he couldn't leave her. They were terrible parents together, just arguing all the time. Fact is, I *saved* both of them."

Natalie and I did a double take on that one. We doubted Audrey, the ex-wife, saw it that way. Then Natalie asked if I were really going to write an article.

"Why not? I could begin by interviewing my ex-shrink." Suddenly, I realized at that moment that my offhand comment might be useful. If I told Kisselstine I was doing research for an article and I needed him as a resource, the article could be my cover. And I was bound to learn something from him—my new "friend."

"Wait a minute," Carla interrupted. "He can't reveal information about his patients."

"No, of course not," I agreed. "But, without naming names, he can give me some interesting material."

Both Carla and Natalie pointed out that even though I'd finished therapy, wasn't there a chance I'd resume it at some point? How could a shrink agree to such a proposition?

"Actually, Kisselstine and I are finished. Therapy doesn't go on forever, you know," I announced airily, expert that I am. "Besides," I said with bravado, "I'm handling this very well. Just because I'm complaining doesn't mean I'm not ready to move on."

Natalie wasn't buying. "If I heard you correctly a moment ago, you were finished with men altogether. Do you call that normal? I don't. I'd say you needed a therapist right now."

I replied in a steely voice. "I said I was taking a break from men; I didn't say I was entering a convent. Ladies, I have a 1:30 meeting and I have to leave. I just wanted to let you know what's going on in my life." I gave each of them a stern look. "And how well I'm handling everything."

Natalie grabbed my arm. "Wait, wait. Just tell me how you're going to survive without dining on shredded eel intestines and loin of bison testicles and all those other fancy, schmancy dinners that Enrique has been stuffing into you at Cascada?"

I stood up and gave them my most severe expression. "There's always take-out."

That was as good an exit line as any. And, of course, it made no sense at all. The last thing upmarket restaurateur Enrique Barranco would want was take-out business—with a pile-up of carelessly dressed customers waiting impatiently for their Moroccan lamb stew, garnished with rosemary infused fingerling potatoes, tucked into Styrofoam containers that would be bleeding sauce all over them before they even hit the street.

So *not* part of the American dream!

# January 15<sup>th</sup>

*I* truly believe there must be something in the code psychologists live by that prohibits total patient abandonment. Besides, doesn't my shrink realize I already have rejection issues—thanks to Renny. Maybe I'm deluding myself, but I think Kisselstine and I have a special connection because he stepped away from his professional role to help me; I know he cares about me enough to have broken a rule. So, if I give him a sensible reason to meet with me that would keep him in his comfort zone, he would probably comply. I miss him.

I worked up my courage and I texted a proposal. Basically, I said that we should meet for a friendly dinner one night next week because I wanted to get his input about the current dating scene in New York—from a psychologist's point of view. I indicated that I was writing a magazine article and I'd really appreciate his insights regarding some of the topics I have in mind. I suggested a sociable dinner for the interview. Bottom line—this would be a business meeting, so I'd put the tab on my expense account. That is, my imaginary expense account.

I was feeling good about my message to Dr. K. I had appealed to his conscience—how could he totally forsake me? And I'd appealed to his offer of friendship—didn't he mean it when he said we could be friends? And I hope I appealed to his intellect—couldn't he give me words of wisdom for my article? It took three days for him to answer, but he did text and agree to meet for dinner.

I think my set-up is rather clever. Except, of course, if he sees right through me.

# January 16ᵗʰ

*I* met Dr. K at a rustic, neighborhood Italian restaurant that was on the far western edge of uptown Manhattan, so obscure and so small that I was certain he chose it to avoid meeting anyone he knew in the psychology trade. When I finally found the place—that is, after my taxi circled a two block area several times—I realized how much he wanted discretion.

The restaurant had an unapologetic red sauce menu. No frills, no foam, no pork cheeks; just hearty portions that spilled over the plate. It was nothing like the artfully presented delicacies at Cascada. Nevertheless, it was very satisfying.

Dr. K relaxed as soon as he downed his first glass of Barolo. "I've never done this before. I'm not sure how this works, actually. When I told you we could be friends I was really thinking that I had to help you get to a doctor as soon as possible. Sophie, I worried you might have a breakdown if you tested positive and I wanted to be there for you. But, I didn't think beyond that."

"Well, I just want to pick your brain." Then I quickly added, "For the article."

"I want to help you in any way I can, but, you must know…this meeting is very unorthodox. And, honestly, I'm no expert on Manhattan men, as you seem to believe. I have to navigate the dating scene myself," he said somewhat sheepishly. "It's not like being a psychologist gives me an edge."

That was intriguing. "Well, how do you meet your dates?"

He shrugged. "Let's see…I met the last woman I was dating for a while at Whole Foods. Don't laugh. I was tapping a watermelon, listening for the right "thumping" sound, so I'd know if it was a good one, when an attractive woman standing nearby said to me, "I think you've got it. By God, you've got it!" The *My Fair Lady* approach," he observed with a grin.

"Very clever of her. So what happened next?"

Dr. K. smiled. "Well, we bantered a bit and then we went over to the Whole Foods Café and had coffee. One thing led to another, and we made a date for that Saturday night." He picked up his fork and started eating his pasta.

"That's it? That's all you have to say? If you were one of my girlfriends, there'd be a story with details."

"The story is that we dated for about six months and I really liked her but she was ready for a commitment and she let me know it. I was not. Simple as that."

"Frankly, I'm surprised," I replied. "Surely, as a psychologist, no doubt dealing with these matters, you have evidence that it's not as simple as that. It would be really helpful if you told me why *you* weren't ready for a commitment. Um, that would be very good stuff for my article."

"Well, I certainly liked her a lot, but I didn't love her and it really was as simple as that. No point stringing her along."

That statement set off alarm bells and I immediately went off script. "Do you think that's why Renny let me walk out of his life? Are you're saying that a man doesn't have commitment issues when he really falls in love? That would mean that Renny wasn't really commitment phobic but just…just not in love with me. Right?" I was leaning forward, both hands on the table, hoping for an answer—at last.

Kisselstine shook his head. "I'm saying I, myself, am not afraid of commitment. I just didn't love this woman." He paused and when he continued, he spoke as a psychologist. "But I do know that some men *can't* fall deeply in love until their commitment issues are resolved."

"I'm confused. What are you saying?"

Kisselstine exhaled forcefully, probably well aware that, intentionally or not, he had directed the conversation toward a therapeutic moment. "Sophie, I wasn't referring to Renny. At any rate, I didn't mean to upset you."

I gave up all pretense that this conversation was about a magazine article. "Are you saying that someday when the right woman comes along, Renny will want to spend the rest of his life with her and no doubt have a litter of kids? And I was just not the right woman?" Why was it so important for me to believe that Renny loved me? I guess it's because I'd like to think that I meant something to him beyond availability, beyond convenience. If he really didn't love me, it would mean that I was truly interchangeable with the next woman who came along.

The psychologist in Kisselstine kicked in, once again. "I'm not saying that it's about you not being the right woman. *It's just the opposite.* Obviously, he cared for you—but I think he was unable to go the distance—meaning fall in love. When a man has commitment issues—as I believe Renny does, although it's speculation since he is not my patient—he's simply not open to permanent relationships. His capacity to love is limited. Impaired. But, when something changes in his life, if he feels a void or if he realizes time is running short— that's when his anxiety lessens and he can open his mind and heart to a lasting relationship. Something has to happen to diminish his apprehension. It could be concern about getting older or a recognition that superficial relationships aren't fulfilling or a sudden longing for permanence. Whatever the catalyst, that's when his commitment issues diminish and he develops the capacity to love. Who knows? Someday, Renny may find himself longing for a stable rela- tionship and he'll be open to loving the next attractive, bright woman who comes along. I just have to assume that Renny cared for you but was unable to go the distance because none of these manifestations had kicked in."

Kisselstine let the words sink in, giving me time to absorb his perspective. Then he said, "Remember what we discussed in my office?" He held my eyes with intense scrutiny. "We've already talked about your own reluctance to get married and how that corresponded with Renny's own preference. Now I'm saying to you that I don't believe *you* were in love with him."

"I didn't love him? You never said that to me in the office."

"Well, that's what I believe and I almost told you that night we were having dinner in New Jersey. I didn't discuss this with you in the office because initially I had to establish the fact that you were averse to getting married and repeating your parents' experience. That was the first order of business. Eventually, I was going to explore the question of whether or not you were in love with him."

Could that be true? I didn't love Renny? "You're confusing me, Dr. K."

"Well, that's something to think about. Take your time, Sophie," he coun- seled, as if he were asking me to decide something as unimportant as whether I would order the tiramisu or the cannoli for dessert.

It soon became clear that Kisselstine had no intention of elaborating on the subject. He had put it out there for me to deal with and he was finished. As he often did in therapy sessions, he gave me homework. Dr. K had definitely switched into therapy mode; I guess he couldn't help himself. I was grateful, if not a little dazed.

I couldn't help myself either, so I decided to ask him a question that was on my mind. I hoped he wouldn't think it was intrusive, but I decided to go for it. "So, are you seeing someone now? Perhaps someone you met in the dairy aisle? Or possibly frozen foods?"

He laughed, even though I think I was a bit snippy, because in an ideal world he'd date casually but bestow the the major part of his attention on needy me. He had just speared part of a meatball and was about to eat it. He put it down and looked up at me. I imagined that our new status flashed before him: should he talk to me as a friend or should he treat me as a cast-off basket case. "Well, let's say right now I have a few very lovely women on speed dial," he replied.

Unlike me, determined to stick with my renewed dating moratorium. Not that I'm complaining. I'm relishing the freedom and the total absence of a requirement to please a man. In a strange way, I feel liberated because I'm not on the dating treadmill: that continuous loop of hunting and flirting, even coddling, that is required when you first initiate a relationship. Of course, this repeat dating suspension has lasted about two weeks...

This meeting with Dr. K turned out to be a fruitful session even though it took place in a restaurant and I didn't ask him all the questions I had in mind. And when the waiter put the check on the table, Kisselstine scooped it up before I had a chance to put him on my non-existent expense account. So, free therapy and free dinner. Plus, he drove me home, thank goodness—so no huge taxi fare to get downtown.

Now all I have to do is figure out if I ever truly loved Renny.

# January 25th

*I* am a January dynamo! I'm feeling confident and productive and I attribute my new sense of well being to the good news I received from Dr. Leah. And as for my relationship with Renny, I believe that Dr. K was right. Neither one of us were in love. Probably the relationship worked because of that; if I did love him, I would have been the only one in the relationship who felt that way and that wouldn't have worked. It's a little strange to be thirty-three years-old and discover I've never been in love, but I'm okay with that.

The bottom line is that I'm healthy. At spinning class, I push a little harder, at the agency I'm more excited about what I do and at the food pantry on Saturday mornings, I volunteer and forget about me—that is, the me who has often worried about trivial things.

I texted Kisselstine to ask him for a referral for Maya as I had promised I would. Just to needle him, I suggested that handsome therapist, James, whom I'd met in the bar. Unless, I wrote, innocently, he wanted *me* to see James. I knew that would irritate him. Much as he insisted he could no longer be my therapist, I sensed he would not be happy handing me over to a colleague who'd obviously shown an interest in me. Of course, I was right. He emailed the name of two therapists: Louis French for me and Wallace DeSisto for Maya. I Googled Dr. Louis French and, no surprise, he was over sixty and had a strong resemblance to Albert Einstein. However, I don't want a new therapist in my life— not even one who could *finally* explain the theory of relativity to me.

I texted Kisselstine and asked him to join me for dinner again and answer a few questions for my article. Yes, I had questions for him that I would have preferred dealing with in the office setting, but since that was not possible, at least I could meet for dinner and use "the article" once again for my benefit. I felt bad about this ploy, but not bad enough to discontinue it. This time we met way downtown at a small Chinese restaurant; the food was good, but the patrons were sparse. How he found it, I'll never know. It seems my shrink is quite good at intrigue. To make it businesslike, I assume, he again didn't offer to drive me there, which was mildly irritating since I had to take two trains. Too many people above ground were searching for taxis because of a gentle but persistent rush hour snowfall and tonight the transit system was my best choice.

I carried a note pad with questions written down to confirm my legitimacy. I pretended to study my outline and then I looked up at him and said, very professionally, "Obviously, I'm including material about bi or homosexual men because my own experience has prompted this article. I think I should be writing about why a man would get serious with a woman knowing that she would never satisfy him."

Kisselstine didn't respond right away and I wondered if he'd call me on this gambit, so, I was actually surprised when he answered with a long explanation. "Clearly, each person is different and I can't give you one answer that will cover it for all bi-sexual or homosexual men. Obviously, certain religious beliefs make it quite difficult to function as a gay man. Sometimes, there's a persistent desire to be quote—normal—unquote and try to partner with the opposite sex. For some men, it's a test to see which part of their nature is the strongest. Often, it's a cultural necessity—as I suspect it is with Enrique, although I wouldn't rule out a combination of factors for him or any other bi-sexual individual. There's no one-size-fits all answer. If a bi-sexual man were in my office, we'd explore his needs and his anxieties until we came up with a way to help him live his life honestly."

I looked down at my pad and I made some notes so that he could see I was using this information for my non-existent article. I could feel my face flush because I felt guilty exploiting him, but I told myself I really needed him and this was the only way we could talk.

Then he surprised me and addressed my concerns. "From what you told me of Enrique, I don't think he deliberately meant to hurt you."

"But he put me at risk," I protested.

"That he did. No question. Based on everything you've told me about him, I'm thinking that he probably had convinced himself that being with you fulfilled his destiny. He might have truly believed that his relationship with Luca was ultimately avoidable. Wasn't he sending Luca to the Los Angeles Cascada when it opened? Perhaps that was his plan to remove temptation."

"Are you telling me to forgive him?"

"Sophie, I'm certainly not saying that. I'm just pointing out that Enrique might have been trying very hard to be faithful to you because he truly cared for you. Nevertheless, he couldn't deny his dual nature. I just don't think he intentionally meant to harm you. You were someone he not only cared about but you were also his ticket to respectability. That is, *his* idea of respectability."

He paused and I could see the wheels turning. He was always thoughtful when he introduced a new concept. "I think you would feel better about your relationship with him if you'd understand that Enrique didn't deliberately put you in danger. He's kind of a victim himself. I'm not trying to get him off the hook, Sophie. I'm trying to help you heal."

Just then, the waitress served our soup and I was grateful for the break. Kisselstine wasn't saying anything I hadn't intuitively known, but he was laying it out for me so clearly that I was able to step away from my anger and consider it. Of course, I was still upset with Enrique, but now I also felt a wave of compassion complicate my feelings.

"Do you think Enrique can ever have a traditional happy marriage? Not with me," I corrected hastily, "but with someone else who wasn't aware of his sexual orientation?"

"From what you've told me, it's doubtful. However, my guess is that he feels so strongly about marriage between a man and woman that he will do all he can to make that happen."

"Dr. K, don't make me feel too sorry for him, please. I'm still angry with him."

"You have my permission, not that you need it, to be as angry as you wish." He paused, gathering his words. "Look, Sophie, I have to be honest with you. If you had tested positive..." He trailed off and took a deep breath and then leaned toward me and spoke with urgency. "I don't know what the hell I'd be saying to you right now. So take everything I've just said with a grain of salt. It's easy for me to be rational about Enrique now that I know you're safe. I was so worried about you."

I leaned into him to reply, close enough to catch the citrus scent of his aftershave, and suddenly, I had a desire to kiss him. For a second, I thought he had the same inclination, but that was not possible. I pulled back, horrified. If I kissed him, I would be just like the patient who'd come on to him and nearly got him disbarred or discharged or defrocked—or whatever they call it when they strip a psychologist of his license. Kisselstine would cut me off completely. As it is, he's skulking around Manhattan, trying to avoid his colleagues—who don't even know me and would have no idea that I am a former patient. But *he* knows and he's obviously grappling with a situation he's never been in.

We both pulled back and retreated into silence, paying more attention to our egg rolls than to each other. By the time our main course came, we were able to segue into a political discussion and I relaxed because I decided my interrogation was over. Frankly, I was relieved that the question and answer portion of the evening was concluded. It was good to have a casual conversation with him and not feel as if I were being manipulative.

It was time for small talk. "So, what does a shrink do on weekends?" I asked, curious.

"Let's see. This Friday night I'm meeting a few friends at Charley T's and then we're going back to my place to play cards. Kind of a boys night out that we do once in a while. I'd compare it to you and Carla having your nails painted together."

I bristled slightly. "Carla and I are not that superficial. I'll have you know that last week, for example, we went to the Metropolitan Museum of Art to hear a lecture about Renaissance painting."

"I apologize, Sophie. I meant it as a joke, but it was patronizing."

I admired him for that. He had said something condescending and when it was pointed out to him, he owned up to it. Renny would have laughed and said something like—"Good for you for keeping up with the art world with the rest of the Manhattan dilettantes!" And the old Sophie Marks would have accepted that.

Kisselstine continued. "On Saturday, I have tickets for a concert at Lincoln Center and on Sunday morning I'm going for a run in Central Park with a running buddy. Later, I'll have dinner with my mother."

I zoomed right in to the important part. "A concert with a date?"

"Yes, a date."

"What is she like?"

He grinned and shook his head. "But enough about me," he said, as if he'd just given me a complete description of his date including age, height, weight, occupation and level of desirability and was now turning his attention to me because he didn't want to dominate the conversation. Then he showed a renewed interest in his chicken and black bean sauce. Clearly, he was reluctant to share; when it came to our biographies, the scales tipped in his favor. He knew way too much about me.

When our fortune cookies arrived, he looked at his watch and frowned. "I need to call a client in a few minutes, so I'll have to say goodbye. I'll walk you out to get you a taxi and then come back here to take care of the check and my phone call."

"No problem," I said.

He hailed a taxi, gave my address and then, before closing the door, leaned in and said, "Take care of yourself, Sophie." I couldn't help myself: I had the strangest desire to kiss him, once again. Instead I gave him a cheerful goodbye wave.

I'd said "no problem" in the restaurant, but that wasn't quite true. The problem was simply that this magazine article scam couldn't last much longer. I'd have to find another tactic or he would be out of my life altogether. At that moment, I couldn't figure out if I wanted him more as a shrink or as a man.

Damn it, I had to untangle myself from this transference business. I needed him back as *Dr. K*, my easy to talk to friend and my one and only shrink.

# *January 29th*

onight, I really did get to see Kisselstine as a friend. I was so relieved that I didn't have to resort to deception about a magazine article. Instead, we were just two pals having a good time. I had no guilt-inducing hidden agenda to push and I resolved to keep as far away from that seductive aftershave as possible. That was the only way to keep him in my life.

One of Dean Hathaway Chung's biggest clients had given two courtside tickets to a Knicks game at Madison Square Garden to a colleague of mine who couldn't use them and I was the lucky beneficiary. That night I texted Kisselstine, figuring that no serious male New Yorker would turn that down. "Friend, have two tix for Knicks game tomorrow night. *Courtside.* Golden opportunity." He texted back within minutes. "Count me in."

Men are such pushovers when it comes to balls that are pitched, slam dunked, kicked or served. Kisselstine was more likely to be recognized at a Knicks game at Madison Square Garden with its eighteen thousand fans, but now he was throwing caution to the winds, taking a chance that a television camera would scan our courtside seats revealing his former patient at his side.

We met at the arena and he immediately bought hot dogs, fries and soda for us. I did take out my wallet to try to pay my share, but he waved it away. This man doesn't understand the rules of friendship.

It was a great basketball game and Kisselstine was ecstatic. The Knicks' star forward hit a three pointer with two minutes remaining to tie the game and then they proceeded to win in overtime by five aggressively contested points. Afterwards, we went to a nearby bar to celebrate and I insisted on paying the tab and finally, he allowed it. That made me feel as if we'd turned a corner and this was a sign of a promising friendship.

Kisselstine was like the proverbial kid in the candy store. "Sophie, that game was one of the highlights of my life. I don't know which thrilled me more: the Knicks' win or the great seats." He raised his beer in salute. "I do know. It was the seats. They made the win even sweeter."

"I'm so glad you had a good time. I did, too." It was nice to see him so relaxed and casual.

"Honestly, I'm surprised. I never would have figured you for a basketball fan."

"Actually," I responded, "I prefer watching the women play college basketball, but I do watch the Knicks occasionally." I didn't mention that the Knicks featured in my past life—with Renny. But even Renny couldn't score such great seats. "You see, I'm a multi-faceted female. Very deep."

"Definitely a Renaissance woman," he said approvingly. "What else don't I know about you?"

I thought for a minute. "Okay, I'll give you a top ten list." I proceeded to tick off on my fingers: "I'm passionate about spinning; outside of class I'd never ride a bike in Manhattan; I really love to cook; I'm a terrible swimmer; I read historical novels; 'I'm sometimes claustrophobic in small elevators; I love to dance; I see all of Woody Allen's movies; I'm allergic to cats and let's see… number ten, I'm so glad we're friends now."

"Sophie, I'm awestruck. I could never put together a top ten list about myself so quickly."

"Well, my friend," I replied, "when I get to know you better, I'll do it for you."

I think that comment scared him, because he immediately thanked me for a great evening and said it was time to call it a night. Once on the street, he hailed a taxi for me and waved me off.

What is the matter with Kisselstine? The moment I express my pleasure in the friendship and tell him I want to know him better, he practically turns on me. Not one of the nine million inhabitants of New York City could identify me as a former patient of his, so why can't he relax? (Obviously, I'm discounting the two New Yorkers who do know about us—Carla and Natalie.) I have come to the conclusion that Dr. K and I could, indeed, be friends, if he would only relax enough to let it happen. I enjoy his calm demeanor, his thoughtful comments, his humor and the occasional therapeutic moment. And I really think that it's wonderful to be with someone who requires no flirting, no compliments, no hand-holding. I can just be myself.

What's more, I'm determined to obliterate any sign of transference on my part. I know my occasional erotic thoughts are a product of our therapist/client relationship and it's rooted in fantasy—not reality. It would embarrass him terribly if I showed an interest in him, because God knows, he would find that repugnant. As for me, I'm in a better place now, no matter what aftershave he's wearing. I've thought about it considerably and I think that we could make this friendship thing work.

Hadn't the girls in my college dorm voted me "Miss Congeniality" in our mock beauty pageant? I have incredibly great friendship potential and he was missing out. It didn't make sense.

# February 1ˢᵗ

*Y*esterday, I finally returned Enrique's phone calls. I'd been avoiding him but Kisselstine had encouraged me to meet with him and talk, even argue, possibly cry. Dr. K said this was important because I had to find some semblance of closure. "Closure" may sound like a cliché but I think it's very meaningful in this context. Enrique and I needed a final conversation to sort things out.

I was concerned about seeing him in a public place because I didn't know how our meeting would play out, so I asked him come to my apartment tonight. When he arrived, he was cautious. He made no attempt to embrace me or use any of his endearments to bring me around. I think he was embarrassed. Once again, I felt almost sorry for him. Almost.

Enrique kept both hands on his coffee mug as if to warm himself in my chilly presence.

I waited for him to make the first move in this relationship chess game. He was intense, speaking more Spanish than I'd ever heard him use, because he prided himself on his grasp of the English language and its connection to his American dream.

"I never meant to give you this pain. Never. *Nunca!* I am so sorry. *Lo siento mucho.*" He reached out for my hand. "Sophia, you must believe my intentions were...I mean are," he corrected, "completely with honor. You are the woman I want to marry."

I withdrew my hand and I could see him flinch. "Enrique, I can't marry a man who has a male lover. Our marriage would be a charade."

"No, no, no," he protested. "I would be most faithful, *muy fiel.* You must know that is the reason I am sending Luca to Los Angeles. I need to break away from that and give myself only to you. I know if Luca is not here all the time I will be stronger." He met my gaze and spoke with conviction. "I must be stronger. *Sero fuerte!*" As if to show how strong he would be, he made a fist with one hand and brought it down hard on the table.

"I think what you really want is Luca. Enrique, you could be having a loving, open relationship with him because— for God's sake— it's the twenty-first century. You can be married!"

"That is not who I am," he said firmly. "*Quero una esposa e hijos!* I want a wife and children. I want *you* to be that wife. I think we have the magic together and we could have beautiful children, Sophia, I am ready for our marriage."

"Enrique, you should follow your heart. I'm just a substitute for Luca because you think I'm socially acceptable. But things have changed and you don't have to deny your feelings.

If you stay with Luca you could still have the family you want. You could adopt a child, you know, or father one of your own with a surrogate." I think I had morphed into Kisselstine somehow and was saying the words he was likely to speak.

Enrique answered passionately. "I want a child with my own wife— a child who has my blood and guts, my heart, my soul. And I want the woman who is my wife, *mi esposa,* to be the mother of my child." He looked at me with the saddest of expressions. "The woman I want is you. *Te amo.*"

*Te Amo?* How could a man who was expressing a declaration of love look so mournful? "I can't be that woman, Enrique. And I really don't think there are many women out there who'll take the deal you're offering." His face darkened. Apparently, he had come to my apartment thinking that he could actually persuade me to resume our relationship.

Wasn't this ironic? I was getting a marriage proposal—at last—that came from a man who couldn't love me unconditionally. And incredibly, he had no idea that I was not in love with him. I said gently, "Perhaps you should consider what you really want and give yourself permission to have it."

Enrique was despondent. He certainly didn't seem like a man who would own up to his nature and embrace it. I didn't tell him about my HIV panic because I sensed that he was awash in self-punishment and there was no point adding to his distress. He left soon after that and we actually hugged goodbye.

That night, I called Kisselstine on his cell and I told him about my conversation with Enrique. He was quite impressed. "Sophie, I had a feeling that you would be empathetic."

"You were right—it was closure for me. I know Enrique can't see himself in an explicit relationship with Luca right now, but he may come around. He deserves to be happy."

"Sophie, I'm so pleased you had that conversation with him. You're feeling alright about it?"

"Dr. K, I'm at peace with Enrique." Yes, it's true. As I write this journal entry, I'm thinking that I hope Enrique can find peace himself by arranging a cease-fire with his competing desires.

"As for me," I told Kisselstine, "I'm taking a time-out from the dating scene. I'm sticking with the moratorium. In fact," I joked, "I'm seriously considering joining a convent." Hadn't I just recently said *the opposite* to Natalie and Carla? Well, a girl has the right to change her mind.

"Let me know just how long that convent gig lasts," Dr. K said with laughter in his voice. "Good night, Sophie."

Okay, maybe not a convent, but I'm definitely continuing this self-imposed moratorium.

Four weeks now! Truthfully, I'm so tired of the dating game that the convent thing—especially the part about abstinence—is very appealing at this time in my life. I can see it now. Cue the Gregorian chants: Sophie Marks, unlucky in love, embraces a life of contemplation and renunciation.

On second thought, ditch the chants. I'm sure I'll fall off the wagon eventually, but, when I do, it will be on *my* terms. Seriously, I've come to a decision: I'm not going to be intimate with the next man I date until I'm quite certain it's something *I* really want. I'll only have sex with someone whom I truly care for.

Someone who will touch my heart—*before he touches me.*

# February 5th

*I* texted Kisselstine and asked if he were free to get together again so I could discuss my article. Although I'd originally set it up as an exploration of dating from the man's viewpoint, I decided I would expand the subject—still from the male perspective. I didn't think that would make Kisselstine unduly suspicious. I wanted to deal with the question on my mind: Why do men stay in unhappy marriages? Of course, I was thinking of my father who had stayed in his marriage when childcare and I believe, money, were no longer an issue. Why didn't he leave?

And why didn't my mother leave the husband who'd cheated on her? One thing I knew: I couldn't bring up the subject with her now. She had told me about the Rita Orloff affair so that I could better understand her and accept her relationship with Edgardo, but she had clearly indicated—no questions.

I knew I wouldn't get an answer that would definitively explain my father, but at least I would get some insight from Kisselstine. So, for purposes of my "article," I arranged to get together with him at my neighborhood Chinese restaurant. That was a very good sign; Kisselstine was no longer hiding me away in faraway localities. It's not like I am wearing a huge scarlet letter on my chest—a "P" for patient—that would give me away. Tonight, Dr. K definitely seemed more comfortable being with me.

True confession: I'm still uneasy when I see him after hours—that is, without his beige and taupe office uniform, his thick black-framed glasses and his shellacked hair. He showed up in his black leather jacket and once again, it was very disconcerting. Civilian Kisselstine is quite good-looking; civilian Kisselstine makes me want to run my fingers through his wavy hair. I mentally readjusted the picture by conjuring "office" Kisselstine in my mind and I kind of merged that image with the actual, living-breathing person in front of me and that was reassuring. *Office* Kisselstine was incapable of triggering embarrassing, suggestive thoughts.

After we ordered, I took out my notebook and opened to a page of notes and questions. "I was interviewing some of the men in my gym and asking them about their marriages. And Dr. K, I was taken aback when a number of them said that the question I should ask is why they stayed in a marriage that wasn't always satisfying."

He looked up from his soup and had a puzzled expression on his face. "That was the response?"

I could feel my face color, so I bent down to study my notes and let my hair fall forward to conceal my features. I would have to dig a deeper hole. "Oh yes. Of course, I spoke to them individually, but over the course of one week, there were, let me see…" I glanced at my notes. "Seven men out of sixteen who said they were staying in a marriage that wasn't all that happy. Isn't that a lot?" I asked innocently.

"I should definitely advertise in your gym," he grinned. "It would be a gold mine."

I forged ahead, ignoring his remark. "So, what would you say? I mean, about them? Why would they stay in unfulfilling relationships?"

He looked at me intently and then he smiled. I smiled back also, wondering where we were going. But then he proceeded to answer without suggesting that my question was self-serving.

"There's always the issue of money, Sophie. It's so incredibly painful to split assets. It's not only money; it's who gets the dog, the painting over the couch, even the blender. Of course, if there are still children in the home, it's terribly hard. It's difficult to break up a family knowing that you're altering the dynamics in a dreadful way."

He was giving me Divorce 101—the basics. I should have framed the issue differently. I should have steered the question toward older men. "Yes, of course. But most of these men were older. Say about forty-five to fifty-five and didn't have young children." *Like my father.*

"Well, the question of assets is always a big issue at any age. But for older people, there's also more inertia and more fear of ending up alone. I find there's greater uncertainty about the possibility of forming a new, viable relationship when people get older. Many people in that age range are unable or afraid to put themselves into new situations in general. Although, statistics now indicate that the situation is changing and more older couples are seeking divorce when they find themselves in unhappy marriages."

I don't know what I was looking for, but inertia, fear of being alone, resistance to change and uncertainty about entering new situations—all of these things might account for my parents' decision to keep their marriage intact. But before I could think of another question, Kisselstine leaned forward and said to me. "Sophie, why do you think your parents stayed together all those years?"

"Oh, I wish I knew! I want so much to understand." As I write this, I have to admit that those words were the first honest ones I'd spoken since we sat down for dinner; I feel bad about my deception.

"Well, In my practice, I've learned that sometimes older couples find peace with their situation and develop common ground later in the marriage. That does happen, you know. Maybe your parents made just enough adjustments to strengthen the marriage. Maybe they decided that being together and working together was preferable to staking a claim on an uncharted lifestyle. You know, it's entirely possible they settled into a reasonably stable relationship after some years and neither wanted to shake things up. Think about the later years, Sophie. Perhaps they were not as unhappy. As you look back, would you say that in time some of the rough edges were smoothed?"

"Well yes, I do think things were better, kind of easier, as the years went by, but Dr. K—my parents were never overtly affectionate as far as I can remember."

"Sophie, many *happy* couples are not overtly affectionate, so that may not be the best yardstick. As I recall, most of the unhappy memories you brought up in the office related to the early years of their marriage, lasting through your high school years. This is just a guess—but it's possible that at some point Rita Orloff left town or got married or joined the army or whatever—and that made things easier. It's conceivable that later on the marriage worked well enough for them. Notice I said "well enough" for *them*. Every couple has different expectations, different needs." He smiled at me and said, "Something to think about, right?"

I loved hearing those words—*something to think about*. I could have been sitting in his office, having this conversation, learning things about myself, feeling comforted. But there was no point letting him know how much this discussion meant to me, so I answered him briskly. "You're right about that. Things were not that tense when I got older." I sighed. "But, Dr. K, I know they weren't passionately in love and that makes me sad."

"Not everyone gets the prize, Sophie." He leaned forward and spoke to me with conviction. "Now that you know more about what was wrong in the past, you shouldn't dwell on it or you'll miss what's right in the present. And that's where you have to be. My job is to keep you in the here and now."

His *job*? Had he forgotten that he had terminated our therapist/client relationship? I waited for him to correct himself, but to my surprise, he didn't catch the slip. So I continued the discussion. "And my mother's 'here and now' is definitely Edgardo," I responded. "Why, that man has catapulted her to the far end of the happiness spectrum."

"I'm going to do the same for you," Kisselstine said with conviction.

I jotted down a few notes in order to look authentic but I didn't ask any more questions. I'd have to face the fact that I'd never get a definite answer about my father or my mother. Perhaps Kisselstine had just come close. That would have to do.

The conversation turned to politics and the latest scandal in Albany and I was relieved that we could transition to other topics. Otherwise, it would have been quite awkward. Then we turned to books we've read. I was pleased to learn that we both had enjoyed the historical novel that had won the prestigious Man Booker Prize in England and we agreed that the television adaptation couldn't do justice to the interior thought process that constituted the bulk of the book. We had a few other books in common.

"True confession," I admitted, "I've not read *Fifty Shades of Gray*. I may be the only woman in Manhattan who hasn't."

He shrugged his shoulders. "I didn't read it either. I decided neither my practice nor my personal life had that obligation." I swear *his* face colored slightly. Now that he wasn't in his sheltered office domain, *he* was the one uncomfortable talking about sex! Go figure.

Kisselstine was a rare find for me: a male New Yorker who read books and not just the sports pages or the *Wall Street Journal*. I don't have a huge stable of men to make that judgment, but of those I know, their reading habits have limitations.

"We should start a book club since we're reading some of the same titles," I suggested playfully.

"I'll take that under advisement."

"Oh," I countered, "That doesn't sound positive. Should I consider your response a *no*?"

"Correct." And he didn't elaborate.

Our dinner was finished and at that point I started to wonder how often I could use the subterfuge about a magazine article I was supposedly writing. I had to figure out a way to see him that seemed natural. And then it came to me. "This Sunday I'm going to a tango competition, courtesy of my mother and Edgardo. These tango competitions get really exciting. Why don't you come along? You might enjoy it."

"A tango competition? I can't say that anyone's ever offered that to me."

"Come on, please say yes," I urged. "You'll see for yourself how hot and steamy it is."

He looked at me closely and I thought he was definitely going to turn me down. Then his face softened and he surprised me. "All right, I'll give it a try."

"Great. I'll text the details and see you Sunday."

When I got home, I wondered if he had seen right through me when I'd asked the marriage questions and just decided to get to the heart of the matter and have a mini therapy session to help me. If so, it was kind of him not to "out" me as a fraudulent article writer. I wish the men I dated were as considerate and caring as Dr. K.

If only he had a brother.

# February 10th

Watching the tango competition, I felt as if I'd taken a detour and wound up in Rio de Janeiro. Olé! The men wore bolero jackets and leather bolo ties and the women were dressed in brightly colored tops and billowing ruffled skirts with petticoats that swirled a kaleidoscope of colors. I'd seen my mother and Edgardo dance in competition before, but it had been a while, and this time I saw a much more polished performance.

Gliding effortlessly to the music, Sarah/Sherri and Edgardo were sinuous and slow at times, displaying intricate steps that were deftly coordinated. When the music picked up, they covered more ground and introduced interesting flourishes. He would hold her close, their bodies entwined, and she would actually bring her bent knee up to his waist and then twirl away from him and quickly spin back into his arms. Imagine that! My mother, limber as a teenager—practically a Radio City Rockette!

At one point Edgardo dipped her very low and to his credit, didn't drop her or look uncomfortable. Not even a quiver. Meanwhile, some of the other men performing the same maneuver were shaky and obviously having trouble with their partner's weight. I was very impressed.

Kisselstine and I met in the lobby before the competition got underway. To my chagrin, he was carrying a bouquet of flowers, tissue-wrapped and beribboned. "For me?" I asked with a little curtsy, although I knew very well that I was not the intended recipient.

"Of course not," he grinned.

"Damn, why didn't I think of that?"

He handed me the bouquet. "No problem. You present it to your mother. It will make her even happier if it's from you."

"Oh, that's where you're wrong, Dr. K. You don't know my mother. If she sees me with a man, any man, she would give *him* the flowers. She probably has a graph in her bedroom that charts my advancing age versus my decreasing fertility. But, I'm going to introduce you as my friend and see if she can handle that." I handed back the flowers. It was sweet of him and why should I get the undeserved credit?

So we settled into our seats and I have to say the competition was entertaining. The music was suggestive, like listening to Ravel's *Bolero* on a running loop, but this time I was not uncomfortable watching my mother and Edgardo display their sensuality in public. I think that's because I felt better about them being a couple. Kisselstine gets credit for that. Every time I glanced at him, he was smiling, thoroughly enjoying himself.

At one point, he turned to me and said, "I'd like to do that."

Really? My shrink—dancing? I couldn't visualize it.

When the winners were announced, Edgardo and Sarah/Sherri were awarded a third place trophy tied with a red, white and blue ribbon. All the finalists held them aloft as if they were on the Olympic pedestal. Who knows? If my mother and Edgardo keep winning trophies, they might get their picture on a Wheaties box, bumping LeBron or Serena or whatever champion has that coveted real estate at the moment.

Dr. K and I applauded heartily when Sarah/Sherri's and Edgardo's names were announced. They were glowing with elation and eagerly embracing their tango friends, but when my mother spied us, she raced over to throw her arms around me.

"I'm so glad you came," she said, and then looking directly at Kisselstine, she smiled broadly. "So, who is this?"

"Mom, this is the friend I told you about…" I hesitated for a moment, realizing I'd never used his first name and never even thought of him *having* a first name. "This is um…Robert, my…um friend." I emphasized *friend* although I knew my mother was not into subtlety.

Kisselstine handed her the bouquet and told her what great dancers she and Edgardo were. Edgardo had his hands around her waist and was still breathing heavily.

My mother was swift. "So, you two, join us for a bite. We're always starving after a competition."

Before I could think or decide one way or another, Kisselstine accepted the invitation. What can I say about our *bite*? It was totally enjoyable but not without a few speed bumps.

Sarah/Sherri: (Not wasting time). "So, your wife—she doesn't like the tango? She couldn't come?"

Kisselstine: (Shaking his head with regret). "Oh, no, I'm not married."

Sarah/Sherri: (Leaning forward, eyes wide). "So, what do you do for a living?"

Kisselstine: (Very quick). "I'm a therapist working mainly with marriage counseling." Obviously, that excluded me.

Sarah/Sherri: (In matchmaker mode). "So how did you two meet?"

Kisselstine: (Smoothly fabricating). "We met at a bar and we've become friends. Sophie and I also have a business relationship. I'm consulting with Sophie on a magazine article she's writing.

Sarah/Sherri: (Totally confused). "So friends? That's what you are?" She wrinkled her forehead, clearly puzzled. "That I never had, a man friend." She turned to Edgardo, quite serious. "So, tell me, did you ever have a woman friend?"

Edgardo: (Responding with the same bewilderment as if he were asked about having a Martian buddy). "A woman friend? I don't think so."

Sarah/Sherri: (Shrugging her shoulders in exasperation). "Well, good luck, you two."

Kisselstine had a hint of a smile on his face as he'd parried her questions, but the last exchange caught him off guard and he couldn't quite suppress his amusement.

My mother pursed her lips and unconsciously nodded her head, taking in the information that this man was not a "live" one. Then she relaxed and we had pleasant conversations. Dr. K was charming, really, and my mother obviously liked him in spite of the fact that he was not a contender for my hand in marriage. We had a wonderful evening. It's really pleasant having a male friend to talk to and laugh with and not worrying about sex getting in the way. Okay, I admit I have an occasional fantasy about Dr. K, but it's mostly pretty tame.

Running my fingers through his hair is hardly the stuff of a porno movie.

# February 16ᵗʰ

*E*ight weeks. That's how much tine I have to find an escort for Carla's April wedding. Once again in my adult life, I faced the prospect of going to a wedding without a date. Not that I'm keeping track, but the exact number is five. Five times I've been seated at a table with a mash-up of stray singles who made small talk while the music pounded and the lucky couples around us gyrated.

No Renny. And now, no Enrique. I might have to interrupt my dating moratorium (six weeks now) and find a suitable escort for one night only. One night only? Maybe the easiest thing is to hire someone. I know there are websites for that—but the humiliation! The anxiety! My escort for hire would probably be a man on parole for God knows what offense. Armed robbery, no doubt. And, my luck, he'd be a terrible dancer.

I briefly considered one man who might qualify—that is, he was alive and within shooting distance. He was on the television team that was working with us print people on the Renegade project. Sam Basinger. But except for a few easy water cooler type conversations, Sam and I really didn't know each other. All I knew about him was that he was taller than I was and nice looking and sported an unadorned ring finger.

No date—that was the bad part. The good part—Carla, in a moment of sanity, was letting me, her maid of honor, wear the stunning dress I'd worn to my mother's wedding. So, I was all set with a dress, shoes and handbag. Everything but a living, breathing escort.

Natalie and I were in the park watching the two older kids, Nicky and Micah, toss a ball I'd just given to them. Each time it hit the ground, it lit up and each time the kids squealed in surprise. "We love it, Auntie Sophie," said Micah. Nicholas added, "Ith tho great."

I was holding sleepy little Alice, Natalie's adorable toddler, whom she fondly referred to as her PTL baby—that is, pre-tubal ligation. Alice snuggled her chubby body into mine and I was intoxicated with her baby scent.

"So, do you have any prospects who could be your escort at the wedding?"

Both Natalie and Carla were treating my single status as a tragedy. "Well, there is a man at work whom I hardly know, and I haven't a clue about him other than he makes a living at Dean Hathaway Chung and doesn't wear a wedding band. Asking Sam to be my date would be a desperation move."

"You really have to go through your Rolodex and get a date, Sophie."

"Nobody uses a Rolodex any more, Natalie," I advised her.

"That's not the issue, my love. You have about six weeks to get a date. Where are the eligible men in this goddamned city?"

Micah clutched the ball to his chest. "That's one of the bad words, Mommy."

Natalie rolled her eyes. "It's okay for Mommy, sweetheart—just this one time. Now, throw the ball to your brother."

I sighed. "There are men, I guess, but the good ones are hard to come by. And truthfully, I haven't really been looking since I broke up with Enrique because I'm in the dating moratorium phase of my life—remember? Enrique kind of took the wind out of my sails."

She raised her eyebrows. "Really Sophie? *Wind out of your sails?* Well, Matey, why not drop anchor and find a sailor who'll kick up his wooden leg with you."

"Natalie, it was just a metaphor. Get over it," I said crisply, suppressing laughter that threatened to bubble over.

"How about asking that Kisselstine guy. Carla says he's nice looking."

"Not a good idea. He knows my deep-down, innermost thoughts. My sex life! He knows more about me than anyone I've ever known. He's seen me cry with make-up running down my cheeks and mucus coming out of my nose. Believe me, that's not the kind of guy you'd want to date." I didn't dare tell her that sometimes I found him so appealing I wanted to shake up the friendship thing; one night I dreamed that I tried to tear all his clothes off. Well, I might not have control of my dreams, but in real life, I know it's best if Kisselstine kept his clothes on. I also remind myself that Kisselstine was still a somewhat reluctant friend and I could lose him with one wrong move. He most certainly wouldn't want to be my escort at a wedding.

Natalie fished into her enormous bag for a banana and kept half for her-self and gave the rest to me. Micah once again clutched the ball to his chest. "Mommy, is that my banana?"

Nicky chimed in. "Ith that my banana?"

Natalie laughed. "Boys, your bananas are safe and sound in this bag. Keep bouncing that light up ball Auntie Sophie gave you."

She continued where she left off. "So what if he knows all about you. You only need him for one wedding. Unless you have a shitload of invitations I don't know about and you'll have to hire a gigolo to get you through the wedding season."

Micah perked up. "Mommy, I heard a bad word again."

Nicky was baffled. "Which one? Which one?"

Natalie clapped her hands. "Play ball, little guys. Let's see that light come on." She turned to me in exasperation. "Jesus, Sophie, I may not be able to express myself until these kids turn twenty-one."

Nicky, obviously frustrated with our grown-up conversation, was now on the verge of tears. He pleaded, "Who ith Jesus?" Natalie, unable to suppress her laughter, grabbed her boy for a bear hug, tousled his hair and released him. He seemed placated. Meanwhile, I turned away so the wouldn't see me laughing. Then, I placed my hand on Natalie's shoulder and said in mock seriousness, "I suggest you take a vow of silence until these kids reach puberty."

She ignored me. "Really, Sophie, don't walk into Carla's fantasy wedding without a date. Even that Kisselstine fellow is better than nothing."

"I'll think about it." Then I remembered Sarah/Sherri. "You know, my mother is invited. She met Kisselstine once and she accepted the fact that he was a friend because I told her we were collaborating on that article I was supposedly writing. But if I brought him to the wedding...." I didn't finish the rest of the sentence. What would my mother do? Interrogate him, I guess, about his family, his interests, his financial picture. She'd get under his skin with queries more suitable for an IRS agent. Would she annoy him with an exaggerated list of my virtues? Probably yes to all of the above.

"It's your call," Natalie responded. "You have to figure out which scenario is worse: date or no date. Anyway, you know how I'd vote."

Micah came up to our bench and thrust his head into the bag and came up with a banana in his teeth. Nicky tried to do the same but was too small to manage it. "Mommy, I can't thee my banana!" He let out a wail that turned heads and possibly suggested there was some form of child abuse going on.

As they say, *little* people, little problems. *Big* people—sometimes *little* annoying, foolish and ridiculous matters that are more irritants than problems. Would it really be so bad if I went to Carla's wedding without a date? Probably not. But I surrendered. That night I called Kisselstine on his cell. "Can you talk," I asked, because I heard music in the background.

"No problem," he said. "What's happening?"

"I need your help; I'm really desperate. If I don't get a real date by April 6th, will you be my escort at Carla's wedding? I just can't walk in there alone."

Silence. And then, "Seriously? You're an attractive woman. You can't get a date?"

"Attractive woman? Are you patronizing me?"

"Now you're being overly sensitive. I'm sure there's a man out there who'll take care of business."

"Are you deliberately trying to humiliate me? Do you think I wanted to ask you to do this? I'm in a bind and I need an escort and you know I've sworn off men. I told you about my dating moratorium."

"Well, I'm not an escort for hire—especially an escort on a contingency basis. If I understand you accurately, you want me to save the date and then the night before you might inform me that you've found a live one—and you'd cancel. Correct?"

"Oh, you're so much in demand you can't schedule one free Friday evening to help out a friend?"

"Well, I'm having a real problem with this friendship thing."

"Damn it, I'm asking you to do me a favor. I don't even want you, but I don't have much choice right now. Why are you being so damned difficult?"

"You don't even want me? Well said, Miss Marks. And let me point out that Natalie and Carla will be there and they know I was your therapist, so it's awkward, to day the least."

"Believe me, they couldn't care less. I have to tell you that you're just not that important to them."

"Well, let me see how many ways you've insulted me in this brief conversation."

"So, is that a no?"

"That's a no."

"What? What did you say? The music is getting so loud I can hardly hear you. Where *are* you?"

"In answer to your first question: That's a no," he said, raising his voice. "And where am I? At the Odyssey Club."

The dance club? "Are you on a date? Are you out dancing?" I asked, my voice also rising.

"Actually, yes."

"Shit!" I hung up immediately and let out a string of expletives worthy of the most hardened truck driver. Too bad Micah wasn't at my side. What a terrific opportunity to enlarge his vocabulary of naughty words and drive Natalie crazy!

# February 17th

When Kisselstine's cell number showed up on my caller ID tonight, I was so relieved. Thank God, he was calling to apologize for his rude behavior last night on the phone. No doubt he wanted to tell me that he would suit up for the wedding and be my escort—if needed— and prevent the two hundred and fifty guests from considering me a tragic figure who was likely to die alone in a cluttered apartment with twenty or thirty cats in residence.

Instead, without any greeting, he said in a stern voice: "What was that all about?"

"What do you mean," I asked warily.

"I mean the cursing. The hang up."

"Christ, you were on a date. You should never have taken my call."

"Don't be childish," he said, sounding exasperated. "What if you had a problem? A crisis? How could I not take your call?"

"Never, never answer my call if you're on a date. *Even if I'm dying.* Is that clear?"

"Your logic escapes me."

"Well, don't worry about it. I'm never, ever calling you again!"

"It's definitely my turn." With that, he hung up on *me*.

Son of a bitch. He was supposed to apologize.

# *February 18ᵗʰ*

*C*arla called me at 10:30 tonight. I'm always up at this hour but Carla's an early bird, so I was surprised. "Hey, what's happening, bride? Change your mind about the big wedding," I teased. "Going to elope?" Not a chance in hell.

"This is serious, Sophie. I need your help. Diane's sister—you know, Maya—just called and woke me up. She's planning to come to the wedding but up until now, she didn't have a date. So I have a favor to ask you."

"Hold on, hold on." I felt shaky, as if I were about to hear something that was categorically not in my comfort zone. Of course, I was correct. "You told me you'd invited Diane and her date to the wedding and I understand that because you work together. But Maya? How do you even know her?"

"Well, uh, it's really a long story."

Carla was embarrassed and I was confused; not a good combination. "Tell me the long story." I uttered "long" with enough *o's* to let Carla know that this conversation was not going well.

"Oh, we've been getting together, the three of us, Diane, Maya and I. She's met Jake, also. We've kind of, you know, had drinks together, some dinners…" She trailed off. "Honestly, she's really a very nice person. Anyway, Maya had stopped seeing Renny, so I wasn't doing anything wrong." Long pause, met with silence. "Right?" she added, hopefully.

"When did this friendship thing happen? You hadn't met her when we celebrated Jake's birthday—or had you?" At that dinner, I'd been blindsided by Diane's comment that Renny "adored" her sister's child. What about the child I'd carried? *Our* child? Imagine if Carla had known at that time about Renny,

Maya and the little girl and had kept it from me? That would have been a terrible violation.

I could hear Carla groaning when she should have been begging my forgiveness. Instead, she told me that she'd met Maya *after* Jake's birthday dinner. "And she's really a very, very nice person," added Carla once again, possibly implying that *I* was the disagreeable one.

I know I sounded sharp, but I couldn't help it. "Bottom line, you're telling me that my ex-boyfriend's ex-girlfriend is coming to your wedding. Did I get that straight?"

"Well, not exactly." She hesitated and that was my clue that something more unpleasant was about to transpire. "Look, Maya's seeing Renny again and she would like to ask him to be her escort unless you object. She told me she doesn't want to hurt you, but she did point out that *you* broke up with him, so she feels you're not the injured party."

"Carla, he broke up with *me*. He discarded me...and our baby!" Okay, maybe I was exaggerating here, maybe *discarded* was too strong a word, but I was definitely correct about Renny ending our relationship and rejecting our baby.

"Oh no, Sophie, I covered for you. I told her *you* were the one who broke up with him! Anyway, you've moved on. I never hear you talking about Renny anymore so I thought he was history."

Really? I did sustain some serious bumps and bruises having something to do with a proposed abortion followed by a break-up and a miscarriage, but perhaps Carla has forgotten this in the flurry of wedding hysteria. Frankly, I was amazed that Carla was asking me for this favor. And I was also surprised that Maya would be so insensitive to assume that bringing Renny to the wedding would mean nothing to me. Certainly it would be awkward.

Carla continued. "Maya said I have no idea what it's like to be the single woman at a couple's event. She must think that I've been under a rock all these years. Of course, I know exactly what that's like and so do you. So, it would be really pleasant for her if she could bring an escort to my wedding, don't you think?"

I had no coherent response. "I can't believe this," I mumbled into the phone.

"Sophie, I don't want to worry about you sitting by yourself at my wedding. So please, ask your ex-shrink to be your escort; I mean, he seems to be the only man in your life right now because of your silly dating moratorium. Natalie and I both think he'd make a good escort. If that's a go and if it's all right with you, I'll tell Maya she can invite Renny."

"Carla, I really, really feel uncomfortable about Kisselstine being my escort and I have no intention of asking him." I refused to admit that he'd already turned me down.

"Of course, of course, I understand completely," she said soothingly. Then she changed gears. "Frankly, Sophie, Diane just asked me to co-broke a penthouse apartment overlooking the East River. If we make the sale I stand to get enough commission to cover the cost of the flowers. So, you know how it is—I wouldn't want to upset her about her sister's dating situation. Of course, you might still want to avoid Renny and I'll understand if he will make you uncomfortable. Although, by now, the past is…well, past." She paused. "But, you're my best friend, so it's your call."

Had I just heard a string of outrageous mixed messages? "I have to think about Maya and Renny, Carla," I replied with clenched teeth, suppressing the anger that would have been my first choice of response. No, it wasn't about anger at that point. It was about disappointment—and that was worse.

"Fine. And don't forget," she said in a reasonable tone as if the person on the other end of the phone (me) was not already distressed, "the calligrapher needs the exact names for the invitations. And he's also doing the place cards for the table seating and you understand I can't figure that out until you let me know if you have an escort. Really, Sophie, I can't keep the calligrapher waiting much longer."

That was the final insult, delivered with just the right amount of self-absorption to make me wonder if our friendship could be repaired. Luckily, I was able to suppress the profanity that would have been my first choice of response. I don't usually swear, but lately I've had more provocation than is customary. "I'll get back to you, Carla," I said brusquely and then I hung up.

At this point, it was totally clear to me that Bridezilla had lost all concept of friendship and loyalty—not to mention sensitivity. Imagine if she had another single gal pal casting about for a wedding escort. No doubt she'd ask me if I wouldn't mind if *Enrique* could do the job. Why not? I don't talk about *him* anymore, do I?

In my heart I believed Renny was seeing Maya again because he was too busy to exchange her for another woman; Maya was just a placeholder until he had time to find a good-looking alternative—certainly one who not only didn't discuss the dreaded "M" word, but one who also had a major aversion to children.

I didn't want Renny's girlfriend replacement to be me—but he could have made an effort to reconnect...to admit that he missed me...to plead that he was lost without me. I know I wouldn't take him back; nevertheless, would it be so dreadful if he declared that he'd made a terrible mistake and couldn't live without me?

On second thought, aren't I expressing mixed messages myself?

# *February 20th*

My desperation plan to get a date for Carla's wedding was to approach Sam Basinger, my counterpart on the television team, to see if he had potential. Since I had only three weeks to the wedding, I had to act fast and be assertive—which is not exactly my style. When print and television finished this morning's session on the Renegade project, I practically ran over a secretary in order to exit the conference room side by side with Sam. Before he could get away, I grasped his arm to get his attention.

"Sam, how about lunch? It will give us a chance to kick around some of the ideas we've been working with."

"Lunch? Hey, Sophie, I was really planning to skip lunch today." He hesitated, apparently trying to figure out what to say next. Then he pulled me aside, because some of the copywriters were still in earshot. "Actually," he said, with a broad smile, "I have to stop by Tiffany's during lunch hour and pick up the engagement ring I ordered. I am beyond excited."

He went on to explain—in one long, excruciating sentence! "Today it's exactly one year since my girlfriend Valerie and I met outside Tiffany's and wouldn't you know, we were both looking at the same window display and I impulsively said to her—a total stranger!—that you'd really have to love a girl beyond all reason before you spent all that money for a ring and she said that with the right girl, the money was well spent and I said maybe you can change my mind and then she said give me a chance and then I said how about coffee and a doughnut and the rest is history."

With breath control like that, he should give up advertising and go for the tenor sax. "Great story, Sam. Congratulations."

I went down to the cafeteria and bought a salad and a low fat muffin to eat at my desk. What was I thinking? I didn't even know the guy and all I had to go on was that he was nice looking and didn't wear a wedding ring. I can imagine Natalie's amusement when I tell her about this.

Tonight, I called Carla to see if she might have reconsidered her request to me about letting Renny come as Maya's date. Not a chance.

"Sophie, just get it over with and ask your Dr. K to escort you. It's no big deal."

I wanted to tell her that, yes, it is a big deal. He has anxiety about being my friend and he certainly doesn't want to escort me to your wedding. In fact, we had a stupid argument and he's no longer in my life. Of course, I didn't say this. Instead, in a gesture of undeserved magnanimity, I said as nonchalantly as possible, "Carla, of course it's okay if Renny comes. I'm a big girl and he's history."

"Oh, Sophie, that's great. Maya will be so happy! And who knows, someone might turn up for you. How about Match.com.? Or that other one—oh, I can't remember the name. Because I really want you to dance at my wedding."

"Thanks Carla. That's so thoughtful of you to think of a well-known online dating service and *that nameless other one* to save the day. No doubt either would provide a suitable candidate on the very first try." But my sarcasm was lost on her.

"Exactly," Carla agreed, her common sense dwindling at a rapid rate the closer she got to her wedding day. "So, work on this escort problem quickly because I do need the complete guest list very soon. The calligrapher has called twice; he's getting antsy."

After we hung up, I wondered if I should have asked her if the calligrapher was single. Now, that's a true sign of desperation. I made a mental note that when I get married, *someday*, I'd never hire a calligrapher. I'd create address labels on the computer for the invitations and I'd have handwritten Post-it notes on a bulletin board, indicating the seating plan. Better yet—open seating—just winner take all when it comes to finding a place to fit your fanny.

It's a sad state of affairs when your mother, your girlfriends *and the calligrapher* worry about you showing up to a wedding without a date.

# *February 23rd*

*I* miss him. I miss him terribly.

He would make me feel better about this wedding nonsense. The rational part of me knows that Carla is simply taking care of business, keeping Maya happy so that her sister Diane will continue to co-broke expensive condominiums with her. If that's the case, and I'm fairly certain it is, why do I need this validated by Dr. K? Why do I want to talk to him if I already know how he would think? Well, I just feel better when I talk to him. He's calm, he's centered...and he's funny without having an edge.

The irony is that I feel as if I've turned a corner and I don't need a shrink anymore. I now know more about my family and myself than when I started and I understand how my relationships were influenced by my parents' marriage. I feel stronger and wiser and I certainly believe I'm in a better place emotionally. I don't have a need to continue therapy with Dr. K or any other therapist, for that matter.

So, why do I miss him? Why am I thinking about him? Sometimes a flash of desire strikes and I imagine what it would be like if he took me in his arms. I could be working at my desk when suddenly, for no apparent reason, I'd want to inhale his aftershave, which seems to have seeped into my pores and introduced a citrus sense memory that I can't shake. I could be lacing up my sneakers for spin class when I would think about brushing my lips against his and wondering if he will sense the electricity—because I am conscious of a current pulsing through my body when I think of him that way.

Sophie Marks—don't think of him *that way*! Don't fall into that transference trap which is totally irrational. Kisselstine would be upset if he knew what I was thinking. He has enough anxiety being my friend because patients are not supposed to convert to companions and I have already ruptured that taboo.

But, perhaps...perhaps it isn't transference at all. Maybe these occasional erotic fantasies are the consequence of my dating moratorium; it could be that I've zeroed in on Kisselstine because there's no man in my life. Isn't that ironic? Kisselstine is the one person who could figure that out for me.

I was having supper in my apartment—with those thoughts interfering with my peace of mind—so I turned on the news in order to turn off my daydreams about Dr. K. It was just me and a plate of pasta and the various weather-related natural disasters, political upheavals and basketball scores on the evening news, when my mother called.

"Edgardo and I haven't seen you in ages. Come to dinner Friday night and I'll cook for you my brisket and sweet potato casserole."

"Mom, Sherri, that sounds wonderful." And then it came to me. "Oh, can I bring my friend, the one you met at the tango recital? He's in-between girl-friends right now and kind of lonely. I can find out if he's free Friday night."

"Really? No girlfriend? He's such a nice-looking boy, so well-spoken, why don't *you* go out with him?"

There are two good reasons and I can't tell you either of them: because he's my ex-shrink and I *paid* him to listen to my problems and now he knows too much about me, not to mention *you* also and he can't be my date because—back to square one—he's my ex-shrink. Anyway, we had an argument and I told him I'd never, ever call him again. So I don't even know if can I pull this reconcili-ation dinner off. That's what ran through my mind. What I actually said was, "Really, we're just friends. But I think he'd enjoy the dinner and the company."

"Fine, fine. Bring him on Friday. I'll make it special and bake Grandma's strudel just for him."

"I thought *I* was the special one," I said with pretend petulance, but she'd already hung up.

I want Kisselstine back in my life, but I think I backed myself into a corner when I said I'd never call him again—*never, ever!* Sophie Marks, you're such a drama queen; you didn't have to go that far. But, did *he* say he'd never speak to me again? That's a crucial piece of information, but I can't remember.

Or did he just say he wouldn't be my escort for Carla's wedding? If I had an emergency, he's surely take the call and help me. Maybe if I told him I was stranded in midtown because a blind date had tried to molest me and then fled when I hit him with my Jimmy Choos? No, even in a fantasy, I'd never waste my Jimmy Choos on a date with someone I'd never met; if I'm going to put mileage on those shoes, it has to be for someone worthwhile. What if I were mugged in a dark alley and my money and phone were taken and I had to borrow someone's cell phone to ask him to take me home? What if I called him at three in the morning and told him I was having an asthma attack and I needed to get to the emergency room and I didn't want to alarm Sarah/ Sherri? What if I let him know that it was the fifteenth anniversary of the loss of my beloved dachshund, Romeo, and I was so heartbroken that I was sinking into a major depression. Ridiculous fictions—except for the part about Romeo. In fact, next week will mark twelve years since his passing and I will cook two hamburgers and put one in Romeo's bowl and place it on top of the brass box that holds his ashes and I'll put mine on my grandmother's good china plate. Romeo and I—didn't we both love a good, medium rare burger. Every February for the last twelve years, I've honored him with this ritual. Tears still stream.

Damn, this wasn't getting me anywhere, so I steeled myself and made the phone call before I lost my nerve. When he said hello, I had a rush of pleasure, hearing his voice. "It's me. Sophie. I'm calling because…because I'm sorry. Really sorry." And after those words, I was lost.

"Sophie, it's okay. Please don't be upset. It's okay." He sounded as upset as I was.

"It's not okay. I ruined everything," I said, choking the words out.

"Sophie, you didn't ruin everything. I lost my cool and I got angry and that was wrong."

"Just tell me you forgive me, please. Tell me we can be friends again."

"Yes, we can be friends again." He paused. Then, "I'll try."

I should have been happy, but I wasn't. Something was still wrong and I wasn't able to identify it. "I have to get off the phone now," I said hurriedly and I hung up because a surge of sadness had washed over me, like a powerful wave flooding my chest and then receding, leaving me hollow inside. And then I knew what was wrong: he'd said, "*I'll try.*"

When I composed myself, I texted him—not taking a chance on a phone call where I might fall apart again. I wanted to approach him calmly because why would he want to be with a friend who was so emotional? I had to salvage this relationship as a grown-up. I let him know that my mother was inviting him to dinner this Friday evening and was preparing her delicious pot roast and sweet potato casserole and there would be homemade strudel. I could use the company, I wrote, and he would enjoy a great home-cooked meal.

He called me back that evening. "Sophie, I'm glad you got in touch. I never want to argue with you again and I'm sorry, really sorry that I made you unhappy."

I was so relieved. "Then you'll come to dinner? Please."

"Yes, I'll come. You know, that's my kind of menu. However, isn't that a bit tame for your enlightened taste buds?"

"Oh no, I'm an equal opportunity eater." Which is true. I haven't experienced a painful withdrawal now that I don't dine on Cascada's elegant fare. It was an amazing culinary three-ring circus for a while, but the quail eggs, the pork cheeks, the monkfish cloaked in béchamel—they are just pleasant memories now that the ringmaster is out of the picture.

"Well then, the earliest I can pick you up is at 6:15," Kisselstine replied. "Considering Friday night rush hour, we'll probably hit traffic and you ought to warn your mother we'll be late."

"Will do. See you then."

He'd never admit it, but I bet he missed me. Sort of.

# *February 26*<sup>th</sup>

*K*isselstine picked me up promptly at 6:15. He actually parked and came up to the apartment instead of calling me on his cell and having me meet him downstairs. I was touched.

"Looking good," he commented. But he didn't smile when he said it, so it sounded strange. I can't remember him ever making an observation about my appearance. This little dinner was not getting off to a good start; something was wrong.

Maybe he was bothered about my outfit. How could I tell him that what to wear tonight was a toss-up: should I dress for him or for my mother? Option #1: for him, jeans, sweat shirt and sneakers. Option #2: for my mother, a silver and black sweater and figure-hugging leather pants and my Jimmy Choos.

My mother had always loved to dress me up, even going as far as following the trends when I was in high school and encouraging me to wear whatever was in style. As I think about it, perhaps that was a substitute for her own unfulfilled desire to dress fashionably. Whether her restraint was motivated by economy or diffidence, the previous incarnation of Sarah/Sherri was never stylish. But I had as many clothes as a Barbie doll. Interestingly enough, my father never complained about the money she spent on me. Thinking about this, I'm surprised that it never came up in therapy.

Anyway, I had chosen option #2, leaning toward sexy—and perhaps this was awkward for my ex-shrink who hadn't yet come to terms with our friendship. Suddenly shy, I threw on my coat and quickly buttoned up as I wondered if my V-neck sweater had more "V" than necessary. Point of information: tonight, my mother sported a seriously deeper V.

Kisselstine programmed his GPS and concentrated on his driving. After a while I realized he simply wasn't talking to me. I tried to get the conversation going but he didn't seem eager to talk. My comment about Syrian refugees didn't elicit a response. A reference to the stock market also failed to take hold. An allusion to the congressman from Alabama who had just been indicted, did not get the conversational juices flowing. I resorted to office gossip, recounting a recent blow-up when a very nice fellow in accounting accidentally sent a video to one of the secretaries that featured a sexy but not naked woman pole dancing. Despite his embarrassed apologies, the secretary had gone to Human Resources charging harassment. Our office was divided on this, I told Kisselstine. I hoped he'd take the bait and come down on one side or the other and we'd get a discussion going, but he was silent.

Finally, I asked, "What's the matter?"

"What's the matter? You tell me."

Honestly, I didn't know what to say. "Please tell me why you're upset."

He practically spoke through gritted teeth. "Sophie, I'm having a hard time with this friendship thing. I don't know. I shouldn't have accepted your invitation for dinner at your mother's house. Frankly, my conduct has been erratic and that's really bothering me." He allowed himself a grim laugh. "I'm a psychologist and I should know better."

"I think you're being unreasonable," I said indignantly. "We like each other. And we've turned a corner because the therapy part is in the past and now we're just two people who enjoy each other's company. Isn't that enough?" I'd never seen him look so miserable. I wanted to turn this around and make him happy but I instinctively realized that I didn't know how to do that.

"Why did you invite me?" he asked. "Are we playing a psychology cat and mouse game? If so, I'm just no good at it."

I didn't know how to answer him. My invitation was just spontaneous on my part because I didn't want to lose him. Well, actually, maybe not totally impulsive. I did think it would be fun for us to be together to enjoy Sarah/Sherri and Edgardo in action and I did appreciate his company, no question. But I had to be honest with myself; I also remember thinking that it would be productive to take a car trip because we'd have time to talk about anything and everything. Of course, I'd find a way to work in the information that Maya was coming to the wedding with Renny. I had been manipulative and he saw right through me.

He continued. "I helped you out initially as a friend when we went to New Jersey, but I'm just not comfortable with…with this friendship business. I'm sorry."

"But, Dr. K, I like being with you—and I thought you felt the same way. That's what a friendship is all about, isn't it? Anyway, when I asked you to come, you seemed all right with the invitation."

"I've had time to think."

All I could say was "I'm sorry." And now, *both of us* were sorry. Kisselstine didn't respond, so the rest of the drive was uncomfortably silent. When we arrived, he parked and cut the engine and turned to me. "Don't worry, I'll play nice."

"You're being unfair."

"No, I'm being realistic. We're going to have a pleasant dinner and I'm going to enjoy the company. Actually, your mother reminds me of my favorite aunt and I really enjoy her. And I relish a home-cooked meal, so this evening should be fine. Just fine."

I had made a mistake. I hadn't appreciated the depth of his reluctance to be friends and I'd pushed him too far and only succeeded in making him unhappy. He handed me a tissue from the box on the visor, just like in the office. I couldn't help but wonder if he kept tissues handy because the women he dated, like his patients, were prone to tearing up.

"But, this is it," he said sternly. "No more tango competitions or dinners at your mother's. I'm available if you need help for your article," he said very quietly without looking directly at me, "but I suspect you have all the information you need."

When we stepped inside the apartment and my mother greeted us warmly, he was smiling and friendly, even taking a wrapped gift out of his coat pocket. My mother was predictably delighted, but honestly, it was a lovely hand-painted silk scarf and she immediately wrapped it around her neck and kept it on all evening.

Kisselstine was serene and engaged as if we'd never had that unpleasant conversation in the car. That made me calm down after a while and I was able to relax and join in the conversation. The evening progressed with random chatter about the tango (Sarah/Sherri: "Such a happy dance, right Edgardo?"), about marriage (Edgardo: "I'm still on my honeymoon with this wonderful woman!"), about cooking (Dr. K: "My mother's pot roast is made with onion soup, just like yours, Mrs. Marks, although I'm thinking you have a special secret ingredient that makes it taste so much better."), about the evening. (Me: "I'm having such a good time tonight. I'm so glad we're all together.") I hoped he would get the message that I still optimistic about our friendship.

Predictably, Kisselstine said that Sarah/Sherri's apple strudel was the best he'd ever eaten—and he'd been to Vienna, the mecca for strudel, and could make that comparison. Edgardo agreed as he and Dr. K bolted down their pastries with enthusiasm. The two of them reminded me of Romeo, who accomplished the feat of eating without explicitly chewing.

What wasn't predictable was the fact that my mother didn't pepper Kisselstine with personal questions or in any way assume he was marriage material. Frankly, I was surprised at her self-control. But, upon reflection, I think it wasn't a matter of restraint. She simply believed that we were friends and didn't bother to get his pedigree or calibrate the potential of this friend I'd brought to dinner.

We said our goodbyes and headed back to the city. The first thing Kisselstine did when we settled into the car was apologize. "Sophie, I'm very sorry I was so difficult on the ride to Brooklyn. I didn't mean to hurt you. It's just that...that this isn't... working."

I wasn't used to him having difficulty expressing himself. Finally, he said, "I do care about you, Sophie, of course, because we've been together for a while, you know, as therapist and client. But, I'm obviously having trouble with this arrangement."

I didn't know what to say. When he wasn't upset with me, he was kind and caring and I didn't want to lose him. He made me feel safe. He fell silent and concentrated on his driving and I took my cue from him, so for the rest of the trip, the entire forty minutes of it to be exact, there was no conversation. He double parked in front of my building, gallantly came around to open the door for me and walked me to the entrance.

"Good night, Sophie," he said softly.

But to me, it sounded like "good-bye."

# March 1ˢᵗ

This morning my secretary told me my mother was on line two. My first reaction was that there must be something wrong because we have an agreement that she would call me at the office only if it were urgent. Otherwise, I'd get frequent notifications about the ten best foods for reproductive health or a newsflash that cousin Linda in California (just one year younger) was expecting her fourth child.

Instead, after my cautious *hello*, she said, "Sweetie, I found him!"

My first thought was that Edgardo had gotten lost—although that was highly unlikely since he stuck to her like jelly on peanut butter. So, I took the bait. "Found whom?"

"Don't you remember? I told you I'd find a nice young man to replace Enrique? So, listen. This handsome fellow moved into our building just last week. He's a blondie—like me! He transferred to the New York office of this bank with so many initials I can't remember and he doesn't know anyone in New York. We met in the basement separating our recycle and so I had him over for coffee and he's perfect. He wants to meet you."

"How did you manage that?"

"Well, for one thing, he thinks you're very pretty, you know, because I showed him your picture, and by the way, he said we could be sisters. Naturally, I told him you were an undiscovered treasure."

"Hold on. You told him I was an undiscovered treasure?"

"Why not? Edgardo thought that was a very smart thing to say." I could see she couldn't be more proud of her verbal invention.

"Mom, the "treasure" part's debatable but the "undiscovered" part is definitely not true. I'm thirty three years old and I've been *found* a few times."

"Always with the answers, Sophie, but I'm willing to overlook. I told him I'd try to set up something for tonight. What do you say? Are you free?"

Free? Yes, indeed. Thanks to my dating moratorium, twelve weeks and counting, I am free—as in liberated. It has actually been a relief to take a break from the flirting, the pretending and the expectations associated with dating the opposite sex. Hard to explain, but I am feeling that I have become a more authentic person since I've been on my own. Slowly but surely, I am finding the genuine Sophie Marks.

"Sweetie, he could be your date for Carla's wedding."

Along with Carla and Natalie, my mother was tuned in to the catastrophe in the making: Sophie Marks showing up at the social event of the year, *alone*, facing two hundred guests, all amazingly coupled up for the occasion and remarkably sorry for me.

"Sophie, are you listening to me?"

"Yes, Mom/Sherri, I'm thinking."

"What's to think about? You'll meet him tonight and you won't be sorry. You want me to put Edgardo on the phone to tell you how nice he is?"

"No, that won't be necessary."

"So, please, for me, say you'll meet him tonight."

"Tonight?"

"Yes, tonight. Please, do it for me. He's a lovely young man who doesn't know anyone in the city. Think of it as a good deed. Besides, I already told him you'd be happy to meet him. How can I explain if you back out?"

Damn. I wanted to tell her that I wasn't backing out—because I'd never *backed in* in the first place, but it was useless to argue. "Okay, okay, I'll meet him."

"So, he'll meet you at your City Diner, you know, the one around the corner from you. I said 7:30. I figured that would give you time to get home and freshen and then walk over to the restaurant."

"Do you mean to tell me you already set this up?"

"Of course. I told him I'd call back by lunchtime to let him know it was definitely on for tonight. You know, sometimes you just have to push."

"Mom, you get extra credit for pushing. I've got to go now. I've got a presentation in ten minutes."

*Irene Silvers*

After I hung up I just sat there wondering how I let her do this to me. But then it hit me—who was I kidding? At this point even I was brainwashed enough to think that getting a date for Carla's wedding was a high priority. I grabbed my briefcase and headed out for the presentation with my print group and the television team. Just as I was passing my secretary's desk, she held out the phone. "Your mother, again."

I hesitated, but then figured I'd better take it. "Yes?"

"Sophie, big shot, you hung up before I could tell you his name. Travis Harper. And he has that gorgeous blonde hair and big brown eyes and he told me that tonight he'd be wearing a navy blue blazer."

Good to know. I just hope the City Diner isn't flooded with Midwesterners who have blonde hair, brown eyes and blue blazers. That could be exhausting. So, I followed orders. Came home, "freshened" as my mother suggested and showed up at the City Diner at 7:40, hoping Blondie would arrive before me. He did. I immediately recognized him; he was indeed blonde and quite good looking, wearing a gold buttoned navy blazer, tan slacks, a pinstriped, button down shirt and tasseled loafers. A very, very tall Midwestern preppie.

He extended his hand for a firm handshake and a very formal introduction. "I'm Travis Harper from Grosse Pointe Park in Michigan. So glad to make your acquaintance. I do appreciate your helping me out on such short notice."

That was confusing. "Helping you out on such short notice?" I repeated.

"Yes, indeed. As you know, I'm new to New York and I'm just finding my way. Not too easily, I might add. I was so fortunate to meet your mother and accept your offer to show me around the city."

My offer? Was I a date or a tour guide? "What did you have in mind, Travis?"

He shook his head and smiled ruefully. "So far, I can go from Brooklyn Heights where I live to the Financial District where I work. After that, I'm somewhat lost. I need some help with the subway system and with...with everything. I had to ask five people about trains and directions in order to meet you here."

"Your company must have dossiers listing different transportation options, local restaurants, clothing stores, medical facilities and so forth. Most big firms have relocation people to help you out." Christ, I was all business, sounding like a human resources exec instead of flirting shamelessly in keeping with the first-date formula for success. In a sweet, breathy voice, I could have said, "Oh Travis, I'd be delighted to show you around. We'll have so much fun together in the big city." I would've accompanied this treacle with batted eyelashes, a dimpled smile and (coup de grâce) hooking my arm through his—letting flesh on flesh seal the deal.

"I did get some information, but I found it overwhelming. New York is more complicated than I ever imagined. I definitely need some help, Sophie."

Maybe this was a date and but he was shy, so he was was downplaying tonight as just a friendly meeting. I could deal with that. It's not as if I planned to drag him back to my apartment and tear off all his clothes in the process of ravishing him. At least, not on day one.

We talked about New York restaurants as we ate our entrees and it was clear that the restaurants he longed for had to serve regular American food. That said as he impaled a chunk of meatloaf and soaked it into the brown gravy on his plate. We talked about New York neighborhoods and by the time we got to dessert—pie à la mode for him, no surprise—he seemed most interested in the Chelsea area, known for its contemporary art galleries.

"So, I take it you're interested in modern art?"

"Oh yes, of course. Well, no, not exactly. I think I like modern art. I don't really go to museums," he said apologetically. Then he brightened. "But this is New York and that's what one does."

I couldn't figure him out but I felt obligated to do my part. "If you happen to be free on Saturday afternoon, would you like to go to Chelsea?" I asked, taking the plunge. "We could visit the galleries and if we have time, take a walk on the High Line. It's a lovely park built on an old elevated train track and it's become a New York favorite."

"That sounds quite delightful," he agreed. "I would certainly enjoy that."

We made plans to meet again at the diner for lunch on Saturday and then taxi to Chelsea. Whether or not *he* would consider our afternoon an official date or a sightseeing expedition, I couldn't tell. Anyway, I was doing this for Sarah/ Sherri. However, if he turned out to be reasonably interesting, I would be doing it for me—because I'd ask him to be my escort for the wedding. In my mind, I could hear Natalie saying, "Interesting? Look if he has the normal complement of ten fingers and ten toes and appears stable, just ask him to the wedding. Who needs interesting if he's blonde and tall?"

I do.

When I came home, I found two messages. My mother had emailed: "So?" I took my cue from her, suddenly a woman of few words and I emailed back, "So—can't tell yet."

Natalie texted: "How would you rate "recycle" guy on a scale of one to ten?" She had laughed uncontrollably when she'd learned that my mother and Travis had met in the basement of their building, separating garbage from recycling.

I fired back. "On a scale of one to ten, he is a ten in the looks department and unfortunately, also a ten in the stiff category."

She texted right back. "Stiff? Isn't that a good thing?"

"Not always. Stiff as in personality, not stiff as in pecker."

This earned me an LOL from Natalie—plus an emoji that was laughing so hard it had tears in its eyes. It suited me just fine. That's exactly how I felt, dealing with this wedding business.

# *March 4th*

*Y*esterday, I had my first and last date with Travis Harper. I quickly realized that his heart would forever belong to the state of Michigan. He might reside in Manhattan and eventually learn a few New York tricks, like how to hail a cab in the rain or get a restaurant reservation at trendy Nobu, but he would never be truly comfortable as a New Yorker. I'm convinced he'll transfer back to the heartland as soon as possible. He's wide-eyed and breathless about the "Big Apple"—yes, that's what he called it—but he'll always be a tourist in Manhattan. I doubt he'll ever get used to the brisk pace here, not to mention the noise, the crowds and the attitudes. Frankly, I sometimes have some adjustment issues myself, but this is my territory and I know how to deal with it.

We took a taxi to Chelsea and his eyes were fixed on the meter for the entire trip, and I could see that he was very uneasy. At one point, Travis turned to me and admitted, with a hint of homesickness, that at home he either drove his own car or walked. Then he turned silent, fixing his eyes on the meter again, each uptick no doubt as dreadful as an actual stab to his wallet.

I sometimes have issues with taxis as well—but only if we're at a complete traffic standstill and there's no possibility that the mess will be resolved while I'm still in my thirties. Absent a major traffic snarl, I consider taxis to be a trade-off for my financial success. I can't navigate the city without them and I've achieved an inner peace by understanding that I have a symbiotic relationship with the driver. He, and it's often a foreign born he, is feeding his family in the United States and probably sending money back home where it's urgently needed, and I am helping him achieve his worthy goals—thanks to the fare plus my regular 20% tip; 25% if I have luggage. Secondly, the driver is getting me to my destination while navigating city streets crammed with trucks, buses, bicycles, jaywalking pedestrians and of course, impatient drivers looking for the holy grail—a legal parking spot. But all this was lost on Travis Harper. I suppose he will eventually accept the taxi as a New York fact of life—or he'll use Uber, which I've resisted so far. I'm in the minority, I know, but I'm being loyal to a constituency that has taken care of me since I finished college.

By the time we arrived in Chelsea, Travis had a fine layer of perspiration on his forehead. I would've liked to lessen his distress but I thought it would be embarrassing if I offered to pay the fare. I decided that when we took a break for coffee, I'd definitely pick up the check.

I soon recognized that Travis Harper really wasn't a fan of modern art. We browsed through the Chelsea galleries and he discovered to his surprise that he didn't care for most contemporary paintings and sculpture. I don't think he had ever been exposed to them before.

"This has been an excellent day for me," he said with enthusiasm, as we strolled along the elevated High Line park. "I can't wait for you to take me to Radio City and the Empire State Building. I have quite a list, Sophie."

"I'm glad you enjoyed our outing," I replied, now convinced that he considered me more tour guide than romantic material—which was perfectly fine with me. "Actually, I have a suggestion for you. There's a group called Big Apple Greeters, sponsored by the city, and for no charge a guide will take you around different neighborhoods and give you their history. I confess they know a lot more about the city than I do."

"Just what I need," he concurred. "I'll certainly take your advice and get in touch with Big Apple Greeters. Sophie, I'll do my very best to become a true New Yorker."

"Good luck, Travis. It won't take long for you to fool the natives." It was a cliché said with a touch of irony, but it breezed right by him. At that point, my services as tour guide were no longer necessary. What's more, I didn't see any romantic possibilities for me with this man. On the positive side, he's tall and good-looking and will probably be successful in his banking career—especially if *earnestness* contributes to professional success in the banking industry.

However, unless he develops a sense of irony and a more amusing outlook, which is doubtful, he'll be a catch for someone else. Am I so jaded that I can't appreciate a really nice, uncomplicated man? I've been thinking about that question as I write this journal. Honestly, I believe there has to be some spark of attraction, be it emotional, intellectual or physical—and for me—nothing.

So, having assessed Travis Harper, I am now releasing him back to the New York dating pond so that an adorable, hopefully Midwestern girl can reel him in and enjoy his sweetness and innocence.

This morning the phone rang so early I hadn't even gotten out of bed to get dressed for work. "So, what did you think of him?" my mother asked with a tone that reeked of satisfaction.

"Not going to work, Mom/Sherri. He's sweet but he's very serious. Believe me, he has absolutely no sense of humor. And honestly, I didn't get the feeling that he was at all interested in me."

I heard a tsk tsk sound—a definite sign of disappointment. After all, what were the chances of her finding *another* handsome, single man hanging around the recycle bin? But, she rallied. "Okay, darling, not to worry. It's a big city. I'll find another one."

"Keep up the good work." And I hung up quickly so that I could give in to my desire to burst out laughing.

I just checked my email before leaving for the office. Travis thanks me for the tour and writes that when his *girlfriend* visits New York this Easter, he'll be ready to *paint the town* with her—thanks to my good advice. Naturally, I forwarded his message to Sarah/Sherri just to prove that my intuition was correct: I was a tour guide.

Enrique? No. Travis? No. Perhaps my mother should consider giving up the matchmaking business since she now has two strikes against her.

# *March 5ᵗʰ*

*R*idiculous! My dating timetable is being dictated by Carla and the calligrapher—both waiting anxiously to see if I can dredge up an escort from the Manhattan dating swamp. Life would be simple if Kisselstine had agreed to escort me. I know I shouldn't have told him that if I couldn't get anyone else, would he be my escort—as if he ranked so low on the list that practically anyone else would do. I'd just assumed he wouldn't want that gig.

I really was saying that I'd release him from his commitment if someone else came into the picture. Of course, Kisselstine took it to mean someone *better*. I confess, what was also in play was that I was terribly embarrassed that I had to beg my ex-shrink to be my date.

And now we'd had this rift that I was determined to mend. What I needed was a peace offering that would at least allow us to talk to each other as adults; I didn't need to define our relationship as "friendship" but I did need to know that we could speak to each other occasionally and still have some kind of rapport.

So, I texted an invitation to come to my place for dinner because we'd parted on bad terms. "We're better than that," I'd written. "Let's not be angry with each other because it makes me sad and I hope you feel the same way." We would come to some kind of acceptable terms thanks to my pork tenderloin with roasted potatoes and Grand Marnier mousse for dessert. If I couldn't get him by way of friendship, I'd get him by way of his appetite for another home cooked meal.

He caved.

After I set the table in my usual fashion, I realized the whole night could be misinterpreted. I always bought fresh flowers from the deli on the corner and used my grandmother's silver candlesticks and her yellow and blue floral china and her embroidered tablecloth and matching napkins as well. I didn't want Kisselstine to get the wrong idea, but the best I could do at that point was get rid of the candles.

And what message was I sending, wearing a scooped-neck blouse and black silk pants and my spiky Jimmy Choos. That wasn't exactly the outfit to cement a shaky friendship. So, I ran into the bedroom and changed into a tailored white shirt, a pair of jeans and sneakers. That sent a better message.

He came in and handed me a bottle of wine. He didn't seem angry at all and I felt relieved. I surmised that deep down, he would always see me as his patient, a rather needy woman who had messed up her personal life.

While I was getting dinner on the table, he browsed my bookcases but didn't ask for a tour of the apartment—which I think would have been tacky. When we sat down to eat, he complimented me on the dinner.

"But you haven't tasted it yet," I protested.

"I'm simply admiring the presentation and the effort. Honestly, I can't think of one woman I've known who could do this. Although, some have tried."

"I do love to cook. And I love to eat."

"In fact, I see you as a very judicious eater. I've watched you savor food and then eat only half of it. I've seen you get dreamy over a dessert and then after a few bites stop cold. You seem to have a lot of willpower—which I admire."

I shook my head. "Not exactly true. I do love food and I need to exercise some willpower, especially with ice cream, but I have to admit that I don't have that big an appetite. In fact, my father used to bribe me with chocolate bars if I'd finish whatever was on my plate."

"Did it work?"

"Not exactly. I'm not a big candy fan. But sometimes, I'd force myself to finish my dinner—or if I were very lucky and he got up to clear the table, I'd stuff my leftovers into a couple of napkins and produce a clean plate. I did it for him because it made him so happy when I ate. I was kind f a spindly kid when I was young, so I guess a clean plate was a victory for my parents."

"I couldn't say this when you were a client, Sophie, but now I can. Your warm and loving relationship with your father and your irreverent spirit has made you a very special young woman. You're a warm and witty person with a generous disposition and a wonderful sense of humor."

It was such a personal and unexpected comment that I blushed and hurriedly changed the conversation. I don't know why. "Please, please tell me about *your* father. I'd really like to know. After all, you know so much about me. Now it's my turn."

Kisselstine smiled broadly. "My father was a dentist with an affinity for dentist jokes—both good and bad. Practically all his patients were on the lookout for dentist jokes and they'd make their contributions when they came in for an appointment. Some were funny, some were cringe-worthy, but he brought them all home, so we had a lot of laughs at the dinner table. He's gone now, four years this June, but my mother is still going strong at seventy-six. She's a retired social worker who walks her one mile every day, twice a day, and keeps busy with reading and knitting. She has her own apartment in Manhattan and runs a highly competitive bridge game twice a week."

"She sounds like a terrific woman."

"Actually, she is, except for one thing: she's a terrible cook. We have lunch or dinner together every couple of weeks and when I can, I persuade her to go to a restaurant or let me bring in take-out, but, she thinks it's her motherly duty to feed me something home-made. Well, your mother is a great cook, so you can imagine how much I enjoyed that dinner. And, I'm enjoying this one as well," he added politely.

"Really? I hope this dinner measures up," I responded, not really fishing for compliments, but seriously wondering if he was enjoying it.

"Absolutely. I'm a very happy man right now."

"Good. That's what cooking is all about." We were both silent because I think we had arrived at a place that he wasn't sure he wanted to be in—a place where he acknowledged he was happy being in my company and was fine with the friendship. He'd been fighting that since January. I couldn't let him linger in that place.

"Okay, I can't let you off the hook," I said enthusiastically. "Tell me one of your father's bad dentist jokes. I want to imagine you as a child, sitting at the dinner table."

He thought for a minute. Then, with a gleam in his eye: "A husband and wife walk into the dentist's office and he says, 'Doc, I want you to pull a tooth. But no anesthesia because there's no time to wait for it to get numb. I have three friends downstairs in my SUV and we're in a big rush because we have a hard to get tee time at one of the fanciest golf courses in town and if we're late we're going to lose our spot, so just yank it out quickly, Doc, and we'll be out of here.' The dentist thinks to himself—what a brave man to pull a tooth without anesthesia! So he says to the husband, 'Which tooth is it, sir?' And the man turns to his wife and says: 'Open your mouth and show him, dear!'"

Then Kisselstine started to laugh and I joined in. "Oh, that's just mildly cringeworthy," I noted. "But you told it with enthusiasm and you get points for that."

"Much appreciated. But be careful, I have dozens more like that."

"Well, I'll take a rain check, for now." He was in such a good mood that I decided to go further. "So, your mother is seventy-six? Well then, I have to ask. How old are you?"

"Thirty-nine and counting. I'll be forty this August."

"Any brothers or sisters?"

"Like you, an only child."

Since he was so willing to talk, I continued. "And you never married again?"

"No. The right woman has been elusive." He quickly changed the subject. "Sophie, did I mention that this dinner is absolutely wonderful?"

I got the message: no more personal revelations, so I brought out dessert. It was time for me to make one more attempt to settle this wedding problem. "Dr. K, my dating moratorium is important to me; it's been three months now and I really believe that I needed it to reclaim my independence. I don't want to be in a position wherein finding a man is the most important thing in my life and I think the dating freeze has helped. That said, I have to say it puts me in an awkward position. I mean, about Carla's wedding."

His face was impassive and I couldn't tell what he was thinking. Then I soldiered on. "Please help me out. It would be difficult if I walked in there alone. Maya is coming to the wedding and bringing Renny as her escort. He means nothing to me now. But, I don't want to be alone at the wedding. You're the only friend I can ask."

He took a deep breath before he spoke. "Look, Sophie, there was no reason to do all this..." he waved his hand across the table. "I'm sorry I let you down last time you asked. But, I didn't need this bribe to do a favor for you."

"It's not a bribe! Whether you say yes or no, I wanted to make up with you. I don't want you to be angry with me."

"I'm not angry, Sophie. It's just that this friendship thing is...awkward. And, I chafed at the thought that I was on standby for this wedding. Look, I'm not a robot. I may be a psychologist from nine to five, but after hours I'm allowed to have personal feelings. I guess that's foolish masculine pride kicking in," he admitted apologetically. "Sophie, I'll be your escort for the wedding and I hope you forgive me for letting you down the last time."

"Oh, Dr. K, thank you, thank you."

Suddenly, I could see his face tighten and I immediately realized I'd said something incredibly foolish. I'd called him by the only name I've used when I've spoken to him—except for the time I introduced him to my mother and then—what choice did I have?

"Rob. It's Rob. Say it." His tone was sharp.

I could hardly meet his eyes. He'd always be Kisselstine to me—or Dr. K. But I did what he told me to do. "Rob. Of course, it's Rob."

"That's much better." Then he smiled for my benefit and said in a lighter tone, "All right, shall we put that behind us? Yes, Sophie Marks," he said with mock formality, "I can indeed be of service. So tell me the dress code for this shindig? Dark suit or black tie?"

"It is black tie because Carla is having the wedding of her dreams. She's going to flutter her way down the aisle in a mermaid dress that's absolutely wrong for her. But I do know that some men are coming in dark suits, so don't worry."

"I happen to own a knockout tuxedo with all the bells and whistles, and that's what I'll be wearing."

"Great. Shall I meet you at the event space at Chelsea Piers? It's called for six o'clock"

"No, that's not necessary. I've been there before and I know there's parking, so I'll pick you up about five fifteen. How does that sound?"

"Excellent." I couldn't stop smiling. My elation must have been contagious, because he smiled as well. And then, Kisselstine surprised me by helping me clear the table and stack the dishwasher after I'd rinsed off plates and cups. We didn't say much at that point, but he whistled a tune I didn't recognize and he seemed quite at ease. When the clean-up was finished, he took his jacket from the closet, gave me a military salute and said, "See you April 12th.

I was so relieved. Now I would have an escort who was not only presentable but also well dressed in a tuxedo. Actually he was more than presentable. He was obviously very intelligent and had a good sense of humor and was easy to be with. I should have told him how happy I was that he was going to be my escort. Maybe my smile was not enough. Oh, but then I might have scared him off if I showed too much enthusiasm.

I texted Carla that it was all settled. I would not be alone; tragedy averted. I omitted everything I really wanted to say to the bride because any hint of how I actually felt would have damaged our friendship and spoiled the celebration. Now, all the calligrapher had to do was spell Kisselstine's name right.

At some point, I'll have to figure out how I'll deal with seeing Renny. As I write this journal entry, I realize I would look foolish, even jealous, if I totally ignored Renny Chapman. I'll have to be cordial and smile and be above it all. And that's exactly what will happen because I'll have Dr. K at my side.

Now I can relax and in my spare time practice saying his first name.

# *March 29ᵗʰ*

*C*arla's wedding is in two weeks and I haven't spoken to or seen Dr. K since our dinner at my apartment. Twenty-four days. That's why I'm starting to worry. I can't imagine that he would stand me up, but I need a word of confirmation.

Carla insists I should just *call* him and firm up the plans for the evening. Natalie says I should *cancel Dr. K* and ask Travis Harper for the favor because the best thing to do is show up with seventy-four inches of blonde handsomeness.

Instead, I *texted* Kisselstine. "Wedding bells on April 12ᵗʰ. I'll be waiting outside. You don't have to park."

My thinking is that Dr. K is too kindhearted to leave me in the lurch. Even if he gives me the silent treatment at the wedding, which is doubtful, he's surely planning to honor his commitment to show up and be my escort. However, I'd feel more comfortable right now if I had a sign that he that he is alive and ambulatory.

I fully expect he'll answer my text affirmatively. Thank goodness I have no more weddings lined up in the near future because my dating moratorium continues: three months now and more to come. I feel good about that.

Weddings are way too stressful for a single girl who has sworn off men.

# March 30th

"Have tux, will travel," he texted.

Excellent response. Short and sweet with a hint of amusement and a willingness to please. Just what I needed for Carla's wedding.

I emailed back. "Have dress, will dazzle."

# April 12th

When I put on my beautiful dress for the wedding, I was transformed into a Disney princess. All I needed was a magic wand and a handsome prince to complete the picture. For a moment there, as I looked at myself in the mirror, I was transfixed. But not for long. Snap out of it, Sophie, I scolded myself. Don't buy into the princess industry's collateral damage: beautiful dresses that imply that the wearer's self-esteem depends on her appearance. And forget about the fantasy that a prince will show up to rescue you. For heaven's sake, you're a grown woman, so you certainly know that you don't need a prince to make your way in the world. In fact, any single woman who can pay the mortgage on her condo, write a check for the monthly maintenance and contribute to charity and still have money left over to buy an extra pair of shoes—does *not* have to depend on a man.

However, as I looked at my image in the mirror, I succumbed. *Just for tonight.* Just for tonight, I said to myself, I'm officially joining the princess line-up and tomorrow I'll revert to the self-sufficient, resilient woman I'm cut out to be. I know Dr. K would not approve, but this stunning royal blue sequined gown with the black net overlay that floats as I move has done its job; I am, indeed, a princess *just for tonight*. I spun around, delighted in my reflection. I must remember to tell my mother once again how grateful I am for her extravagance.

The evening was so mild that all I needed was a shawl around my shoulders. When I stepped out of the elevator, I received a thumbs up from Roy, the night doorman.

"You're killing it, Sophie," he said with enthusiasm. "So, who's the lucky guy? Renny?"

"No. I've got new blood, Roy. He's probably double parked out there, so I'm on my way."

Probably? Definitely! I was ten minutes early, but to my relief the Lexus was parked nearby and he was standing by the passenger side of the freshly waxed car. My first thought was that he looked terribly handsome in his tuxedo and then I reminded myself that every man looks 100% better in a sleek black tux with that adorable bow tie.

He looked me up and down without any embarrassment and gave me a lovely compliment. "You will definitely outshine the bride." Said with a big smile.

"That's not my intention," I replied, "but thank you."

Suddenly, I knew I was going to be safe and it really didn't matter if Renny was there with Maya. He was Maya's problem now. Dr. K had shown up, ready to escort me and he was smiling, so I knew that he was going to see to it that everything went smoothly. I was going to enjoy Carla's wedding. And, what's more, I forgave my old friend for everything. After all, she waited years to be a bride and years to finally marry Jake, so she was entitled to a full measure of wedding madness.

Carla had arranged for the cocktail hour to be held first and between bites of hors d'oeuvres we mixed and mingled. I knew Kisselstine was probably enjoying the opportunity to see the cast of characters I'd talked about in therapy. They were all there, except for Enrique. When Renny and Maya came over to say hello, I had a brief moment of panic that I might have told her my shrink's name, but then I remembered: of course I'd not revealed it to her.

Neither one of them would suspect that Dr. K wasn't a legitimate date. And to be sure, I introduced him as Rob, a man who didn't bear the burden of a last name. *Rob.* His name slipped off my tongue as easily as my own. When I said it, I swear he winked at me.

We were so civilized—just your typical laughing foursome. When Natalie and Warren joined us, she raised her eyebrows and pursed her mouth, signaling how much she appreciated what a rational situation this was. She steered me aside when she had the opportunity and said, "Your Dr. K is a hunk. Good work, Sophie."

"Yes, he cleans up nicely," I replied, rather casually. I could've said, "Yes, isn't he handsome?" but I restrained myself.

Then my mother and Edgardo joined us. "Such a beautiful wedding, isn't it? The best! Just what I want for my lovely Sophie." She turned to Kisselstine and narrowed her eyes. "So, what do *you* think, Rob? Does this affair put any ideas in your head?"

I hadn't seen that coming.

Natalie, Warren, Renny and Maya swiveled their heads in unison to look at Kisselstine and await his response. I could feel the color rising in my cheeks. Kisselstine nodded his head in agreement and said, "You're absolutely right, Sherri, this girl of yours deserves the best. There's nothing *medium* about her." And he put his arm around me and gave me a lingering kiss on the mouth. How clever he was about reminding me about my Christmas morning computer mistake. But there was no mistake about that kiss. I found myself kissing him back.

When he released me, all I could do was plaster a smile on my face. My mother was beaming, Natalie looked perplexed, Maya showed surprise and Renny was frowning. Of course, Warren had no clue. Just at that point, the guests were ushered into the adjoining room for the ceremony. Before I joined the bridal party, I turned to Kisselstine and said, "What was that all about?"

"Hey, just doing my job. Being a good date."

"Have you had too much to drink?"

"I've had a few. You might want to catch up."

I just shook my head in amazement and left him there because I had my maid of honor work to do.

The ceremony was perfect. I sailed down the aisle, carrying my bouquet, keeping my eyes on Jake, who was standing by the altar, fidgeting slightly. But when Carla came down the aisle, her pretty face glowing in a cloud of white veiling, Jake brightened as he watched her do the deliberate "Here Comes the Bride" two-step toward him. We attendants, Natalie and I, had tears in our eyes. This was a long time coming, but it surely was worth the wait.

After Carla and Jake had their first dance, the guests were encouraged to join them on the floor. Kisselstine led me to the dance floor and put his arms around me and at first we had at least five inches of space between us. After a minute or so, he held me closer and the space disappeared. He lowered his head and he buried his face in my hair.

I discovered that underneath that tuxedo there was a solid, muscular physique. There I was, experiencing in real life the tired cliché in a bodice-ripper romance novel: this man had a *hard* body. He had definitely put in some serious gym time. Why did I ever think he was *medium*?

"What are you doing?" I asked as he pressed my body into his. I mean I knew what he was doing, but I was surprised he was doing it to *me.*

"Well, I'm being a good date and dancing with the sexiest woman on the floor and I might as well enjoy it. Just for tonight, I promise."

When the music changed to rock, he released me. The evening was turning out to be full of surprises. He was a very good dancer and he looked sexy and comfortable on the dance floor. I had no idea this would be so much fun—dancing with my therapist. Okay, technically ex-therapist. I should have known he liked to dance because hadn't I called him one night on his cell when he was at the Odyssey Club—dancing? That reminded me. "What happened to the date you took to the Odyssey Club, you know, that night I called you?"

"Ah yes, the night you hung up on me. Not very nice."

"Well, I was terribly embarrassed. You were on a date, after all. Anyway, what happened to her?"

"Nothing happened to her. I'm still seeing her occasionally."

"Oh."

"If you remember, Sophie, I called you the next day, and then I hung up on *you.* That was very sophomoric of me."

"That's exactly what I thought!"

Then he pulled me to him as if the music had changed to slow dancing. But it hadn't. Everyone else was gyrating to the band's rendition of a Beyoncé song, but he was holding me close. "Isn't this better?" he whispered in my ear. And then he kissed me. I closed my eyes and once again I kissed him back. I'd fantasized about his kiss and now—here it was again. I wanted more. There we were in the middle of the dance floor, acting like a couple of teenagers. When I opened my eyes, the first thing I saw was my mother and Edgardo dancing next to us. They both were smiling—and to my surprise, my mother didn't make any comment—other than her smug expression—which, I suppose, was commentary enough.

I pulled away from my escort, because there was no point in confusing my mother and Edgardo. As for me, I was terribly confused. "You'd better think about sobering up," I whispered to him. I said that because I felt it was the right thing to say, but I really wanted him to kiss me again.

We sat down for dinner and enjoyed a lively conversation with Natalie and Warren and two couples who were Carla's cousins that I've known for years. Kisselstine was very comfortable with this tableful of strangers, but he did refill his wine glass a number of times. Every once in a while he draped his arm over my chair and rubbed my bare shoulder. I felt it acutely; my shoulder had turned into an erogenous zone.

He whispered in my ear, "Just for tonight. Just for tonight." Like a mantra. But I didn't understand what he meant. I really had to concentrate on what people were saying and pretend that nothing was happening as he kissed my neck and then continued his conversation. Natalie regarded me with raised eyebrows, shooting question marks at me.

Between courses, Natalie and I went to the ladies room. She pounced. "Are you kidding me? Are you telling me you're not involved with him? And, he's damn good looking which you never mentioned."

"Nat, he's my therapist or more accurately, my ex-therapist. I'm not supposed to think of him that way." (I was embarrassed to admit to her that I did fantasize about him—*that way*). "Natalie, I've told you that a shrink knows humiliating things that you'd never tell anyone in real life. Remember, I said he's seen me being bitchy and foolish and angry and teary and I don't know what else. Sometimes I'm ashamed when I think of the things I've revealed in therapy. You know, about sex." I shuddered and whispered, even though we were alone. "Orgasms, Nat."

"Cut the crap, Sophie. He's all over you, so nothing you said or did has stopped him. So, what's going on?"

"Truthfully, I don't know. He told me he was just doing his job. Being a good date, that is."

"Well, I'm pretty sure you're going to figure things out before the night is over. You're a smart girl." She paused. "Well, you used to be."

Natalie had asked the right question. What was going on? He had been burned once with a client who had made sexual advances that he'd rejected and he could have lost his license. Would he consider a romantic relationship with an *ex-client*? No, I warned myself, this must be all about too much wine. Oh, screw it, I thought, I'm a princess and I'm having a good time and he can kiss me all he wants, *just for tonight*. Don't overthink it, Sophie!

There I was in this elegant ladies room with huge mirrors. There was nothing else to do but check my reflection—and feel elated. It's nice to be called the sexiest woman in the room even if it comes from a man who's doing you a big favor and also has had too much to drink. As I was leaving, I ran into Maya. "Sophie, I'm happy for you, really. Your date seems very nice."

"Thanks, Maya." I nearly wished her good luck, but stopped just in time. I knew she needed luck with Renny, but it was not my place to tell her that. Instead, I told her I was happy for her as well and I guess I really was. Maybe Renny would settle down and be good for her. God knows, he wasn't good for me.

When I returned to the table, Kisselstine stood up and pulled my chair out for me. Still standing behind me, he placed both hands on my shoulders and rhythmically stroked them as he continued his conversation with Warren. No-load index funds seemed to be the topic. Normally, I'd be interested in that, but I was too aware of his hands on my bare skin to concentrate. Then he leaned over and burrowed his face in my hair and kissed my cheek. He was making me dizzy. I briefly considered the possibility that my 'G' spot had migrated to my face.

When we got up to dance again, Renny and Maya approached us on the dance floor.

Renny drew near and said, "Shall we change partners for this dance?" And without waiting for an answer, he deftly guided Maya to Kisselstine as he took me in his arms and we glided away.

"Who is that guy," he asked, sounding annoyed.

"He's my date."

"Is this serious?"

"Renny, it shouldn't matter to you if it's serious or not. You're with Maya now."

He shook his head. "Honestly, I'm doing her a favor. She asked me to come because she didn't have a date and I couldn't turn her down."

I was incredulous. "You're not back together?"

"Maya's a wonderful woman and I really like her but we're never going to be a couple and she knows it. Look, I tried it with Emma, you know, the "father" thing, because I felt so guilty about…about your baby. But it just didn't work for me. I miss you, Sophie. We were good together. We had three great years and we could have more. Seeing you here tonight, I realized how much I want you back."

Recently, I've been getting very disagreeable propositions from the men in my life: Enrique proposes marriage, even though he's bi-sexual and stands a good chance of being unfaithful to me; and Renny offers me sporadic cohabitation, mainly in my apartment—not his—without the possibility of children and with the probability that it won't be a lasting commitment.

Well, my perverse wish came true; Renny wanted me back. And then, I understood that it gave me no pleasure to have him reach out to me. It was no longer about my pride or vanity. Even though he initiated the break-up, the bottom line is that it was best for both of us. So I smiled at Renny and just shook my head—no. After all, I'm a princess, just for tonight, and according to the fairy tales, I will have a happy ending someday. *Someday Sophie*—back in business.

Just then, Kisselstine and Maya materialized as if on cue. Kisselstine smiled at Renny.

"Shall we put these women in their proper places?" he said smoothly as he gently handed off Maya and drew me close to him.

"I rescued you, princess," he said, "I'm your knight in shining armor."

"I can't believe you said that!" I could hardly stop laughing. "I have a confession to make. When I put this dress on, I suddenly knew what little girls feel like when they wear their Disney gowns! Silly of me, I know, but I felt that "princess" vibe."

"I think you're really happy and that makes me happy," he said softly.

When the music changed and the dance floor became crowded with all the couples who had waited for the slower songs, he did it again. We were so close

I could feel his body grinding into mine; he leaned down to me and kissed me as his hands gently worked their way up and down my back, sometimes more "down" than was suitable in a public space. I could feel my breathing coming faster.

Natalie was right. What was happening? But, wasn't he a wonderfully kind, intuitive, intelligent and appealing man that any woman would want? Except for that annoying detail that he was my ex-shrink. I was not supposed to feel this way. Nor was he.

The evening became a blur. I know I gave a good maid of honor speech, delivered with the right pauses and inflections, getting the laughs I'd hoped for as I drew on the wonderful memories that Carla and I have shared: our first furtive glass of whiskey stolen from my father's cabinet when we were twelve (we hated it); the blind dates we went on together (hated them, too); the fire in her mother's oven because we forgot about the cookies we were baking (we cried and were forgiven); the race to see who would get her period first (she did); the time in our twenties when we forgot our bathing suits and skinny-dipped at midnight when we were on Cape Cod (a policeman scolded us and kicked us off the beach). How could I stay angry with Carla, my long-time comrade in arms? In spite of temptation for the easy laugh, I never once mentioned that Carla was in a fairly constant skirmish with her strapless gown, trying to keep its bounty in check, just as Natalie and I had predicted.

When I sat down and it was Natalie's turn to give her toast, I could hardly concentrate because my date was intermittently running his hand up and down my thigh. I say intermittently because I would remove his hand and he would smile at me and then, after about fifteen seconds, replace it.

And that's how the evening went. I didn't know exactly what was happening, but it didn't take me long to realize how much I wanted him. He was kissing my neck when my mother came over to say goodnight. "Sophie, a wonderful speech. You're the best maid of honor. Right, Edgardo?" And Edgardo concurred. I have come to appreciate Edgardo because no matter what my mother says or does, he is completely supportive.

My mother turned to Kisselstine. "I see you're having a very good time, Rob. I'm so pleased." And Edgardo actually saluted him in a gesture of male bonding. When they left, we both burst out laughing and I only stopped when he kissed me on the mouth.

It was midnight and the wedding was over and I doubted that my escort could drive, but he had anticipated that. "Don't worry, Sophie, I'm leaving my car here for the night and I've called a taxi because I've got a buzz on. You might have noticed," he grinned, without apology. "Come princess, your chariot awaits."

In the back seat of the taxi, he put his arms around me and kissed me. Then, he pulled me close so that my back was nestled into his chest, with his arm tight around my waist. He slipped his free hand down my dress and caressed my breasts. When I didn't resist, he dropped his arm from around my waist and slipped it under my dress. We were both breathing heavily. I know I was supposed to push him away because he was my therapist, rather ex-therapist, but he smelled so good and he felt so good that I just gave in to it. And I didn't let myself think of future consequences when he came upstairs with me. I just knew that I wanted him. I could barely get the key in the lock because he was caressing me and when I finally managed to open the door, he scooped me up in his arms and carried me into the bedroom. We undressed each other in the dark—with only a dim light coming from the hall. As much as I wanted him, I needed the darkness to protect me from the reality of what was happening. In the dark, we were just a man and a woman who were passionate about each other.

He kissed my hair, my eyelids, my face and my breasts and worked his way down my body with sweet tenderness. I was the object of a desire so gentle that everything fell away and I was his, completely. He didn't require anything from me because it was all about giving me pleasure.

And when it was over, when we both shuddered into submission, we curled up as if we were an old married couple and this was just the right thing to do. Within minutes, he fell asleep, his arm around my waist, our legs entwined. I knew what I had to do and suddenly I also knew it was entirely possible. I had to erase "Dr. K," the therapist, from my mind and replace him with this strong, smart man in my bed who wanted me. Because I wanted him. I wanted him because I cared about him in a way that was so much more than friendship. I had deceived myself, thinking that my attraction to him was simply transference, thinking that he couldn't possibly be interested in me as a woman because he could only see me as a *patient*. I was wrong. Very wrong.

I drifted into sleep, elated with that thought. When I woke up sometime during the night and I felt his body next to mine, an explosive desire overwhelmed me. The Dr. K who had been my therapist had indeed vanished. In his place was this ardent man who had awakened something in me that I'd not known before. Passion. Love-struck passion that made me ache with desire. I didn't recognize myself; I was hungry for him, for his kiss, his touch. And I suddenly understood that I wanted him to want *me* forever. If he wanted me, I would be happy.

Just like a fine-tuned race car, he went from sleepy to stimulated within seconds. I became his collaborator and I gave him what he hadn't asked for the first time—my intense participation. I felt an urgent need to have him; it was as if I'd lost all sense of self and had no reticence or shame. I heard no inner voice commenting on the proceedings—something that often accompanied my sexual encounters with the handful of men I'd seriously dated. I was floating above my consciousness, only aware of pleasure.

I wanted to have him desire me above all others and to need me beyond all rationality. I'd never had an intimate experience like this before because I'd never cared so deeply about the person I was with. And when we collapsed into each other, our breathing reduced to sighs, our faces touching, our bodies no longer burning, he whispered my name tenderly as he kissed my bare shoulder. And just hearing "Sophie…Sophie… Sophie…" had a hypnotic effect on me. It made me feel as if my name had never been spoken properly until that very moment.

He had been there all the time, within reach, and I had been unable to see how much he meant to me. Just in time, he rescued me. I remember quite clearly that he had promised he would help me find happiness. And he did.

But when I woke up in the morning, he was gone. He'd left a note on the kitchen counter. "Sophie, I'm so sorry. I had too much to drink, as you are well aware. Please forgive me." And he signed it "Dr. K." To make matters worse, he'd crammed that message on the back of his business card. That made me think that he was so desperate to get away before I woke up that he didn't dare take time to look for note paper—an easy find in my apartment. I have note pads in every room—even the bathroom—should I get a spur-of-the-moment idea for an ad campaign I'm working on. He'd just grabbed a card from his wallet, dashed off the message and disappeared. The only thing that would have made it worse was if he had left a $100 bill on the dresser.

I kept re-reading the note, first in shock and then in dismay. So, in the light of day, he had become *Dr. K* again. And he was claiming inebriation as an excuse for making love to me. How could I have confused him with a knight in shining armor? Was I a fool, mistaking our lovemaking for...what? Something much more than a carnal misadventure driven by alcohol?

He had been so loving, so caring that I simply couldn't believe it all added up to too much wine on his part. Surely, it must have meant something to him. It meant something to me. *He* meant something to me.

But, he didn't call me the next morning. I wanted him to have a change of heart and admit that the night we'd spent together was wonderful. More than wonderful; it was a revelation that we were meant to be a couple. But he didn't call. Not in the morning, not in the afternoon, not at night.

Instead, I got a call from Natalie, a call from my mother and even a call from the bride, who was leaving for Hawaii later in the afternoon. Carla said, "Look, I don't have a graduate degree, but I'm telling you that man didn't act like your shrink. Just saying."

Thanks for the news, Carla, I thought to myself. She continued, "My advice is run, don't walk, back to his couch. He does have a couch in the office, right?"

Wrong. There's no couch and there's no office either because I've been banned from the premises. How I wish I could sit down in that comfortable chair and tell him, *as a patient*, that I have a serious problem. I would confess that I'd had an erotic encounter with a man I really cared for but whom I'd thought was just a friend and it turned my thinking about him upside down. I'd discovered that he was too important to lose and I had no idea how to get him back.

Natalie weighed in. "He was all over you last night. Did you sleep with him?" I was in no shape to have that conversation with her, so I lied. "Of course not. He was just doing me a favor."

She snorted. "Sophie, a favor is you asking your neighbor to hold on to your newspapers while you're on vacation. He wasn't doing you a favor. He was *doing* you."

"Good bye, Natalie. I can't talk because I'm nursing a hangover."

Sarah/Sherri was ecstatic. "You know, I was always hoping he was more than a friend because he's the best one you've ever gone out with. Something about him is very special. Sweetie, I think you have a keeper."

Yes, I thought to myself, something about him is very special. Unfortunately, he turned me on and then he turned me out. 'I don't think so. Mom/Sherri, just hang in there."

"What does that mean, Sophie? Just hang in there?"

"It means...it means..." I trailed off and sighed heavily. Then, I decided to be honest with her. "It means we're not a couple."

"So run after him. Don't sit back and wait. Make him a couple with you."

"That's not what he wants. Please, please believe me."

"Sophie, my baby, I love you." And she hung up without trying to change my life.

I was relieved that it was Saturday morning and I had the rest of the weekend to regroup. I put on a robe, made some tea and then went back to bed. I wondered if my mother was right. "Go after him," she'd said. Isn't that what she'd done to get my father? And that turned out to be a mistake. I was not going to repeat her history. Anyway, *he* didn't want me.

The note on his business card said it all.

# *April 13ᵗʰ*

*I* planned to stay in bed all weekend, except for time-outs for the bathroom and possibly getting a pizza delivery. And that's exactly how
Saturday played out. I thought Sunday would be a repeat, but that's not what
happened.

On Sunday, my mother called around lunchtime. "So, are you free today?"

Free and alone. I was hesitant. "Why are you asking?"

"Is that an answer to give a mother?"

"Okay, I'm free."

"Good. Edgardo and I will bring lunch. We just happened to be in the
neighborhood and so we'll pick up some Chinese food. See you soon." And she
hung up before I had a chance to respond.

Really? These two Brooklynites just happened to be in my Manhattan
neighborhood? They arrived about twenty minutes later with seven cartons of
food and they bustled about the kitchen, getting plates, silverware and glasses.
I'd thrown on jeans and a tee shirt, but I hardly looked presentable since I hadn't
showered in two days and I still had leftover make-up smeared on my eyes and
no semblance of a hairstyle. When my mother didn't comment on my appearance or mention the pizza crusts and dishes in the sink, I suspected she had big-
ger things on her mind.

Nevertheless, I discovered I was hungry and very grateful that someone was
taking care of me. After a few forkfuls of sesame noodles, I stood up from my
chair and went over to my mother and gave her a hug and a kiss.

"Thanks, Mom/Sherri. This is just what I needed." She was touched. I
didn't do that often enough—show her affection.

"You know, Sophie, you should call me "Mom." I think I'd like that best."

"I love you, Mom."

With that, Edgardo jumped up from his seat and put his arms around both of us. Damned if we weren't starting to look like a family. Then we sat down and had a round robin with the cartons, passing them back and forth, all of us eating too much. When we slowed down and were just picking at the remains on our plates, my mother began. "So tell us about Rob."

"Not much to tell," I mumbled.

Edgardo put his hand on mine. "I can tell you something about Rob. He's in love with you. This I know for certain."

I put down my fork. "Edgardo, tell me how you know that?"

"I know this, Sophie. I know the way he touched you and how he danced with you. I know the way he looked at you. I look at your mother that way."

"He had too much t drink at the wedding and it was all about the wine. At least, that's what he told me."

My mother was surprised. "He told you that?"

I sighed. How much could I tell them? I couldn't divulge the therapy part because I didn't want my mother to think I was some kind of desperate basket case. And the rest—the friendship—part was much too complicated.

"Yes, he told me that."

Edgardo said, "That's just an excuse. He denies his feelings." Edgardo wagged a finger at me. "But I know for certain that he is a man in love."

My mother went further. "Are you in love with him?"

I was honest. "I think…I think I do love him but it's so confusing. Until the wedding night, I considered him my friend. I didn't realize how much…how much I cared for him. I always knew he was important to me, but I couldn't figure out what that meant."

I wasn't making much sense. How do you explain to your mother that you have no idea how to process your own feelings? "He was doing me a favor, you know, escorting me to Carla's wedding. But then, at the wedding, everything got mixed up. Now, I think he's just walked out of my life and it's too late."

"Something's missing here," she said. "You're not telling us the whole story. How can we help you without the whole story?"

"I understand you're trying to help me but there's nothing you can do, believe me. Right now, I can't talk about it anymore. Please understand."

My mother was thoughtful for a while. "You slept with him," she said and it was a statement, not a question.

"Oh, God," I moaned.

"I think that's a yes." She turned to Edgardo. "Does that sound like a yes?" Edgardo nodded his head affirmatively and said, "Yes, yes! He couldn't help himself. Our Sophie is so smart and beautiful."

My mother rubbed my hands. "And it was good," she said. Again, a statement, not a question.

If I hadn't been so miserable, I'd never have answered her, but I just felt defenseless. What's more, she was rubbing my hands; I was safe with her. I rested my head on the table because I couldn't meet her scrutiny and I whispered "yes."

Edgardo patted my shoulder as if to say "don't worry, it will all work out."

"So, what's this Rob's last name?" my mother asked in a conversational tone—but the question was anything but innocent. Was she planning to arrive at his doorstep and perform an intervention?

"I can't talk about this any more. I have to work it out in my own mind. But thanks for coming and being supportive. I really am so grateful." I gave my mother a hug and then I turned to Edgardo. "Thank you," I said. And he took me in his arms and gave me a kiss on my cheek and whispered, "No te preocupes."

To my surprise, there were no more questions and no more unsolicited advice. They told me to rest and I crawled back into bed while they packed up the leftovers and placed them in my refrigerator, cleaned up the kitchen and called out their goodbyes.

I briefly thought of calling Maya, because she, of all people, would understand my despair, but I scratched that idea right away. The best thing to do was to stay in bed, burrow under the covers and sleep until the alarm woke me up Monday morning. But before I did that, I reached for my iPad to translate *no te preocupes*. *Don't worry*. Oh, Edgardo, I can't help myself, I thought—but thanks for the encouragement.

Monday morning was hours away. The beginning of a new week and the beginning of a new life—without him.

# May 26ᵗʰ

*I* needed just one lost weekend to hit bottom and then on the Monday morning after Carla's wedding, I rejoined the land of the living, sad but functional.

I threw myself into spinning class and concentrated on my work. I was newly charged with introducing millennials to *Hollywood Heels*—a line of multi-colored, floral patterned footwear designed by a Los Angeles television actress. Her energetic love life was chronicled in a reality show that hooked women in the eighteen to thirty-five demographic—our target audience. I was well aware of the fact that at age thirty-three, I was on the cusp of having my membership withdrawn from that exclusive club. No matter, because the heels were five or six inches high and skinny as straws; I could wear them only if I were carried from place to place at all times.

On Saturday mornings when I volunteered at the food pantry, I was given a dose of a different reality that reminded me to put things in perspective. I had my health, my family, my work, my home. I would persevere.

I went about the agenda of my life all the while dealing with the insistent ache of his absence and I missed him more than I thought possible; missed him in a profound way that I'd never experienced before. What could I do? If he couldn't tolerate the friendship, he certainly couldn't bear an intimate relationship. I told myself that his passion the night of the wedding was fueled by too much wine and I would be terribly wrong to regard it as more than that. I comforted myself with the knowledge I'd gained in therapy that this, too, shall pass. After all, hadn't Kisselstine mended my broken heart after I lost the baby? Unfortunately, my shrink didn't teach me how to recover if *he* were the one to break my heart.

I missed him until last night. That's when he turned up—about six weeks after we spent the night together, six weeks after he left me with a terse note on the back of his business card. I had come home from work and rounded the corner from the elevator to my apartment and there he was, leaning against my door, reading a newspaper and holding a bouquet of yellow roses. I saw him first. My sharp intake of breath must have alerted him because he looked up and smiled when he saw me. I nearly ran up to him to throw my arms around him. Don't be a fool, I thought to myself; those flowers may be an offering of apology and not a sign of affection. I opened the door without a word and he came in and we faced each other.

"I've known for months that I was in love with you. Sophie, I always cared for you, probably too much when you were my client, but when you were no longer in therapy, I just couldn't help myself. I fell in love with you and the bright, funny woman in the journal." He brushed his finger across my cheek. "But you always saw me as Dr. K, even after we became friends. You could never get past that. And I was always hopeful that we could mean more to each other. That's why I had such a hard time being friends with you."

I had to sit down because I felt as if I were spinning.

"Sophie, I never intended to go that far the night of Carla's wedding. I promised myself that I would hold you and kiss you, just for that night." He shook his head. "I'd deluded myself into thinking that "just for tonight" would not include going back to your apartment and making love to you. I needed the wine to help me loosen up, and honestly, I thought I'd finally have you in my arms, something I'd wanted for a long time and then, I'd...I'd disappear. I was so conflicted about having a relationship with you. And it never seemed possible anyway, because you just wanted to be friends and I was always *Dr. K* to you. So, basically, it was *my* problem. But once we kissed...once we were in the taxi...I didn't keep my promise to myself."

I've heard people say they didn't know whether to laugh or to cry. I never knew what that meant because it seemed so irrational, but now I understood. I felt myself tearing up.

"Sophie, I've been told by a higher authority that you have feelings for me and that changes everything."

"I don't understand."

"I love you and I came back to see if you could love me. Sophie, I haven't come back to be your friend and I definitely haven't come back to be Dr. K."

"I'm so glad you came back." I felt dazed and happy and yet, tears were spilling out of my eyes. I couldn't help myself. He handed me a handkerchief from his jacket pocket, just like old times. And then he said, "I was wrong to disappear. I should have told you how I felt, even if you didn't feel that way about me."

"But I didn't know how *I* felt. I thought it was my fault having those...those forbidden thoughts that I assumed were transference. You had told me about the patient who came on to you—and how terrible it was. Well, I didn't want to be like that woman. I didn't realize until the night of the wedding how much you meant to me and then you left that dreadful note."

"Sophie, I woke up in the morning and felt horribly guilty because I'd taken advantage of you."

"It's not true that you took advantage of me," I protested. "I wanted you. I would never have made love to you if I didn't care about you. How could you not know that? I'm not the one who had too much to drink. I knew exactly what I was doing."

"That's what I was hoping you'd say."

"I've missed you so much. But...will our being together cause trouble for you—I mean, professionally? I don't want you to have a problem because of me."

"Sophie, I'm not supposed to have a romantic relationship with a client just after she's discharged from therapy; there are rules about that. But..." He trailed off. "Look, the only way I can be accused of any impropriety is if *you* bring up the charges." He added with mock solemnity, "So, I promise to do your bidding for the rest of my life. You'll probably make me your sex slave, but that's a risk I'll have to take."

"Mmmmm, sex slave. That means I'll definitely have to cancel my dating moratorium." And I nestled into this arms and we kissed—until something clicked in my mind. "Wait a minute. Did you just say you were *told* I had feelings for you—by a higher authority?"

"I was wondering how long it would take for you to ask me about that," he replied, smiling.

I pushed him away. "Tell me."

"Well, the Monday after the wedding, my secretary booked an appointment for me with a new client, a Jane Smith. I had no time in my schedule for the next two weeks and then I went to a conference in San Francisco, so my practice was pretty full because I was playing catch up when I came back. I finally saw Jane Smith yesterday."

I had no idea where this was going.

"Jane Smith turned out to be your mother."

"How in the world? How did she find you? I'm certain she didn't know your last name —not that she didn't ask me."

"Your mother told me that she and Edgardo had come to your apartment on the Sunday after the wedding and they'd brought lunch and while they were cleaning up the kitchen she found my note, written on the back of my business card. She saw the name Robert, she saw that I was a psychologist and she put two and two together because I had told her I was a marriage counselor. And so, she copied the phone number and made an appointment."

"I can't believe it."

"Sophie, believe it. You should know by now what your mother is capable of. So, she arrives at the office with about two pounds of apple strudel and a thermos of coffee and sits me down for a chat. Really, she sat in *my* chair and took over. And she tells me, "My Sophie is *almost definitely, very probably* in love with you. And then she said I should be a man and admit I love you and do something about it. So here I am.""

"Please tell me you weren't seduced by her apple strudel."

He kissed me again. "Let's just say I'm into the whole package. And, by the way, I had to promise her that I would make her a grandmother as soon as possible." He assumed a most serious expression. "And I never go back on a promise."

"I'm so happy that we both want a child."

"Yes, my beautiful Sophie, I want to marry you and have children. I know I made your mother very happy when I told her that. Of course, she let me know how lucky *I* was that she came to the office and set me straight."

I shook my head in amazement. "Damned if my mother didn't tell me she was going to do all the heavy lifting and find me a man in New York."

"I'm your man."

"She was right." I kissed him again. "I do *almost definitely, very probably* love you," I teased.

"Let's clarify that. Whom do you love?"

I knew exactly what to say. "I love you, Rob. I love *you*, Rob, now and forever. I love you, Rob Kisselstine."

"Make sure you put that in your journal. I categorically want that in writing."

And that's exactly what I did.

# Acknowledgements

Thanks to Kevin A. and Will G. who saved a damsel in distress when it came to technology. Cheers to Heather Zavod, master of commas, agreement, spacing, quotes and anything else that has to do with the written word. Since I added material to the story *after* Heather edited it, I assure readers that any errors are entirely my own. And a round of applause for Andrea Fassler, who specializes in encouragement. Many thanks to New York City Image Consultant Amanda Sanders for gracing the cover of *Shrink Wrapped* and a shout-out to Leah Casto for the cover photograph and Joan Gordon for Amanda's make-up. Point of information: on the back cover of my *next* book, which is already written, but still in the editing stage, I will have Leah take my picture and go for the glamour shot. Lastly, credit is due to my wonderful husband, Allen, who not only was a good listener when I tried out various plot points on him, but also, was a patient man when I disappeared into my office to write late at night when my creativity was most vigorous.

# About the Author

Since I'm rather disorganized, I cannot find all the short stories I've written; some didn't survive the switch from PC to Mac. Those that did are in folders somewhere in my office. The one thing these stories have in common is that they've never been submitted for publication. Bottom line: I confess that it takes courage to admit to yourself that you're a legitimate writer.

Then, one day, the idea for *Shrink Wrapped* came to me: a novel in journal form that traced the actions of a smart, sassy New Yorker who was unlucky in love. When I started, I was definite about two points: the beginning and the end. Then, a remarkable thing happened; as I wrote, the story took shape. Characters arrived as needed, unexpected events ensued and plot twists surfaced. It was as if these characters, who existed only on the page, had assumed a life of their own and were directing the storyline.

Prior to writing this novel, I've taught English in high school and worked in radio, writing advertising copy and doing on-air voice. I've also written extensively for non-profits, creating brochures, newspaper articles and fundraising material.

My adult children are delighted that they are not represented in the book, although my husband has expressed his hope that he is the role model for any sex scenes in the story. Muji, the family dachshund, is most supportive.

If you would like to get in touch, I welcome your feedback.
Email me at irenesilvers2@gmail.com